Finally it was T...

He eased down into one of the chutes near Jo's seat, this time facing her. She could see his intense concentration as he wrapped the rope around his hand and settled his mouthpiece. The bull stood still as a statue except for its mule ears waving like antennae.

A slight nod and the gate swung wide. Gunslinger erupted into the arena with all four feet off the ground, changing direction in midair. Cameron still clung to the bull's back, but off center so that the next spin shot him off like a rock out of a slingshot. He struck the metal panel directly below Jo's section with a crash and lay still. The eight-second buzzer sounded.

Madison Square Garden went dead quiet. Someone's cell phone brayed, harsh in the silence. Two men from the sports medicine team and one of the bullfighters ran to the spot where Cameron lay. Jo heard someone say, "Hey, Tom—can you hear me?" An indistinct response. "You want to walk out?" A grunt of assent and Cameron climbed to his feet. The crowd cheered as he left the arena supported by two of the medics.

Jo sank back in her seat.

Dear Reader,

Thanks for joining me for the second book in the Cameron's Pride series. I hope you'll enjoy reading about Tom Cameron and his trials and triumphs both in and out of the professional bull-riding arena. I've done my best to take you into the heart of the competition along with journalist Jo Dace as she profiles an athlete involved in the most dangerous eight seconds in sports.

I'd love to hear from you if you enjoy *The Bull Rider* or if the story piques your curiosity about professional bull riding. Feel free to contact me at helen@helendeprima.com. Enjoy the ride!

Helen DePrima

HEARTWARMING

The Bull Rider

—

Helen DePrima

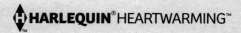
HARLEQUIN® HEARTWARMING™

Recycling programs
for this product may
not exist in your area.

ISBN-13: 978-0-373-36792-4

The Bull Rider

Copyright © 2016 by Helen DePrima

Printed in U.S.A.

Helen DePrima grew up on horseback on her grandfather's farm near Louisville, Kentucky. After spending a week on a dude ranch in Colorado when she was twelve, Helen fell in love with all things Western.

She spent wonderful weeks on the same ranch during her high school summers. After graduation she headed for the University of Colorado to meet the cowboy of her dreams and live happily ever after in a home on the range. Instead she fell in love with a Jersey boy bound for vet school. She earned her degree in nursing and spent four years as a visiting nurse in northern Colorado while her husband attended Colorado State University.

After her husband graduated, they settled in New Hampshire, where Helen worked first in nursing and then rehabilitating injured and orphaned wildlife. After retirement, she turned again to earlier passions: writing and the West, particularly professional bull riding.

Books by Helen DePrima

Harlequin Heartwarming

Into the Storm

Visit the Author Profile page
at Harlequin.com for more titles.

To my husband for keeping my eye on the prize.

Acknowledgments

To my agent, Stephany Evans, for her
encouragement and hand-holding.
To Dana Grimaldi for her deft editorial touch.
To my First Reader, Melissa Maupin, for her
enthusiastic involvement and feedback.
To Earlene Fowler for her prayers and sanity.
To Will Georgantas for his interest and timely gift.
To Carrie Weir of Tennessee Children's Services
for the valuable information she provided
regarding adoption procedures in her state.
And especially to everyone involved with the
Professional Bull Riders who make this series a
labor of love.

CHAPTER ONE

MADISON SQUARE GARDEN had gone cowboy crazy this Sunday in January, with wall-to-wall boots and jeans, denim jackets and wide-brimmed hats. Joanna Dace reflected with wry amusement that her black turtleneck, leggings and ankle boots marked her as a newcomer to the sport of professional bull riding.

A plump blonde wriggled into the third-row seat next to Jo's and smoothed the fringes on her red satin shirt. "Aren't these great seats? My husband says get the best you can buy—that's your Christmas present." She patted the knee of the burly man seated next to her.

"Whatever makes you happy, babe," he said with a grin.

"So who's your favorite rider?" she asked Jo.

"Well, I…"

"Me too—I love 'em all. I hope you don't mind if I jump around and yell—I wait all year for this. Just kick me if I get too noisy."

A raucous horn sounded while *Warning* flashed on the advertising banner boards.

Her new friend tapped her arm. "You'd better cover your ears now if you don't like it loud."

Jo obeyed as the lights went down. Men with fuel cans traced a pattern in front of the bucking chutes and then darted away. Jets of fire shot up accompanied by ear-splitting explosions as flames spelled out letters in the dirt. More pyrotechnics and then the announcer's shout: "Hello, New York City! This is the one and only PBR!"

"HEY, TOM—A GAL grabbed me up on the concourse. She wants to meet you." Deke Harkens fished in his shirt pocket. "She gave me her card."

Tom Cameron buckled on his plain blue chaps without looking at the card. Women often sent bull riders phone numbers and hotel keys, sometimes underwear. He wasn't interested— not now, not like that, never again.

"Wrong Cameron," he said. "Luke's the bunny wrangler."

"Nope, she said Tom Cameron. And this one's no buckle bunny—at least she's not dressed like one."

"She say what she wants?"

Deke shook his head. "Just she'd like to meet you. You want to grab a look? Brown hair, late twenties, I guess—third row, right next to the chutes."

Not the cheap seats. Tom adjusted his belt and stuck the card in his pocket. "Maybe after the event." Bad luck to plan beyond his next ride.

A claxon sounded in the arena. He settled a black Stetson over his brows. "Showtime."

He followed the other cowboys through the echoing corridors under the Garden and mounted metal stairs in darkness to the center pedestal above the bucking chutes. When the spotlight blinded him, he raised his hat to the sold-out arena as the announcer intoned, "Ladies and gentlemen, the current number-one bull rider in the world—Tom Cameron!"

He stood in place during the introduction of the bullfighters, including his brother, Luke; the invocation imploring protection for the riders and the bulls; and then the national anthem sung by an army sergeant with a powerful baritone. When the lights came up, he climbed down and headed toward the locker room, stopping when a woman's voice called his name.

"You're leading in the event, Tom." The color commentator thrust a microphone in his face.

"Will you pick Gunslinger again in the championship round?"

"I guess I'll decide when the time comes," he said. Lisa was a good sort, but he wasn't big on being interviewed—he'd rather let his riding speak for him. She understood he wasn't much of a talker and let him go with good wishes for his next ride.

He continued to the locker room while the first bulls were run into the chutes; shed his hat and chaps; and switched from boots to sneakers before making his way to a deserted space behind the bulls' pens. He closed his eyes for a moment and then began to stretch and strike almost in slow motion, the movements becoming faster and stronger until sweat soaked his collar. He finished the kata and dropped back to cool-down mode until his pulse steadied. At every venue, he managed to find a hidden corner like this, not because he minded the ribbing from the other riders but because it interfered with his concentration. The exercises improved his balance during the ride, and he was able to land on his feet more often than not.

As they always did, the exercises left him feeling loose and peaceful. He'd keep moving until it was his turn to ride, wandering through the maze of pens and chutes holding the bulls for the afternoon's competition. They were undemanding company, some moving restlessly in their pens, others relaxing in the sawdust bedding. A massive cream-colored Brahman sidled over to the fence and poked his wet muzzle between the metal rails.

Tom scratched behind one floppy ear. "Gunslinger, you're a phony," he said. "Some tough guy." The fence creaked as the bull leaned into the caress. Tom had straddled this bull three times already, always coming up short. No shame in that—no one had made the eight seconds on Gunslinger.

"How about it, buddy?" He tugged on the bull's ear. "You want to dance again today?"

Tom returned to the locker room and was pulling on his boots when Arlie Johnson's bull rope with its bell attached crashed against the metal lockers. The tall blond Arkansas cowboy followed and kicked the trashcan twice before dropping to a bench with his head in his hands.

"Son-of-a-gun blew up when he was supposed to spin," he said. "That's the last time I ask an owner how his bull bucks."

Tom listened with halfhearted sympathy. Arlie was new to the big time. He'd learn a lot of hard lessons before he got much further, like not trying to second-guess more than half a ton of muscle and meanness.

"You've got two good scores for the weekend," he said. "That'll probably get you into the championship round."

"Yeah, and get stuck with a bull nobody else wants, like Gunslinger." Arlie's glower smoothed out. "Say, these New York gals sure like cowboys. I was swatting them off like flies in Times Square last night."

"You just keep swatting 'em, sonny," Nick Ducharme said; his soft drawl bespoke Cajun country. He'd made the eight seconds on his bull. "Or you'll go home with a souvenir you can't show your mama. Besides, the girls you were hanging with in Times Square are a bunch of tourists just like you."

Tom tightened the thong around the wrist of his riding glove and shrugged into his safety vest. "Don't worry about picking Gunslinger," he said. "He's mine."

BY THE TIME she heard Tom Cameron's name announced, Jo Dace was half-deafened by the racket in the Garden and stupefied by the raw violence of the sport.

Her new friend elbowed her. "Don't you just love Tom Cameron? He makes riding bulls look so easy. And you watch his brother during the ride—he hovers like a mother hen."

Jo could see only Cameron's back as he climbed down into the bucking chute, but the giant overhead screen showed him wrapping the rope over and around his hand and then sliding forward to a seat directly over his fist. A shiver of apprehension trickled down her spine. One cowboy had already been carried from the arena on a stretcher. What if—

The gate flew open and the big brindled bull shot forward, covering at least a dozen feet in one jump and snapping Cameron's head back so that his hat brim almost touched the animal's rump. Next a vertical leap followed by a feint to the left slung his rider far to the outside of the spin. Jo closed her eyes so she wouldn't have to watch Cameron slammed to the dirt. The buzzer sounded, almost drowned out by cheers, and she opened her eyes in time to see Cameron sail through the air to land on his feet. The bullfighters wove between the rider and the bull that scampered through the exit gate with a final flourish of its heels.

The announcer's voice boomed. "How about that ride, folks? Tom Cameron's gonna be pretty happy with his score—89 points! That should give him first pick for the championship round."

Cameron raised his hat to the crowd. As he passed her seat, she saw a thin scar running from his right cheekbone to the point of his chin.

The next three riders bucked off; two more made the buzzer but with scores lower than Cameron's, ending the round.

"What's happening now?" Jo asked Cindy—by now Jo and Satin Shirt were on a first-name basis—as men set up ramps to the circular steel structure in the middle of the arena. The shark cage, Cindy had called it earlier.

"The fifteen riders with the most points for the weekend get to pick their bulls for the championship round. Now you'll see some real bucking."

Tom Cameron climbed the ramp first. He said "Gunslinger" into the microphone, and the crowd roared with approval. The next thirteen riders chose from the diminishing list, leaving a bull named Booger-Butt for the luckless fifteenth.

When the action resumed, Jo understood what Cindy meant by real bucking. These bulls appeared to have studied at some elite school for mayhem—some kicked so high their backs went almost vertical, others spun so fast her own head swam. Most put their riders in the dirt in only a few seconds. Finally one cowboy hung on for eight seconds, but the announcer commented, "That won't be much of a score, folks—Whirligig had an off day."

And finally it was Tom Cameron's turn. Again he eased down into one of the chutes near Jo's seat, this time facing her. She could see his expression of intense concentration as he wrapped the rope around his hand and settled his mouthpiece. The bull stood still as a statue except for its mule-like ears waving like antennae.

"I knew he'd pick Gunslinger," Cindy said, leaning forward. She cupped her hands around her mouth and yelled, "Ride him, Tom!" Her husband chuckled.

A slight nod from Cameron and the gate swung wide. Gunslinger erupted into the arena with all four feet off the ground, changing direction in midair. Cameron still clung to the bull's back, but off center so that the next spin shot him off like a rock out of a slingshot. He struck the metal panel directly below Jo's section with a crash and lay still. The eight-second buzzer sounded.

Madison Square Garden went dead quiet.

Someone's cell phone brayed, harsh in the silence. Two men from the Sports Medicine team and one of the bullfighters ran to the spot where Cameron lay. Jo heard someone say, "Hey, Tom—can you hear me?" An indistinct response. "You want to walk out?" A grunt of assent and Cameron climbed to his feet. The crowd cheered as he left the arena supported by two of the medics.

The announcer said, "Folks, Tom's gonna be just fine. Doc Barnett will check him out, but you can see he's up and walking. That makes the score 4–0 in Gunslinger's favor." Jo sank back in her seat. She'd gotten more than her money's worth for today's ticket, and she'd seen enough to believe that bull riding was indeed the Toughest Sport on Earth. Other rodeo competitions like riding broncos and roping made sense—they were cowboy skills carried to a professional level, but this… What use was riding a bull? Still, the magnificent foolishness fascinated her. Too bad Tom Cameron had been injured. She would have to revise her plan.

She was exchanging social media information with her new friend ("Maybe we'll see you at another event—there's one in Allentown this fall") when she heard someone call her name.

The cowboy to whom she'd given her card hailed her from the arena floor.

"Miss Dace? Joanna Dace? Tom said he'll be out in a few minutes if you want to wait."

He had to be joking. "Won't he be going to the emergency room?" she asked. "He could barely walk."

The cowboy hooted. "Naw, he's okay. If you'll follow me…" He showed her where to climb down at the end of the aisle and led her through the clanging confusion of the pens and chutes being dismantled. The last bulls were disappearing toward the stock trucks waiting outside the Garden when her guide stopped outside the locker room.

"I'll tell him you're here," he said before he disappeared inside.

She backed against the wall to make way for men dragging heavy electrical cables and pushing massive sound equipment crates. Several other women waited nearby, some with small children who ran forward yelling "Daddy!" as their fathers emerged. The hallway gradually emptied and she waited alone, shivering in an icy draft from some unseen door left open.

A slight man in khakis and a distressed leather bomber jacket hesitated at the locker room door. The light caught his face and she recognized Tom Cameron from the scar on his cheek. He saw her at the same moment and said "Miss Dace?" just as she spoke his name. They both laughed.

"I have to ask," he said. "Are you Joe Dace's daughter?"

The pain and anger brought on by hearing her father's name hadn't died over the years, but it rarely ambushed her as it did now. "Yes," she said. "I'm named for him. You must be an auto racing fan."

"Not so much now, but I got to meet him when I was eleven or so—the biggest thrill of my young life. My brother and I sneaked under the fence at the speedway when my mom took us to visit her grandmother in Talladega. He autographed my cap—I still have it. I wonder if I saw you there."

"You might have—Mom and I traveled with him whenever I wasn't in school."

"When I heard about the crash, I felt like I'd lost kin. Kids take things like that hard." He flushed. "Stupid thing to say, like you wouldn't know."

"It's okay—ancient history," she said, keeping the anger out of voice. "Should you be standing around like this? You took an awful hit."

"Not so bad—just knocked the wind out of

me and scattered my chickens some. My dad will have me out hauling feed and riding the fence line when I get home tomorrow. Which reminds me." He took his phone from his pocket. "Excuse me—I need to do this right away." He tapped in a quick text and stuck the phone back in his jacket. "Sorry—today's event won't be broadcast until this evening so I always let my folks know Luke and I are okay." He grinned. "But I don't give him the results."

"Where did you finish in the event?"

"Second in the event, but I'm still leading in the overall standings. I haven't got Gunslinger's number yet—maybe next time." He looked at his watch. "I have to be at the airport in a couple hours, but I always treat myself to a piece of real New York cheesecake after the last go-round. Want to join me?"

She agreed, and he led her out a back exit just as the last cattle truck pulled away. A few fans had lingered; one teenage girl squealed and pointed. "Tom! Can we get a picture?"

He shrugged an apology to Jo and put his arms around the shoulders of the two girls while a third took their photo.

Jo tapped her arm. "Want to be in the picture?" She captured a shot of Cameron with all three and handed the phone back as a young couple with two boys asked for a photo, as well.

Ten minutes later Cameron waved goodbye to the fans and rejoined Jo. "Sorry," he said, "but I can't just walk on by when folks wait out in the cold."

A few minutes later he ushered her into a booth at the Tick Tock Diner two blocks from the Garden. "Okay," he said after they had ordered cheesecake and coffee. "What can I do for you?"

Now that she had Tom Cameron seated across from her, she hesitated. He seemed so self-contained that her usual pitch to vanity seemed superficial. Because her father linked them in even a small way, she honored him with the truth, or most of the truth.

"I'm a freelance journalist," she said. "I grew up on the stock-car racing circuit, and I'm still trying to figure out what motivates competitors like my dad. He saw friends get killed—he knew it could happen to him. I've interviewed athletes in other high-risk sports and followed them around and written about what I learned. I'd been planning to do a profile on a mountaineer who climbs ice cliffs, but he broke his leg…" She grinned in spite of herself. "He fell off a ladder stringing Christmas lights on the roof."

"Ain't that just the way," he said. He touched the scar on his cheek. "Nothing to do with bull riding. I was mending fence a year back when a rock turned under my boot and the barbwire whipped me across the face."

He laid down his fork. "So your mountain climber got shot out from under you and now you want to dissect a bull rider instead."

She winced at his turn of phrase. "To explore bull riding from one cowboy's perspective. A guided tour, so to speak. After watching today, there's no question in my mind it's the most dangerous competitive sport going. This was my first event, but if today was typical—"

He laughed. "Actually, today was pretty tame. Cory Brennan—he's the rider who got carried out—he'll be good to ride next weekend. But why did you pick me?"

"Two reasons." She ticked off points on her fingers. "You're leading in the current season after coming in second for the championship twice before—I figure that makes you hungry. Plus your brother's being one of the bullfighters is a great angle. I saw him up close when you got bucked off. Are you twins?"

"We get asked that a lot," he said. "Luke's

just eleven months older than me." He scraped up the last fragments of cheesecake. "Okay, send me a list of questions—"

She shook her head. "I do in-depth research, more than just asking questions." She took a manila envelope from her purse. "I've printed a couple of my features to give you an idea of how I work." She leaned forward and gave him her best smile. "I promise I'm not planning a hatchet job on bull riding."

He frowned. "This doesn't really sound like my kind of thing—"

"Just think about it, okay?" She took a fresh card from her wallet and wrote on the back. "Here's my personal email address and phone number. Please read what I've given you and then decide."

CHAPTER TWO

TOM STUFFED HIS carry-on into the overhead bin and eased into his aisle seat. He'd downplayed his wreck to Jo Dace, but the bruised back muscles would probably seize up during the long flight from New York to Albuquerque. With luck, he'd be able to loosen them up in the hotel's hot tub before he and Luke drove north to Colorado the next morning.

Luke stuck the in-flight magazine into the seat pocket. "Deke told me you left the Garden with a woman—you gotta be careful with these big-city girls."

Tom snorted. "You're warning me? I saw the blonde with you in the elevator last night."

Luke grinned. "You got a dirty mind, little brother. She was a physical therapist kind enough to work on my sore shoulder after that bull ran all over me. So tell me about the bunny you took off with."

"You're not going to believe this—she's Joe Dace's daughter."

"Our Joe Dace? Be-damn! What's she want?"

Some instinct kept Tom from repeating Jo's proposal; he wanted time to turn it over in his mind before letting Luke track all over it. "She had some questions about bull riding. This was her first event."

After takeoff, once Luke had reclined his seat and tipped his hat over his eyes, Tom pulled out the pages Jo Dace had given him. He began with the feature on Chris Baker, the winningest jockey currently riding. The compelling writing plus his own insider knowledge of Thoroughbred racing immediately sucked him into the article. His uncle was a track vet in California. He and Luke had visited a few times, following Uncle Tony on his rounds at the track. Jo's account brought back the sounds and smells of the stable area as if he were handing his uncle instruments from his mobile clinic or eating his lunch with the grooms and hot walkers seated outside the horses' stalls.

He put the first article down and began reading about the sailor who raced solo around the world. The ocean was a foreign element to Tom aside from a few trips to the beach with his aunt. Jo's writing dropped him squarely onto the tilting deck of the sleek racing yacht; he could almost hear sea birds' cries and wind whistling in the rigging.

Tom laid the pages on his lap. The lady could write, but the strength of her work depended on digging deep into her subjects' lives. She wouldn't settle for a few interviews and seats above the chutes at a couple of events.

Luke levered his seat upright. "What are you reading?" He grabbed the horse racing article and read silently for a few minutes. "Say, wouldn't Shelby like this! I'll bet she knows some of these people."

"She left the Thoroughbred scene a long while back, but yeah, she probably would enjoy it." His stepmother had spent most of her childhood at Acadia Downs in Louisiana, following at her grandfather's heels while he cared for the horses and working as an exercise rider when she was a teenager. "I'll have her take a look when we get home."

"So now Joe Dace's daughter is interested in bull riding?"

"I guess." Her reasons for asking him made good sense, but he could think of a dozen riders with stories just as compelling and with more colorful personalities.

He reclined his seat with a soft groan, trying to ease his back, and closed his eyes.

ROLLING NORTH THROUGH New Mexico the next
morning in Luke's Explorer lifted Tom's spirits;
turning homeward always cleared his mind. He
enjoyed New York City, a world removed from
his natural habitat, but the gray winter skies
and slushy sidewalks always made him home-
sick for the clean vistas of the Southwest. He
sang "Thank God I'm a Country Boy" under
his breath.

Luke glanced at him from the driver's seat.
"What are you so happy about?"

"Just glad to be heading home. Did your
physical therapist get all the kinks out of your
shoulder Saturday night?"

Luke laughed. "Oh yeah—I was real loosey-
goosey by the time she left." He sobered. "I
read that other article Jo Dace wrote, the one
about the sailor. If that's her formula, she's not
looking to write about bull riding. She wants
to profile a cowboy—you, right?"

Tom shrugged. He still wasn't ready to talk
about it; Luke would try to buffalo him into
agreeing before he'd thought it through.

Luke punched his arm. "I reckon she could
pick worse."

Tom laughed. "Don't try to turn my head
with compliments. I'll run it by Dad and Shelby

before I make up my mind. We could all get sucked into the project."

THEY DROVE INTO Durango close to noon. Luke turned onto the main street. "Let's grab lunch at the Queen," he said. "Dad's going to put us to work the minute we get home—we might as well fuel up first."

Tom had no objection; breakfast at the hotel buffet was a distant memory, and the ranch lay an hour's drive farther west. Luke parked near the Victorian storefront of the Silver Queen Saloon and Dance Emporium. Most of the tables were occupied, but they found seats in the booth nearest the kitchen. Tom lowered himself into his seat a little stiffly; his back had cramped up again on the long ride from Albuquerque.

"Well, look what the cat drug in." Marge Bowman stood at Luke's elbow and pulled a pencil from her white topknot. "What's your pleasure, boys?"

Luke circled her stout waist with one arm. "Sweetheart, you're my pleasure. What's today's special?"

"Anything you want, lover." She lifted his hat and planted a smacking kiss on top of his head.

"See why I can't find a girl to suit me?" Luke

said to Tom. "Marge has me spoiled for ordinary women."

"My heart about stopped when you hit that fence yesterday," she said to Tom. "Would you please get that bull rode so you can stop picking him?"

"I'm working on it," Tom said. "Next time for sure."

"Chicken-fried steak for both of you? And I just took a peach pie out of the oven. It'll be cool enough to cut by the time you finish your meal."

Luke clapped a hand over his heart. "I think I've died and gone to heaven. Bring it on, darlin'."

Maybe Tom should be scornful of Luke's glib tongue, but he secretly envied his brother's gift of gab. If he agreed to Joanna Dace's proposal, he'd likely end up playing a supporting role to Luke's grandstanding. He'd always been the boring middle kid. No teacher had ever phoned his folks about his grades; the sheriff had never given him a warning for underage drinking. Luke had supplied enough drama for the two of them, and now his younger sister, Lucy, with her dreams of stardom, had picked up where Luke left off.

His phone rang and he limped to the men's

room before answering. He checked the caller ID. "Hey, Shelby."

"Hey, yourself. You okay after yesterday?"

"My back's pretty sore, but nothing's broken." Shelby understood bumps and bruises, what was and wasn't serious. She'd been thrown more than a few times by skittish Thoroughbreds and still took an occasional hit while green-breaking horses.

"You want ice or heat when you get home?" she asked.

"Heat first, I think," he said.

"Have you reached Durango yet?"

"We're having lunch at the Queen," he said. "You need something from town?"

"As long as you're there, see if you can talk Marge out of a peach pie for your dad."

"Do my best," he said, and then he keyed off. He stuck his phone in his pocket, thankful anew that Shelby had drifted into their lives a couple years after his mother's death. She was as different from his mom as a prairie falcon is from a happy barnyard hen, but her arrival had glued them back together as a family.

He returned to the table just as their food arrived, and they left after their meal with the remaining three-quarters of the pie Marge had cut for them.

An hour later Luke steered below the ranch sign with *Cameron's Pride* burned into a weathered plank. Luke braked in the least muddy spot near the back door of the rambling log house. A dog as tall as a weanling calf rose from a sunny spot by the barn and approached with a stiff gait.

Tom climbed out of the car and rubbed the dog's ears.

"Looks like we're both moving a little slow today, old buddy," he said. Stranger was starting to show his age. The big dog had arrived a few years ago with Shelby as her protector and sole companion. The welcoming grin on his grizzled face would be sorely missed when he was gone.

Luke grabbed his bag and Tom's from the backseat as Shelby Cameron opened the kitchen door. Tom handed her the peach pie, struck as always by his dad's rare good luck in his second marriage. Shelby's long hair shone like a blackbird's wing while her skin seemed to gather the winter sunlight.

"I know Marge just fed you up," she said, "but I made beignets this morning. Luke, come have a few before you ride out. Your dad found a section of fence down when he and Lucy checked the heifers this morning. I know they would appreciate your help."

She turned to Tom. "I've got the chair heated up. Sit—I'll bring you coffee."

Luke rolled his eyes in mock disdain; although next time he might occupy the big recliner with its heat and massage after taking a beating from the bulls. He left the kitchen and returned a few minutes later dressed in faded jeans and a blue plaid flannel shirt that had seen better days. "Here's that article for Shelby," he said and handed Tom the pages from Joanna Dace.

"Take the rest of the beignets along," Shelby said, handing him a paper bag. "And make sure a few get to your dad and your sister."

Luke grinned. "You're a mean one, Step-mama." He grabbed a flannel-lined Carhartt jacket and a billed cap with earflaps from a hook by the door on his way out.

Tom relaxed and closed his eyes. He'd be pulling his weight by morning and ready to straddle another set of bulls next weekend, but just now he never wanted to move from the chair with its comforting heat penetrating his sore muscles.

Shelby began chopping onions and green peppers for dirty rice, a favorite of both Tom and Luke's. An hour passed and Tom levered the chair upright and stood, twisting his shoulders and back experimentally—still sore, but good enough for now.

"I'll get some of the barn work done before the others get back," he said. "Is Dad behaving himself?"

"As long as I'm watching him," Shelby said. "I know he does more than he should as soon as he's out of my sight, but Lucy helps me keep after him when she's home."

"You mind if I ride Ghost this week? His gaits will be easiest on my back."

"I wish you would," Shelby said. "I don't work him as much as I should. I spent all day Saturday doing a 4-H workshop in Grand Junction, and I'll have even less time when Lucy goes back to Boulder day after tomorrow." She reached into a jar above the sink and handed Tom a few licorice drops. "Apologize to him for me."

Tom changed into rubber paddock boots and headed for the barn. Shelby's gray stallion must have heard him coming or maybe smelled the licorice, his special treat. Ghost stuck his nose over the top rail of his corral and blew a loud breath. Even furred like a teddy bear in his winter coat, his fine legs and delicately shaped face hinted at his Barb ancestry. He'd already sired a nice string of foals that Shelby trained and sold for ranch work.

Tom fed him the candy and scratched along the curve of his jaw. "You feel like working, buddy? We'll check the south fence line tomorrow, maybe stop in for lunch at the Bucks's." He grinned in anticipation. Auntie Rose, a distant cousin, made the best fry bread in La Plata County.

The sun was already sliding toward the western horizon—no sense for him to saddle up now to help the fence crew. He worked his way through the barn, mucking out Ghost's stall and freshening his water bucket, finishing the repair on a partially mended cinch strap in the tack room and forking down fresh hay for the half dozen horses in the corral next to Ghost's. A tall chestnut mare ambled over for special attention. Sadie had some age on her, but she was still everyone's first choice for hunting; he'd shot over her head ever since he was old enough to handle a long gun.

He leaned on the gate, gazing out along tracks left in the snow by his dad's and sister's horses, followed by the hoofprints of Luke's mount. A narrow path branched off to the knoll where the Camerons had laid their dead for more than a hundred years. He and Luke and Lucy had learned to read from the grave markers while their mom tended the flowers planted there, tracing the letters and numbers on the stones: Husband and Father, Beloved Wife, Infant Son; 1888, 1914, 1985... Memorials to Cameron men buried in France in 1918 and lost at Guadalcanal. His mother's grave was the most recent one.

Ghost let out a brassy neigh; Lucy's mare Goosie answered. Three horses emerged from the willows along the creek and crunched through the snow toward the barn. Tom swung the corral gate wide for them and took the horses' reins as the riders dismounted.

"Nice to see you're done goofing off," Luke said. "Now that we've done all the work."

"Timing is everything," Tom said. "I plan to check the south fence line tomorrow."

Lucy Cameron pulled off her knit cap, allowing red-gold curls to frame her face. "I really thought you were going to make the eight on Gunslinger this time."

Tom pulled on one curl. "Next time, Red—I promise."

"Don't call me Red." She slapped his hand away. "I'll be so glad to get back to my dorm."

"Heads up, Boulder," Luke said. "Hurricane Lucy on the horizon!"

Jake Cameron pulled the saddle off Butch, his dun gelding. "Good event, son. I see you're still leading in the national standings."

Tom shrugged and tapped on the corral rail for luck. "Doesn't mean much this early in the season."

They finished unsaddling and turned the horses loose for their hay as the sun dipped below the horizon to the southwest. The aroma of Cajun spices greeted them from the kitchen when they entered the back door and kicked off their boots in the mudroom.

Shelby turned from the stove with a wooden spoon in her hand. "Supper in ten minutes," she said.

"Yes, boss." Jake swept her hair aside and dropped a kiss on the back of her neck; her hand curved around his cheek.

Lucy put together a salad while Tom set out plates and Luke carried roast chicken and a bowl with the dirty rice to the table. They ate mostly in silence until Shelby served bowls of bread pudding with bourbon sauce for dessert.

Tom handed around Joanna Dace's features. "I'd like you guys to read these."

Jake looked up after he'd finished both articles. "What's this about, Tom?"

"She wants to write about a bull rider next."

"Our Tom, to be exact," Luke said.

Lucy clapped her hands like a five-year-old. "You'll be famous!"

"Your brother's already pretty well-known where he needs to be, Luce," Jake said, "although I expect his sponsors would be pleased." He turned to Tom. "Could you stay focused on your riding with this lady practically living in your back pocket?"

Tom spooned the last drops of sauce out of his dish before answering. "I don't know. She's a helluva writer—I'd kind of like to see how she puts her work together." Plus he still felt bad for his dumb comment about her father's death. He wondered if she'd seen the crash. "But like you say, Dad…"

"Never back away from an opportunity out of fear," Shelby said. She laid her hand on her husband's arm.

Jake covered her hand with his. "Shelby's right, Tom. Find out what she has in mind and then decide."

CHAPTER THREE

JO'S PHONE RANG as she unlocked her apartment door while juggling two bags of groceries. She shoved her way inside and checked the caller ID: area code 970, wherever that might be.

"Miss Dace? You said to call after I read your articles."

The connection was poor, probably a weak cell phone signal, but she recognized Tom Cameron's voice. She'd only half expected to hear from him.

"I've thought about what you asked," he said. "If you want to show up Friday night in Oklahoma City, we'll give it a try. Come a couple hours early." He gave her a cell number. "Call Paula when you get to the arena. I won't be able to meet you before the event, but she'll take care of you."

They chatted a few minutes longer about the weather in New York and Colorado and then he rang off.

Jo stood holding her phone, amazed he might

agree to her proposal. Angus, her Maine Coon cat, leaped to her shoulder, waving his plumy tail. She smoothed his fur. "Looks like you'll be spending the weekend with your grandma, pal," she said. More than one weekend if things worked out.

"A BULL RIDER? Who's crazy enough to ride a bull?" Anna Dace stirred honey, a shade lighter than her short curls, into her tea and pushed up the sleeves of her NYC sweatshirt. "How useless."

"So true," Jo said, "and the cowboys take terrible risks every ride, but there's a crazy magnificence about it."

"Please don't try to ride a bull, like you did that race horse."

"A retired Thoroughbred, Mom, and we weren't racing. Chris Baker just wanted to give me the feeling of hitting the head of the stretch with that much horse under me."

"I blame your grandfather for turning you and your cousins loose with his horses." Her mother sighed. "At least you won't be hundreds of miles out on the ocean in a tiny boat."

Jo grimaced. "You wouldn't believe how seasick I was the first few days." But she hadn't backed out, not even when Kevin McCloud had offered to set her back ashore.

"So how will you tackle bull riding?"

"Same as always—soak it all up until a pattern starts to form." She gave Angus a good-bye smooch. "Behave yourself—no eating plants. And don't let him talk you into too many treats," she told her mother.

Jo stood outside the arena entrance in Oklahoma City and punched the number Tom Cameron had provided into her cell phone. A tall black woman in fancy stitched boots and a red pearl-snap shirt waved to her from inside and motioned for her to enter through a side door.

"Jo Dace? I'm Paula," she said. "Tom asked me to show you around." She handed Jo a badge to hang around her neck. "We're starting a VIP tour in a few minutes. You'll get a good idea of the backstage operation, and Tom reserved a seat for you above the chutes to watch the event."

No more than the tourist package, but if Tom had read her articles, he knew she'd need more depth. She wouldn't rush him—let him set the pace. She followed Paula to join a group of a dozen or so fans: a couple with two preteen sons, several wannabe cowgirls in tight jeans and fancy shirts and two gray-haired couples who spoke with familiarity about past events and retired riders.

For the next hour they wound through a maze of pens and chutes, up and down stairs more like ladders, listening to and asking questions of riders and judges and bulls' owners. Jo didn't try to remember most of what she heard, simply storing sensory impressions—the clatter of metal platforms underfoot, the smells of cattle and fresh sawdust bedding, the surprisingly silky skin of one bull that invited petting. The details would fall into place if Tom Cameron agreed to invite her into his world.

Paula took Jo aside when the tour ended. "You'll be sitting right beside the TV broadcast booth," she said. "We don't usually put fans where they might interfere with the live feed, but Tom said you'd be okay there." She led Jo to a high canvas director's chair overlooking the bucking chutes. "Enjoy the show."

The arena filled as Jo watched, a sold-out performance, as New York City had been. The spectators here were a different breed though, men who wore boots and wide-brimmed hats with a natural authority, women whose Western finery said this wasn't their first rodeo and many more children, including babies in arms.

Twenty minutes until showtime. Jo started snapping ranging shots with her iPhone, gathering images to prompt her recollections when she started making notes after the event.

A voice broke her concentration. "Hey there, writer lady—glad you could make it."

A man stood beside her seat. He had Tom Cameron's same dark hair and brown eyes but no scar on his cheek.

"You must be Luke," she said. "I saw you in New York."

"Yes, ma'am, number-one son," he said with a grin. "I had to meet the gal who could lure my brother into the spotlight. Shy as a deer, our Tom." He looked over the railing. "You got the best seat in the house—any closer and you'd be straddling a bull." He glanced at his watch. "Time for me to get suited up." He threw his chest out. "Keep your eyes on me—bravest of the brave."

The event opened with pyrotechnics as it had at Madison Square Garden; again Tom was introduced as the rider ranked first in points. A willowy blonde in a sparkly shirt sang the national anthem, drawing wild cheers when her voice soared a full octave above the high note.

Paula had given Jo a sheet listing the order in which the cowboys would ride, matched against

bulls with names like Sidewinder and Top Gun.
Tom had drawn Texas Twister tonight. Jo hoped
the bull wouldn't live up to his name, or rather
that he would. She'd done her homework since
last weekend. A rider wanted a bull that could
almost but not quite buck him off; an easy ride
wouldn't yield a high score. Jo wasn't planning
to write a detailed treatise on bull riding, but
she needed more than casual knowledge of the
sport to do Tom Cameron's career justice.

Her vantage point above the chutes gave her
a bird's-eye view of the action. Riders wearing
colorful fringed chaps and heavy leather vests
plastered with company logos clattered along
the walkway below her and climbed down onto
the bulls' backs. She had only a limited understanding of their elaborate preride rituals
and jotted questions in a pocket notebook. Why
did some wear helmets while others wore cowboy hats? What was the purpose of the second
rope around the bull's belly? What was the man
hunched above the chute watching for?

She also paid close attention to Luke and his
fellow bullfighters as they darted between the
bulls and the downed riders. The three men
seemed indestructible, bouncing up like rubber
balls after being butted, trampled underfoot and
tossed into the air like toys, but a long scrape

marked Luke's cheek after a bull slammed him against the chute gate.

She recognized most of the cowboys' names from New York City and the arena announcer supplied a few words of introduction for each one: Cody from Tennessee, Sean from Georgia, Harve and J.W. and Mike from Texas, Ben from Australia and Silvano from Brazil, thirty-five in all. According to the day sheet, Tom Cameron would be one of the last to ride.

Thankfully all the cowboys in this round were able to leave the arena on their own feet, although the Sports Medicine medics did have to help a few. Not many stayed on the full eight seconds. "We've got a great pen of young bulls tonight, folks," the announcer said.

At last she saw Tom below her on the walkway. She leaned forward but didn't call his name, recalling his expression of intense concentration before he rode in New York City. He climbed down into the chute, eased onto the back of a black-and-white bull with a wide spread of horns. He took a quick wrap around his hand with his rope and nodded. The gate swung open.

The bull exploded in a frenzy of bucking, swinging its head from side to side. One horn swept Tom's hat off before a wild leap ended in a stumble that yanked him forward so that his face collided with the top of the bull's head. He slumped sideways and landed flat on his back with an audible grunt. The bull regained his feet and capered out the gate.

The Sports Medicine team reached Tom as he climbed to his feet, gulping for breath; one pressed a gauze pad over his bleeding nose. Luke retrieved his hat and brushed the dirt off before setting it on his brother's head.

Tom waved to the crowd and limped toward the chutes, holding the compress to his face. He paused to peer at a paper in an official's hand and then nodded.

"Reride option," the announcer said. "Looks like Tom Cameron will be getting on another bull."

Jo started from her seat in protest. She'd sought an athlete in a high-risk sport, but this was insanity. She sat back, smoothing the day sheet she had crumpled in sweating hands, trying to recapture her objectivity.

Two more riders left the chutes but neither rode for the full eight seconds.

"One more to go," the announcer said. "Tom Cameron's reride on Widow-maker."

CHAPTER FOUR

TOM SHIFTED THE ice pack across his eyes and nose. "How much longer am I stuck here?"

"Till I'm satisfied the bleeding has stopped," Dr. Barnett said, glancing at him over his half glasses. "Unless you don't plan on riding tomorrow night, in which case you can leave anytime you want. Maybe I should have kept you off your reride bull, but you weren't concussed, and it's your nose."

Tom leaned back and closed his eyes. Doc could be a pain in the butt, but every cowboy on the tour took his advice as gospel. If Doc Barnett said he should sit one out, he might complain but he'd obey; there was no appeal to a firm "No way."

A whistled chorus of "Friends in Low Places" alerted him to his brother's presence. "Hey, kid," Luke said, "maybe you should stop beating up bulls with your face." He lifted a corner of the compress and whistled. "Cute."

Tom grunted. "Thanks. Listen, you gotta help me. I promised to meet Jo Dace—"

"All taken care of. I told her you'd be tied up for a while so I'd check on you and then walk her home."

Tom struggled to a sitting position. "The hell you will."

"Relax." Luke pushed him down against the backrest. "I'll treat her like an old-maid schoolmarm. Besides, she ain't my type. Keep him here as long as you want, Doc—there's nowhere he's gotta be."

A COUPLE HOURS LATER, Tom sat in his hotel room, listening to the Weather Channel report on the latest snowstorm barreling down out of the Southern Rockies. This one didn't sound like it would be as dangerous as the one last spring, but he called home anyway.

"There's only about six inches predicted for here," his dad said. "We've got the heifers in the lower pasture and hay already out, so we're all set. Stop worrying and ride your bulls."

Shelby took the phone. "We're fine here—everything's under control, including your father."

Reassured, Tom hung up and took another bite of the half-eaten ham sandwich from room service. A bottle of Coors gone flat sat on the bedside table.

He had grabbed a quick look into the hotel bar after Doc had finally let him leave Sports Medicine but had seen no sign of Luke or Jo Dace. Now the bedside clock read 11:42 p.m. Where was Luke? He and his brother generally got separate rooms because of Luke's social life, but half of Oklahoma and part of Texas had hit the town for the bull riding this weekend, so they'd been forced to bunk together.

He took a swig of the beer and swore as the bottle tapped against his teeth. His whole face hurt and he had a headache to match. He wasn't waiting up any longer—Jo Dace was a big girl, who'd probably fended off guys more determined than Luke. He limped to the bathroom and scrubbed at the bloodstains on his shirt soaking in the basin before peeling out of his sweaty undershirt and jeans. The door clicked open as he turned on the shower.

Luke tossed his hat on the bed. "You still up? I figured you'd take a handful of Advils and turn in early."

Tom bit back a dozen questions and stepped under the spray, wincing as the hot water hit his face.

"Jo didn't know to book a room here, so I walked her back to her hotel," Luke said. "It was just a few blocks."

"And you stopped for a drink." Tom kicked himself for commenting.

"Well, sure, the night being young and all. I knew you weren't up for partying. We talked quite a while. She's a pretty cool gal, sailing like she did all the way to South Africa on a boat no bigger than a gooseneck trailer."

"Sounds like you guys hit it off," Tom said. "Maybe she should write you up instead of me."

Luke laughed. "That's what I told her, but she said she profiles athletes, competitors, not poor working stiffs like me. I sweet-talked the desk clerk downstairs into finding her a room here for the rest of the weekend. She wants to write about bull riders, she should be smack in the middle of the action. She wanted to check to see if you were okay. I told her you wouldn't be fit company tonight but you'd have breakfast with her downstairs around nine. You'll have time before that truck dealership meet-and-greet tomorrow at eleven."

"I don't recall hiring you as my social secretary," Tom said, "but since you're being so helpful, rustle me another bucket of ice for my nose."

"Will do, and I brought your sunglasses up from the truck. Maybe you can go with the celebrity look tomorrow instead of short end in a bar fight."

Tom grinned and then grimaced—even smiling hurt. Luke could wear on him sometimes, but they always counted on each other, in or out of the arena.

TOM LOOKED INTO the mirror the next morning and swore—two black eyes with major swelling across the bridge of his nose; his upper lip had puffed up overnight like a sausage.

He sighed and dug in his weekend bag for a tube of Dermablend. Getting banged up was part of the job, but he'd try his best not to scare the little kids who were bound to show up at this morning's meet-and-greet. He shaved and then smoothed the concealer over the bruises, wincing when he touched his nose. Broken again—one of these days he'd get it fixed, after he quit riding for good. Of course, it might get busted again if his horse went squirrely on him chasing a calf, but that was the risk of cowboying, like the barbwire catching his cheek.

The phone rang; Luke answered. "Hey, Jo," he said. "Yeah, he's almost ready—just putting on his makeup." He yelped and dropped the phone as Tom whacked him with a towel.

CHAPTER FIVE

"I THOUGHT LUKE was joking," Jo said, trying to keep dismay out of her voice. Bruises around Tom's eyes extended beyond the edges of his Ray-Bans and showed like muddy stains through the concealer. "You really were putting on makeup."

He gave her a wry grin and pulled his hat brim lower. "Too bad my sister isn't here—she'd have done a better job on my face. She's studying acting in college. I mean theater arts."

Jo dragged her eyes away from the damage. "Congratulations—I know you won the round last night, but what happened with your reride? I didn't have a good view from my seat, just the medics going out again."

"Heck, they run out like that every time somebody stubs a toe," he said. "Widow-maker likes to sling his head. He gave me a little tap with one of those big horns on my way down—just bad luck it started my nose bleeding again."

She bought time by sipping the coffee the

waitress had already poured. Her job was observing and reporting on athletes' careers, not passing judgment on the wisdom of their decisions. She framed her next question with care. "Would a helmet have helped?"

"It might have, but one of the worst wrecks I ever saw, the rider was wearing a helmet and he came close to dying from a concussion that would have killed most people. I rode with one for a while, but it messed with my peripheral vision and screwed up my balance on the get-off. The younger riders have to wear them, but old-timers like me still get to choose."

He picked up the menu. "You ready for breakfast?"

"Is Luke joining us?"

"Naw, he's out running—keeps him one jump ahead of the bulls, he says. Then he's doing a workshop for high school kids who think they want to be bullfighters."

They both chose the breakfast buffet. Jo picked up fruit and a biscuit with honey, trying not to stare at Tom's heaping plate: scrambled eggs, bacon, home-fried potatoes, biscuits with sausage gravy…

He caught her glance and grinned. "I'm catching up. I don't eat much before I ride, and

I didn't want much by the time Doc cut me loose last night."

"So you saw a doctor?"

He laughed. "Not just any doctor, our doctor. Doc Barnett travels with the tour. He's a trauma specialist and orthopedic surgeon. He wouldn't let me leave Sports Medicine last night till my nose stopped bleeding, and I'll have to take a concussion test before he clears me for the next go-round."

"Do you really have to ride tonight? Couldn't you—"

He laid down his fork and took off his sunglasses. "Look at me," he said. "Welcome to professional bull riding. Now that you're staying at this hotel, you're going to see guys younger than me hobbling around like old men."

She looked away from his battered face, hot with shame at her rookie blunder. "I'm sorry I questioned your decision. It just seems foolish—"

He frowned. "I appreciate your concern, but this arrangement isn't going to work if I have to debate you every time I get beat up a little. You wanted to dig into this sport—this is what it looks like. We're all freelance competitors. We don't have team contracts with guaranteed salaries. If we don't ride, we don't earn any money. We'll sit out a round or an event if Doc Barnett tells us to—he has veto power if he thinks riding is too big a risk. Otherwise we suck up the pain and get on our bulls."

He replaced his glasses and sopped up the last smear of gravy with a fragment of biscuit. "I have a meet-and-greet for a sponsor in about an hour." He grimaced. "If they're not afraid I'll scare the little kids."

She laid her napkin on the table. "I can improve on your makeup if you like."

"Lady, I'll take all the help I can get." Tom scribbled his room number on the check and led the way through the lobby, stopping several times to pose with fans and sign cowboy hats and T-shirts. If being waylaid irritated him, he hid it well, asking where they hailed from and if the kids planned to be bull riders. "See you all this evening," he said with a final wave as he and Jo stepped into the elevator.

He fished for his room key outside his door. "Let me make sure Luke's not in the shower."

No Luke—the room stood empty and disordered. "Go clean that stuff off your face," Jo said. She opened the drapes and pulled a chair close to the window. "Then sit here."

Tom emerged from the bathroom carrying the tube of Dermablend and sat. Jo flinched on seeing the full extent of the damage but this time made no comment. She tipped his head back.

"Close your eyes," she said and tapped dots of the concealer over the bruises, blending them together with a tiny sponge she took from her purse.

She stood back and surveyed her work. "Go look in the mirror." She followed him into the bathroom.

"Whoa! Not near so scary," he said, peering at his image. He touched his swollen upper lip. "Nothing you can do with this, I guess."

"I don't think so. Besides, it gives you kind of an Elvis vibe."

"Thank you, thank you very much," he said in a credible imitation of the King.

She giggled, surprised by his whimsy.

Luke appeared behind them, wiping sweat from his face with a red headband. "Am I interrupting something?"

"Just consulting with my..." Tom looked to Jo. "What's that fancy word?"

"Esthetician?" She turned to Luke. "How does he look?"

"Pretty close to human. You better hustle," he said to Tom. "The van's here. Take Jo with you. It'll be part of her education—she'll get a good look at the fan base."

THREE HOURS LATER Jo wished she'd eaten a breakfast like Tom's. He and two other cowboys sponsored by Bass Pro Shops sat at a table signing shirts, hats and programs, and other memorabilia. Many fans also wanted a photo with their favorite rider, which frequently involved hunkering down with small cowboys and cowgirls. Jo made herself useful by fetching fresh Sharpies as they ran dry and keeping bottles of water at the riders' elbows.

In between, she chatted with the fans lined up to the door, hearing about how Grandpa rode bulls in his youth and how four-year-old Jason, wearing miniature chaps and vest, watched every televised event seated on his toy rocking bull.

When the store manager finally announced it was time for the riders to leave, Tom and the other cowboys made their way along the line of fans still waiting, giving everyone a chance for a quick photo or autograph.

Tom sank into his seat in the van and turned toward Jo. "How's my war paint holding up?"

"Still looking good," she said.

"How'd you rate your own makeup artist?" Len Haley asked.

Tom had introduced her to the other riders,

but apparently they assumed she was part of the support team.

"Jo's not staff," Tom said. "She got interested in bull riding at the Madison Square Garden event so I invited her for this weekend. She took pity on me when she got a look my face this morning."

Okay, he wasn't advertising their exact arrangement; she would play it his way.

The van dropped them back at the hotel and the other riders excused themselves with a touch to their hat brims. Jo stood in the lobby with Tom, trying not to drool at the aromas of food wafting from the dining room. Her stomach grumbled.

Tom laughed. "Sounds like I need to feed you. Now you see why I stocked up earlier—a cowboy never knows when he'll have time for his next meal."

"I'll remember that," Jo said. She followed him to the hotel dining room and halted in dismay. Although it was nearly two o'clock, every table was filled.

"We should be able to seat you in a few minutes," the hostess said. "If you care to wait—"

"Tom!" Len Haley waved from a booth near the buffet. "Come sit with us. I called ahead for Sophie to get us a table."

"Thanks, don't mind if we do." Tom ushered Jo into the booth and slid in beside her.

The young woman with Orphan Annie curls reached a slender hand across the table to Jo; her thumbnail sported a dramatic bruise. "Hi, I'm Sophie, Len's top hand when he's on crutches."

Jo pegged Sophie's accent as one of New York's outlying boroughs, or maybe North Jersey. She introduced herself. "Sounds like you're a long way from home," she said.

Sophie laughed. "You've got that right—I'm a Hackensack cowgirl. I visit my folks when the tour hits the East Coast and then hightail it back to Texas where I should have been born in the first place."

Len grabbed her hand. "See this? She can stick this little paw into a mama cow and turn a stuck calf like a real pro." He kissed the blackened thumbnail. "But the squeeze chute still bites her sometimes."

Sophie punched his arm. "You're so romantic."

Jo was already learning that the world of professional bull riding held many stories beyond a single athlete's profile. "How did you come to marry a bull rider?" she asked.

Sophie giggled. "What do you think? I was a

buckle bunny. We met three years ago in New York at an after-party."

"First time I saw her twitch that cute little bunny tail, I was a goner," Len said. "It took us a few more stops on the tour to make it official, but I knew right off I caught me a good 'un."

A waitress appeared to take their orders; they all stuck to the buffet. Sophie and Jo made their selections and returned to their seats while the men were still loading their plates.

"So how did you meet Tom?" Sophie asked. "He doesn't party much."

Jo opted for a nonspecific version of the truth. "Tom was kind enough to answer some questions about bull riding after the Madison Square Garden event. He said I was welcome to come this weekend if I wanted to learn more."

Len set his heaping plate on the table. "Okay, you gals can stop gossiping about us now." He forked an extra shrimp onto his wife's plate. "What's on your schedule for this afternoon?"

"Betsy Wolf is babysitting all the kids so a bunch of us can go shopping. Sheplers is having a big sale."

He groaned. "Sheplers is always having a sale."

"Speaking of sales, is there somewhere nearby I could buy a pair of boots?" Jo asked.

She stuck a foot out to display her plain russet ankle boots. "These are fine for New York, but they don't fit in here very well."

"Come with us," Sophie said. "Unless you have other plans."

"You should go," Len said. "The gals can tell you a lot about bull riding. Some of it might even be true."

"Oh, you!" Sophie slapped his arm. "Save it for the bulls tonight."

They finished lunch and Sophie told Jo to meet her and the other wives in the lobby. "We'll pile into Lou-Ann's SUV and hit Sheplers like a swarm of locusts."

"Guess I better make a money ride this evening to pay for your loot," Len said. "At least I'll enjoy a nice quiet afternoon without your yammering." He countered his statement by planting a loud kiss on her cheek before they headed to their room for Sophie to grab her coat.

"What about you?" Jo asked Tom as they waited in the lobby.

"I didn't sleep real well last night—it was kind of hard to breathe through my nose—so I'm going to laze around this afternoon."

"Will I see you for dinner?"

He hesitated. "I don't eat a full meal before

I ride, just some protein snacks. You could graze your way around the concourse before the event—soak up the atmosphere, watch the fans. Paula will take you to your seat again."

"So, tell me," she said. "Do you enjoy the fan stuff?"

"Mostly I do. Sure, there's times when I just want to sneak past and crawl up to my room without being bothered, but except for the fans, we'd be home chasing cows or maybe wild-catting on an oil rig. Once you get west of the Mississippi, a trip to a bull riding event is a real big deal for kids and their folks too. They might live out in the middle of nowhere, so a chance to meet their favorite rider means a lot to them." He hesitated. "Like I'll never forget how nice your dad was to Luke and me."

CHAPTER SIX

THE ELEVATOR DOORS opened before Jo could respond and Sophie swept into the lobby trailed by two blondes, a brunette and another redhead. She grabbed Jo's arm and towed her along. "All right, let's shop! Don't worry," she said over her shoulder to Tom. "We'll bring her back safe."

Sophie introduced Jo as "Tom's friend from New York" as they rode another elevator down to the parking garage. The blondes were Susie and Barbara, Mara was the brunette, and auburn-haired Lou-Ann owned the Dodge Caravan with Oklahoma plates. Last names had come at Jo too fast to remember.

The women chattered about babies' teething, 4-H projects and weather conditions on the northern Great Plains. "Snow up to your you-know-what," Susie (or Barbara) said. "Being in OKC for the weekend is like a summer vacation."

"Unless a blue norther blows in from the

Panhandle," Lou-Ann said as she whipped around an EMBARK bus. "Then you'll wish you were back in Montana." She pulled up with a flourish in front of the sprawling building whose sign proclaimed Sheplers—Western Stores since 1899. "Everybody out," she said, "and shop till you drop."

"Stick with me," Sophie said to Jo. "I need to buy boots too."

Having Sophie as a guide, someone intimately involved with the world of bull riding but with an outsider's view like her own, suited Jo. She led the conversation by being a good listener as they browsed the racks of boots ranging from plain workaday footwear to styles embellished with fancy stitching and metallic finishes.

Sophie pulled out a pair with brown lowers and intricately embroidered ruby-red uppers. "These look like me. I've beat up my old ones till they're not fit for polite company." She stuck out a battered boot for Jo to inspect. "I'll retire these for work around the ranch and get a new pair for dress. Have you seen any you like?"

"I don't know where to start—too many choices."

"What will you be using them for?"

Jo hesitated. Some of the less ornate styles

would work in Manhattan, but she wanted a
pair more like Sophie's, for future bull riding events if Tom decided to keep her around.
"Mainly walking around arenas at bull riding
events," she said. She picked up a sister pair
to Sophie's but with turquoise uppers. "How
about these?"

"Perfect—Justins are good Texas-made
boots but not too high-end. Once those get too
disgusting, you can buy a fancier pair for dress.
Believe me, once you start wearing cowboy
boots you'll throw away all your other shoes."
She looked sideways at Jo. "So you plan to be
around awhile?"

Jo ducked the question. "We'll see how it goes."

Sophie nodded. "Best way to play it. As
long as you're buying boots, maybe you should
get some real jeans." She looked with pity at
Jo's skinny leggings. "You've got the figure
for those, but they're so buckle bunny." She
grinned. "I should know."

Sophie left Jo trying on jeans while she bought
shirts for her husband. Forty-five minutes later
Jo carried her purchases into the ladies' restroom to change, excited as a child about her new
look, almost a new identity. Besides the boots
and jeans, she had bought a tooled leather belt
with a modest silver buckle and a pearl-snap

plaid shirt in soft autumn shades of rust and smoke-blue. She was zipping her new Wranglers when she heard the restroom door open and two women enter.

"So what do you think of Tom's new girl-friend?" Jo recognized Sophie's voice. "Quite a change from the last one—Traci something."

"That must have been before Bobby came up to the tour—I've never seen Tom with a girl." *Lou-Ann*, Jo thought.

"Maybe two years ago, I guess—not long after Len and I got married," Sophie said. "She hung all over Tom, and she treated the rest of us like a bunch of dumb hicks. What a joke—I know what big-city looks like, and she wasn't it. I felt bad for Tom when she left, but I can't say we were sorry to see her go."

"They had a big fight?"

"Not a clue," Sophie said. "One day she was flashing a diamond and the next—poof, she was gone. Even Luke didn't know what happened—I asked him."

"Are you sure Jo is Tom's girlfriend?"

"I'm not real sure—she said she wanted to learn more about bull riding. Maybe she's working on some kind of research. I guess we'll find out soon enough."

Jo waited until she heard two stall doors

close and then made her escape. She would have to come to some understanding with Tom about her status. She hadn't faced this problem while researching her earlier features when everyone had known about her goal and focus. Bull riding was more like an extended family, close and gossipy.

Still, she had gained some insight into Tom's personal history by her inadvertent eavesdropping. She filed the information under "interesting but probably not relevant."

"I almost didn't recognize you," Sophie said when Jo joined the others still waiting to pay for their purchases. "The colors in that shirt are perfect for you. Are your eyes blue or gray?"

"Yes," Jo said, and the others laughed.

"You need some turquoise to dress it up," Mara said. "You can pick up some nice pieces in Albuquerque. If you think you'll be at that event."

"She hasn't planned that far ahead," Sophie said, taking Jo's arm. "Bull riding takes getting used to, right?"

They piled back into Lou-Ann's vehicle with their shopping bags. Jo's cell phone rang just as they reached the hotel; she recognized Tom's area code but a different number.

"You about done with the hen party, Jo?"

Luke asked when she answered. "Meet me by the desk and we'll go fetch your gear from the other hotel."

Luke did a comic double take when Jo walked into the lobby. "Excuse me, sugar," he said, tipping his hat. "I'm supposed to meet a gal from the big city." He peeked into her Sheplers bag. "You got her hid in there?"

Jo did a runway turn for him. "Did I get it right? I had lots of advice from a panel of experts."

"Well, I guess! I might just take you home and teach you to mend fence and pull calves. Judging from your article on horse racing, you're already a heck of a rider."

Luke drove Jo to the hotel where she retrieved her bag from the luggage room. She checked in at the Marriott while Luke signed autographs in the lobby. Apparently the bullfighters had their own contingent of fans; Luke's were mostly young, female and wearing tight jeans, the buckle-bunny look Sophie had scorned.

"Want to grab an early supper with me before the show starts?" Luke asked as he carried her bag to her room. "Tom means to meet you for the after-party—as much as he plans anything before he rides—but he'll be getting into game mode right now."

Jo ran a comb through her hair and collected her purse. "How does he prep for his rides?"

"He does this kung fu routine—hides out behind the bulls' pens and kicks the air for maybe half an hour. Some of the guys were calling him Mr. Miyagi, but they stopped laughing when he started riding rings around them. A bull fell with him a few years ago and busted him up pretty bad—the hardware in his left hip drives airport security nuts. A physical therapist taught him tai chi to get his balance back, and he went on from there into martial arts."

A great detail for her profile if Tom didn't mind her using it. "Is he self-conscious about it?" she asked.

"If he is, you'll never know it—he never lets on about anything. He could be dying and wouldn't give a hint till he keeled over. Me, now, I take all the sympathy I can get." He grinned. "Girls love a wounded hero—a few scrapes and bruises attract chicks better than a cute puppy on a string."

Jo had to laugh. She doubted any woman would hold Luke's interest long, but he'd show her a great time while it lasted. She wondered if Tom viewed women with the same cheerful hedonism. Somehow she doubted he did, guessing his emotions ran deeper and with a stronger current.

"Tom suggested I cruise the concourse for supper and check out the fan action at the same time."

"I'll get you back in time to see the sights, but I'll feed you better than that. You like a good steak?"

"What's not to like?" she said, following him to the elevators.

AFTER A TEN-MINUTE DRIVE, Luke parked his Explorer in front of a nondescript building with a red neon sign identifying it as the Cattlemen's Steakhouse. A blonde hostess in tight black slacks and a ruffled tuxedo shirt led them to a booth under an Old West mural.

"I saved your favorite table, Luke," she said, leaning close to position his napkin and water glass more precisely.

"I figured you would, Debbie." He circled her waist in a brief hug. "This is Jo Dace from New York City, here to learn about bull riding."

"This cowboy knows the sport inside and out, honey," Debbie said. She turned back to Luke. "Will you be at the after-party? I can get off early."

"I'll be there—come along and take a number," Luke said with a grin.

"Oh, you!" She smacked him lightly with the big leather-bound menu. "Enjoy your steaks."

A waitress set salads on the table; Luke smothered his with blue-cheese dressing and speared a tomato with his fork. "You must get paid pretty fancy for your writing if you can afford to live in New York City," he said.

"I couldn't swing it on my features alone," she said. "I also write copy for an ad agency in Manhattan, and I edit other writers' manuscripts to prep them for publication. Plus I work part-time for my mom. She's a stager for real-estate agents. She pretties up homes before they go on the market so they'll sell faster." She flexed her arm to make a muscle. "Painting and scrubbing and lugging furniture around keeps me lean and mean."

"Got a roommate? Boyfriend?"

Jo laughed. Maybe she should find Luke's questions invasive, but he was so open with his nosiness she couldn't take offense.

"I live with my mom, sort of. She sold the family farm to my uncle after my grandfather died and bought a hundred-year-old fixer-upper in Brooklyn. I helped her rehab it—we're both pretty handy. She has an apartment plus an office on the ground floor and I have my own living quarters upstairs."

"Sounds like a good deal—I still live with my folks. I guess I could build somewhere else on the ranch if I ever get married, but that won't happen till I can find somebody who cooks as good as my stepmom." He smacked his lips. "Cajun-style—Shelby's from Louisiana."

"The arrangement with my mom has worked so far," Jo said. "I don't throw loud parties and she doesn't go through my underwear drawer. Plus she takes care of my cat when I'm on the road."

They dug into their steaks; Jo sat back at last with a groan. "I won't eat for a week," she said.

Luke chuckled. "I thought you were going lick the plate after you finished your pie."

"Please! I won't be able to zip my new jeans if I keep eating like this. But everything was delicious. The best steak I ever tasted."

"We keep the good stuff for ourselves west of the Mississippi—you should taste the beef my dad slaughters and ages himself." He snapped his fingers. "Hey, that's a great idea. Come visit the ranch. You can see what a first-class grazing operation looks like."

Luke's enthusiasm was contagious, but Jo held up a hand. "I'm not sure if Tom would be thrilled about my following him home. I don't know yet if this project is even a go."

His face fell. "Well, dang! Seems like you'd fit right in—I just figured…"

Jo looked at her watch. "You probably need to get back, and I want to get some writing done before I go over to the arena."

"Yeah, you're right." The grin resurfaced. "I'll blow you a kiss from the dirt."

CHAPTER SEVEN

"WHERE IS SHE?" Tom stuck his phone back in his gear bag. Paula, the staffer, had already called twice wondering if Jo planned to sit above the chutes again tonight.

"Can't tell you," Luke said. "I dropped her off at the hotel maybe two hours ago. She said she needed to work on her writing." He strapped on his protective vest and covered it with his electric-blue jersey. "She knows how to tell time—she'll turn up before the show."

Tom's phone rang.

"All's well," Paula said. "She was up on the concourse talking to fans and lost track of the time. Good luck tonight."

Tom muttered a curse and keyed off. His dad had warned him taking on this project might be a distraction, but he hadn't known he'd have to keep track of Jo like a strayed calf. Be-damn if he'd let her break his concentration. As winner of last night's round, he would ride late in this evening's competition—he still had plenty of time to loosen up after the opening ceremonies.

He put Jo Dace out of his mind, almost, but he couldn't help flicking a glance up toward her seat next to the broadcast booth when it was his turn to ride. She hadn't seen him climb up to the walkway, so he took a moment to study her as she leaned over the railing, her face alive with interest. From her articles and in the short time he'd known her, he had come to admire her intensity; she approached her work the same way he went at bull riding—flat out, with nothing held back.

She turned toward him as if she felt his gaze and gave him a thumbs-up for luck.

He saluted her with a touch to his hat brim and climbed down to straddle Bovinator, a bull with the ugly trick of flinging his head up as soon as his front feet hit the ground. Tom had ridden him a couple of years ago when he'd still been using a helmet with its face mask, but his hat wouldn't be much protection if the bull decided to pull that stunt tonight. He put the thought away from him; fear led to disaster.

He nodded for the gate just as he heard Luke say, "Be ready to move in, guys."

The next seconds were a blur, a balancing act between staying centered on the bull's back and avoiding the massive head that slammed toward his face like a wrecking ball. He didn't even hear the buzzer and loosened his hand only when Luke yelled at him to let go. Bovinator flung his head up one last time, actually brushing his cheek with a long ear as Tom dove to one side. The dirt came up hard; Luke leaped over Tom's body and smacked the bull on the nose to lure it in the other direction.

The crowd's roar almost drowned out the announcer's voice as Tom climbed to his feet, dragging air into his lungs.

"How's that for a 90-point ride, folks?"

LUKE CUFFED TOM'S shoulder as they passed in the locker room shower. "Good ride, little bro—you got something to celebrate at the after-party. You do remember you promised to meet Jo there, right?"

"I guess." Tom skipped the noisy bar scene more often than not. "I don't suppose you—"

"Not me, buddy—I stood in for you last night, and I'm already triple booked if Debbie from Cattlemen's Steakhouse shows up."

Tom knew Luke's refusal was only fair—his project, his responsibility. His mom had been raised in Georgia and had drummed gentlemanly behavior into him and Luke. He sighed and pulled on a fresh blue-and-red plaid shirt and jeans not decorated with bull slobber and arena dirt.

He didn't immediately spot Jo seated just outside the hotel's cocktail lounge; in her new boots and jeans and pearl-snapped shirt, she could have been a ranch girl from back home. She looked up with a quick smile and slipped her phone into her shoulder bag.

"Still a fan of bull riding?" he asked as she rose to meet him.

"Oh yes! I was just texting my mom about it. But I have so many questions. Why do some of the bulls have horns and others don't? What breeds are they? How many countries do the riders come from? Why do you wear spurs? How many—"

"Whoa, that's way more than we can cover right here. Let's hit the party. I'll sign a few autographs and then we'll find someplace quiet where we can talk."

Tom escorted Jo into the lounge and spotted a dozen or so other riders inside, all surrounded by fans. Luke stood by the bar with a beer in one hand and his arm around a curvy brunette. A woman in jeans and a fringed vest scurried forward, her smartphone at the ready, and Jo stepped aside while Tom signed her program and then posed with her for a photo.

He hung in for nearly an hour until the crowding and chatter and loud country music became unbearable. To escape, he pulled out his phone like he'd received a call, holding it to his ear as he headed for the elevators. He crowded in with his hat brim tipped down and punched the button for the eighth floor. When he reached his room he dropped his hat on the bed and rubbed his face with both hands.

"God, I'm tired," he said.

"Should I leave?"

He spun on his heel, nearly stumbling as his boot heel caught the bedspread.

Jo stood just inside the door. "You mentioned finding someplace quiet, but if this isn't a good time…"

"Dang, I'm sorry!" Intent on his getaway, he'd completely forgotten about her. "I sure didn't mean to run out on you. These three-day events get kind of intense—sometimes I just head for the high country. We can talk now. We'll raid the minibar and you can ask your questions."

They took two Bud Lights from the little fridge and settled at the round table by the window.

"You've got a great view of the city," she said.

He glanced at the lights below and shrugged. "I guess, but the sun setting over Mesa Verde would look a lot better to me. I like seeing different places, but my favorite view of bright lights is in my rearview mirror."

"I'm just the opposite. I love the city—the energy, the variety... I could live there the rest of my life and never be bored."

"*Bored* isn't a word you'll ever hear on a ranch—there's always more work than time." He took a swig of his beer. "What did you want to ask me?"

"Stuff I can probably Google for myself. Tell me about your ranch."

He leaned back in his chair and stretched his legs. He never minded talking about Cameron's Pride. "Our family has held the land since 1867 when Jacob Cameron came west after the Civil War. Carpetbaggers cheated him out of his holdings in Virginia so he named his new spread Cameron's Pride after his plantation back East. He was headed for California, but a grizzly spooked his horse and dang near scalped him—he would have died right there except some Ute girls found him and dragged him back to their camp."

He laughed. "He kept his hair—their medicine woman sewed his scalp back on. By the time he was healed up, he'd fallen in love with one of the girls who found him. They rode down to Taos in the dead of winter and got the priest there to marry them so there'd be no question of their sons' right to the land. We've been in the same spot ever since." If he closed his eyes, he could almost see the log house snug under the cottonwoods with wood smoke rising from the chimney and light streaming from the kitchen windows into the winter night.

"So you're part Ute?"

"Way back," he said, "but it's complicated—I can never keep the connections straight. Old Jacob and his wife had three sons. One died young, one married a schoolmarm come West from Kentucky and one married back into the tribe. They also had sons but none of those boys married Ute girls so the bloodline got diluted with more Scotch-Irish and some French—my great-grandfather served in France in World War I and came back with a war bride. Funny thing, one Cameron in every generation shows up with red hair and blue eyes like the first Jacob. My dad's hair was red till it turned gray early, and my sister got it this go-round."

"My mom's family has a couple branches like that," Jo said. "My great-uncle married a Japanese woman and his son brought back a Vietnamese bride. My grandfather thought it was a great idea. He raised prize sheep—he always said bringing in new blood improved the flock."

Tom laughed. "Something like that. Our ranch backs up to Ute land, so Luke and I grew up hunting and fishing and scrapping with our Ute cousins just like Dad did and his dad and his dad. Jacob's sons stocked the ranch with stray cattle they drove north from the old Spanish land grants in New Mexico—rustled them, more like it. Now we run Red Angus cow and calf pairs and my stepmother raises ranch horses."

"Are ranch horses a special breed?"

"Just whatever cross produces smart, tough horses good for working cattle," he said. "Shelby has been breeding quarter horse mares to her mustang stallion and getting some top-notch cutting and rein horses. She's got this two-year-old bay filly in training right now who's going to burn up the arena in reining competition."

He pulled out his cell phone. "Okay if I make a quick call home? My folks can watch some events live, but the satellite reception is iffy."

"I remember—you let them know you and Luke are okay. Please, go ahead."

He hit Send and waited, then said, "Hey, Shelby, did you guys…" He laughed. "Me too—I was ducking and weaving for all I was worth. That bull's mama goes back to Bodacious—I think she passed along all his tricks."

He listened for a moment, frowning. "How much do you expect?" More listening while he rubbed the bridge of his nose and jerked his hand away. "Just don't let Dad..."

He smiled. "I know you will." He glanced at Jo. "Yeah, she's here—she's getting a triple dose of bull riding this weekend. You guys take care. We'll be home by Monday morning."

"Everything all right?" Jo asked.

He sighed. "I guess. They're expecting some snow, and that always worries me when we're this far from home. My dad had a heart attack last spring during a blizzard—he was just forty-six."

Tom still had trouble believing it had happened. Except for the dark time between their mother's death and Shelby's arrival, Jake had always been the rock they all looked to for shelter.

"There'd been a couple days of rain, and then the wind swung around out of the north," he said. "The western slope of the Rockies got hit with three feet of wet snow right at the beginning of calving season. Dad was out gathering all the heifers into the home pasture where he could get feed to them. My stepmother was pitching down hay for the horses when Dad's horse came in without him—luckily there was already enough snow on the ground she could track back to where he fell. She got him to the hospital in time, but the storm wiped out half our herd in one weekend, all bred heifers and new calves. At least we didn't lose any horses—they sheltered in a big shed attached to the barn. Some folks had stock freeze to death right in the corral."

"How terrifying for your stepmother, dealing with that all alone."

He gave a wry chuckle. "You don't know Shelby—not much she can't handle. When my dad met her, she was hitchhiking because she told the guy who gave her a ride she'd rather walk than sleep with him. She jumped ship in the middle of nowhere with snow coming on. She says this won't be much of a storm, just six inches or so."

He'd been able to replace some of the dead cattle with last year's winnings, but Cameron's Pride was still drowning in red ink from the blizzard losses, plus Jake's medical bills. After much soul-searching, Tom had concluded that lightening the financial pressure with his prize money would help his dad more than if he worked at the ranch full-time.

"You and Luke were on the road when it happened?" Jo said. "You must have been frantic to get home."

He nodded. They'd watched Weather Channel coverage of the storm from inside an airport nearly two thousand miles away, unable to get a flight even as far as Albuquerque.

"When we finally got to Durango, we checked on Dad at the hospital and then headed out to the ranch. The ice and drifts were so bad we had to go in by snowmobile the last ten miles. And then we started looking for our cattle."

Bitterness rose in his throat at the memory of finding the cows, most of them raised at Cameron's Pride, dead with their calves lifeless inside them or frozen at their sides. They'd had to burn the carcasses, and the stench of scorched hair and roasting meat had hung in the valley for days.

"Is your dad doing okay now?"

He turned to her with a start; he'd been living so deeply in the past, he'd almost forgotten her presence.

"So the doctors say. You'd never know he almost died, but Shelby still rides pretty close herd on him." Yet another reason to bless her presence in the family.

He yawned, almost cracking his jaws, and flushed. "Dang, I'm sorry," he said a second time. "I guess my battery's running low."

A lot of unmarried riders partied after the event, blowing off adrenaline with booze and the ever-willing girls who swarmed around the cowboys. He didn't care much for drinking—the loss of control scared him—and he'd never again settle for sweaty sheets and girls whose names and faces ran together in a blur. Usually he walked for a couple hours to step down from the high of riding; tonight talking with Jo about home had drained away the tension. Too bad Traci had never been interested in hearing about the ranch.

Jo smiled. "Sounds like a cue to call it a night. What's the schedule tomorrow?"

"The event starts at one," he said. "I'll be downstairs for breakfast around nine if you'd like to join me."

"Why don't you stop by my room first? I can help with the concealer again." She stood just as the door opened.

Luke stopped short. "Hey, I can come back later…"

"Jo's just leaving," Tom said. "I've been boring her with Cameron family history."

"Far from it," she said. "I could listen all night."

"And he could yammer on about the family legends till you want to stuff a sock in his mouth," Luke said. "Best take it in installments."

"Thanks for listening," Tom said, although she'd probably considered it just part of her work.

"Anytime," she said with a smile, gathering her purse and the day sheet from the evening's competition. "I'd love to hear more about your family and the ranch."

For a moment, he pictured her at Cameron's Pride and then banished the image. He was a job to Jo Dace, nothing more—they'd have no problem as long as he kept that in mind.

CHAPTER EIGHT

JO OPENED THE door to Tom's light knock and did a quick survey of his face. The swelling had subsided but the bruises around his eyes still gave him the look of a raccoon's mask. She waved him to a chair by the window and opened the tube he handed her.

"Did you have a better night?" she asked. "You look rested."

"I slept like a baby with a clear conscience." He set his hat brim up on the table and closed his eyes.

She studied his face, the tiny lines at the corners of his eyes, the firm set of his mouth, the scar running down one cheek—innocence and maturity oddly blended in his unguarded expression.

"So you're a hardcore city girl," he said as she dotted the Dermablend over the bruises. "Where did you learn to ride enough to gallop a race horse at Churchill Downs?"

"I didn't grow up in New York City," she

said. "My mom and I moved to my grandfather's farm in upstate New York after my father died." The old ache stirred but without the usual stabbing pain. "My grandfather took in retired police horses and my cousins and I rode them, mostly bareback."

She feathered the tinted cream around his eyes, smoothing the makeup with the sponge. "Now you can face the world."

They walked together to the hotel dining room. Riders, some with their wives and small children, occupied many of the tables. Sophie Haley waved for Tom and Jo to join them.

Sophie inspected Tom's face. "Either you're a fast healer or Jo's a wizard with makeup," she said. "Len looks like he's been beat up for days after he takes a hit like you did."

Tom grinned. "I'm thinking about signing her to a contract."

"Or you could wear a helmet," Len said.

"Now you sound like Doc," Tom said.

Jo kept her gaze resolutely on her plate.

The conversation turned to anecdotes about bulls and riders, some humorous, others grim. Jo tried to absorb it all for the copious notes she would write that evening on her flight back to New York.

"We saw you above the chutes last night,"

Sophie said. "Why don't you sit with us this afternoon? There's a free seat in our section—Lou-Ann had to leave early. Someone left a gate open at their ranch and now they've got bred heifers spread across half of Custer County."

Jo looked at Tom. "I've really enjoyed watching from the chute seat, but…"

"Sit with the wives," he said. "You'll get a different view of the action and pick up a lot of good background for your writing."

Sophie punched her husband's arm. "I told you she was a writer." She turned to Jo. "I'll bet you're working on a novel. Will you put me in it?"

Her husband ruffled her red curls. "Of course she will—you're a sure-enough character."

"Not a novel," Jo said with a laugh. "I don't have that kind of imagination. I'd planned to do a magazine feature, but the short format couldn't do bull riding justice." She looked at Tom and took the plunge. "I'd like to do a book, as well, if I don't wear Tom out with my questions."

Tom smiled. "I reckon I can put up with you for a while anyway." He signed for their meal. "For helping with the makeup and letting me bend your ear last night."

He stood and beckoned. "There's someone I want you to meet before the event starts."

She followed him to a rear entrance of the arena and into the maze of pens and alleys holding the bulls for the afternoon's competition. He stopped beside an enclosure in which a massive cream-colored bull stood half-asleep.

"That's the bull that bucked you off in New York, isn't it?" Jo asked.

"Good eye, city girl. Yep, this is Gunslinger. He's one of the great ones—he's been on the tour for three years and never been rode. I plan to be the first." He reached through the bars. "Get over here, you big baby, and let the lady pet you."

Gunslinger snorted and stuck his nose between the metal rails.

Jo put a tentative hand on the huge head and then scratched behind an ear. The bull closed his eyes and rocked on his feet.

"He'd purr if he could. Want to ride him?" Tom asked with a straight face.

"You're joking, right? Do I look crazy?"

"Safe as sitting on a pet pony. Safer—ponies are tricky little rascals. He'll stand just like this until he feels the bull rope tighten up."

"Will you try to ride him again today?"

"If I get to choose first after the long round.

I'll keep picking him till we get it right." He gave the bull a final scratch. "Later, buddy."

"I've heard jockeys talk like this about special horses," she said, "but they're a team trying to win together. The bulls try to keep you from winning."

"Well, yeah—but a good bull makes the rider look good, and there's no feeling in the world like making the buzzer on one like this. To tell the truth, I'd ride for free, with no one watching. When everything's flowing, it's the best eight seconds of your life." He glanced at her from under his hat brim. "You going to put that in your article?"

"I'd like to. Would you mind?"

He shrugged. "I guess not." He checked his watch. "It'll start getting busy back here so I'm kicking you out. But we'll see you before we head back to Colorado." He walked her to the exit and then turned back into the maw of the building.

Jo FOLLOWED SOPHIE down the steep steps to the fifth row near the chutes and took the seat between her and Mara. Susie and Barbara waved to her while other women one row below turned to look with curiosity. Jo guessed Sophie had already spread the word she was gathering material for a book.

"These are better seats than front row," Sophie said. "You can see over the rail and you're not as likely to get dirt kicked in your face."

"OKC is one of the best events of the season," Susie said. "Oklahoma is real bull country—you're seeing all the best buckers here."

"Including Gunslinger," Mara said. "My husband is hoping to get on him today."

"Not my Len," Sophie said with a laugh. "He's too smart. He'll pick a bull he's got a better chance of riding—let someone else go for the glory."

"Luis can forget about Gunslinger, Mara," Susie said. "If Tom gets first pick, he'll grab him again. Right, Jo?"

Jo shrugged. Even if everyone knew she was here to research a writing project, the wives seemed to assume a more personal relationship between her and Tom Cameron.

The lights went down and the now-familiar ceremonies began. Jo was beginning to recognize individual cowboys as they paraded into the arena, especially those whose wives clapped and whistled. Len Haley was among the leading five riders introduced individually as was Mara's husband Luis Veira. Jo applauded and cheered when Tom appeared, still ranked first after the first two rounds, although Luis was close behind.

As the competition proceeded, Jo watched her companions as much as she did the riders, the tension on their faces before their husbands rode and then relief and disappointment or elation after the buzzer sounded. When Tom's turn came late in the round, she found her own hands sweating, her heart pounding as he climbed down into the chute and settled his mouth guard into place.

"We got any Tom Cameron fans here?" the announcer asked, and the crowd roared. "He's drawn Sidewinder—used to be a short-round bull and still has the stuff to deliver a 90-point ride. Tom makes the whistle, he'll get first pick in the championship round."

Sophie elbowed Mara. "There goes Luis's ride on Gunslinger."

"Unless Tom bucks off." Mara flushed as the other women hooted. "It could happen."

But it didn't. Jo was starting to appreciate the finer points of technique; Tom sat the bull with an easy swinging rhythm of his upper body while his free arm wove a pattern in the air like a Balinese dancer's. When the buzzer sounded, he loosened his hand and let the bull's final buck catapult him to land on his feet.

"Just one thing wrong with that, folks," the announcer said over the cheers. "Tom Cameron makes it look too dang easy. Kids, you want to ride bulls, watch a video of that ride."

Picking bulls for the championship round was an anticlimax; everyone knew Tom would choose Gunslinger.

"Luis will be disappointed," Mara said, "but I'm just as glad. Now he's got a real chance to make a money ride."

Although there had been no injuries during the long round, Luke and the other bullfighters had been busy with close calls. Now he trotted over to the fence and called Jo's name.

"We're heading out right after the event," he said, "but we'll drive you to the airport." He turned away without waiting for an answer.

"Looks like you've got the Cameron boys right in your pocket," Susie said. "You're breaking a lot of buckle bunnies' hearts."

"It's not like that," Jo said. "They're just helping me with research."

"Uh-huh," Barbara said. "Good luck with that, but they're both rope shy about women. Tom's awful picky, and Luke loves 'em all."

"You won't likely see many rides this round,"

the announcer said. "Best bulls in the country right here, folks. Here's Deke Harkens leading off on Wooly Bully."

As predicted, only one rider hung on for eight seconds. Len Haley managed to cling to the bull's side during the last heart-stopping seconds to earn wild applause from the crowd. "He won't get much of a score," the announcer said, "but he deserves a 90 for grit. Now we got one last ride—Tom Cameron on Gunslinger."

The crowd went berserk; this was what they'd come to see.

Gunslinger's stillness in the chute was more dramatic than the other bulls' plunging and bellowing. Watching the big overhead screen, Jo could see Tom yank his hat brim down and settle his mouth guard into place before he nodded.

The bull's explosion was cataclysmic, a rearing leap followed by a nearly vertical kick. Tom rocked forward and then back, in complete control. Five seconds, six... Gunslinger spun, changing direction in midair. Seven seconds... Jo was on her feet yelling along with the crowd.

And then the feint to the left. Tom hit the ground with an audible grunt and lay still for a moment. All action seemed to stop: the rider motionless in the dirt, Gunslinger's great bulk suspended above him, the bullfighters frozen in position to leap forward.

The bull's hind feet landed within inches of Tom's head. He rolled to one side and the bull-fighters darted in to lure Gunslinger in the opposite direction. Tom climbed to his feet and raised his hat to the fans and then to the bull trotting out of the arena.

"How's that for bull riding!" The announcer had to yell above the bedlam. "Seven point two seconds! Nobody's ever taken Gunslinger that far. Let's show Tom what we think of that ride."

Tom swung his hat again and disappeared through the exit gate.

Jo turned to Sophie. "So who won the event?"

"Len did, since Tom didn't make the whistle in the championship round." She jigged a few dance steps in the crowded space while Susie and Mara hugged her. "Dang, I could have bought more at Sheplers!"

LUKE PULLED UP to the departures gate at the airport and climbed out; Tom stepped out, as well, and lifted Jo's bag from the backseat.

"I'm sorry we can't take you out to dinner," Luke said, "but we need to start driving west so we can chase the daylight."

"Thanks," she said, "but I wouldn't have had

time before my flight anyhow. I can't believe you're driving and not flying."

"It's too easy to get grounded this time of year," Tom said. "A big storm anywhere in the country screws up flights everywhere—we learned that the hard way last spring. We'll drive straight through and be home for breakfast."

"I really thought you had Gunslinger this time," Jo said.

He grinned. "Me too, till he faked me out by looking right and then going left. Dang, I love that bull!"

She laughed. "I'd think you would love him for steaks and hamburger. By the way, how much did Len win? Sophie was over the moon."

"A little south of forty grand—not bad pay for thirty-two seconds' work."

Jo pulled up the handle on her rolling bag. "Thanks for a wonderful weekend. Is there an event next week?"

"Every weekend through May, except for Easter," Tom said. "You mean you haven't gotten your fill of bull riding?"

"Are you kidding? I'm hooked." She hesitated. "How about you? Was I too much of a pest?"

He smiled, a slow smile that started in his

eyes. "I suppose I can answer a few more questions if you want to show up again. I'd like to see a good book about bull riding."

"Then I'll see you next weekend."

Luke whooped. "Well, all right!" He planted a loud smacking kiss on her mouth. "Welcome to Team Cameron."

CHAPTER NINE

"I'LL DRIVE," TOM SAID.

Luke climbed into the passenger seat and tipped his hat over his eyes. "Wake me when we get to Amarillo."

Tom was grateful for his brother's easygoing company. Like he'd told Jo, the three-day competition pushed his upper limits for big-city bright lights—forget about the five-day circus in Las Vegas for the finals—plus he couldn't help worrying about the weather in southern Colorado. Post-event relief kicked in as soon as the OKC suburbs fell behind them and I-40 stretched ahead into the sunset.

Images and sensations rambled through his mind as he drove: Widow-maker's horn coming at his face on Friday night, Jo's look of consternation on seeing the damage the next morning, her fingers gentle on his skin as she applied the concealer, how good she looked in her new boots and jeans… Something stirred in his chest, a spark he'd thought long extinguished.

"Don't even think about it!" he said aloud.

Luke grunted and opened his eyes. "Say what?"

"Nothing."

Luke closed his eyes again.

Since he was old enough to walk, his dad had taught him to face his fears head-on. *Here's a flashlight—crawl under the bed and chase that bogeyman out. He's likely just as scared of you.* With Luke hanging out of the upper bunk yelling, *Get him, Tommy!* Great preparation for bull riding, but the first time fear climbed down into the chute with him, he would hang up his rope for good.

Jo scared him. He'd felt an instant connection sitting across from her in the noisy New York diner but had put it down to having met her dad. Having her around this weekend had been better than just okay—a pleasure as long as he kept in mind he was no more than a subject for her writing. He would take pride in helping her write that book, and they'd do fine if he remembered her life lay a world apart from his.

He drove into the winter twilight, taking pleasure, as he always did, in the homeward journey. At Amarillo, he steered down the off ramp and parked in front of a Golden Corral.

He poked Luke's shoulder. "Chow time." The food here didn't measure up to Marge Bowman's cooking at the Silver Queen or to Shelby's at home, but it was cheap and plentiful and just off the interstate, a winning combination when driving straight through.

Luke shook himself awake and they entered the noisy buffet restaurant. Even past eight on a Sunday evening, most of the tables were filled, but they found seats near a couple with three children. The oldest boy of about twelve whispered in his father's ear. A low-voiced conversation followed and they all turned to look at Tom and Luke.

The older boy stood. "Excuse me, sir, but are you Tom Cameron?"

For a split second Tom wanted to blow the kid off. The weekend with all its obligations lay behind him; he was just a tired cowpoke on his way home.

He couldn't do it.

"You got me, cowboy." He held out his hand. "What's your name?"

"Jimmy Thornton, sir." The boy pumped his hand. "We're on our way home from the OKC event. You signed my vest Saturday morning."

Tom snapped his fingers. "That's where I know you from. You riding already?"

"Just mini bulls, but I aim to start riding professionally as soon as I turn eighteen."

"And graduate high school," his mother said.

"Jim, you might think about college too," Tom said. "There's some good rodeo scholarships up for grabs."

Jimmy's mother shot him a look of profound gratitude. "Let Mr. Cameron finish his supper, Jimmy. He's got a lot farther to drive than we do."

Tom touched his hat to her and resumed eating. The family finished and rose to go. Jimmy's father stopped for a moment at Tom's side. "Thank you, son. Jimmy's getting to that age he don't think much of my opinion, but he'll remember what you said like it was the voice of God. You boys drive safe now—watch out for that new snow north of Albuquerque."

TOM HAD SLEPT between Amarillo and Albuquerque, but he was back at the wheel as they headed north toward Colorado. A full moon turned the bluffs and ravines into a surreal study in black and silver. The snow had stopped, but the wind kept the flakes aloft, blinding ground blizzard one moment lapsing to shifting eddies across the blacktop like foam on the surface of a dark sea.

"I really didn't think you'd agree to go ahead with this writing project," Luke said. "The way you duck publicity."

Tom shrugged. "Jo seems like a good sort, and a book like she could write would be good for the sport. I can always back out."

"Yeah, like you'd do that after she spends time and money chasing you around the country." Luke laughed. "Me, maybe, but not you."

Tom frowned. "Stop making me sound like some wimpy do-gooder."

"Hey, every family has to have one trouble-free kid—looks like you're stuck with the job."

TOM AND LUKE arrived at Cameron's Pride in time for breakfast and picked out chores from the to-do board as soon as they finished the pancakes and sausage Shelby set before them. Tom opted for fence repair; elk had damaged another section not far from the one they'd replaced just a week ago.

"How about I take Banjo?" Tom asked Shelby. "You could ride along and see how she looks with another rider."

"Good idea," she said. "Luke can ride into

town with your dad—we need to pick up a big order of feed at the Exchange."

Jake looked up from his plate. "I don't need—"

"The two of you can get the feed loaded faster than one man alone."

He grinned. "Yes, boss." He folded his napkin and laid it beside his plate. "Looks like you get stuck babysitting the old man, Luke."

An hour later, Tom rode out on the bay filly; Shelby was mounted on Butch, Jake's cutting horse.

"Banjo has come a long way since the last time I rode her," he said. "You going to try her working cows pretty soon?"

"I'll use her to move some of the older mamas into the upper pasture—they won't give her a hard time. I'm glad to see someone else ride her—I can tell where she needs more balancing."

They reached the downed section of fence and hitched the horses to a fallen aspen while Tom stretched new wire and Shelby hammered fence staples into the posts.

"That should hold till the next bull elk starts rubbing his butt on it," Tom said as he stuck the hammer back into his saddlebag. He mounted and reined Banjo back toward the home ranch. They rode in silence until the ranch buildings appeared in the valley below them. He had asked Shelby to ride with him so he could ask her advice, but he couldn't think how to open the conversation. He cleared his throat and then lapsed again into silence.

"Will your journalist friend be at this weekend's event?" she asked, as if she'd read his mind.

"As far as I know—guess I'll find out come Friday." He half turned in the saddle. "I've got a problem. Jo hung out with the wives last weekend. They know she's planning a book about bull riding, but I guess they also think she's my... I mean that we're..." He rubbed his face in frustration. "I don't want anyone to get the wrong idea."

Shelby rode without speaking. Tom had come to her because she always listened with absolute concentration and then thought before answering. Truth be told, he and Luke had both been half in love with her when she first showed up five years ago. She was older than them by a few years but closer to their age than their dad's. Luckily they'd never gone beyond admiring her in silence; she'd been Jake's and his alone. Now they regarded her more as an honored older sister than a stepmother. He'd probably fallen for Traci because she looked a little like Shelby. Too bad the resemblance had been only skin-deep.

"So should I say—?"

"If anyone asks you straight out, tell them it's strictly a professional arrangement. How you both act will speak more loudly than what you say. She sounds like a smart lady—follow her lead."

Tom relaxed a little. "I can do that—I just don't want to come off like a coward."

Shelby smiled. "Tom, you ride bulls for a living. Nobody's going to think you're a coward."

CHAPTER TEN

JO LEFT HER agent's office flush with excitement and a rank case of nerves. Jessica McIntosh had jumped on her idea for a book with such enthusiasm Jo would be ashamed to back out.

"The Sunday editor is panting for your feature," Jessica had said. "They'll hype it based on your previous profiles, and you can use it as early buzz for the book. I'll start hitting publishing houses as soon as you send me a proposal with reader stats—no, scratch that, I'll research the stats—you just concentrate on writing the book."

Jo hit the speed dial on her cell phone and sighed with relief when her mother answered.

"Are you free?" she said. "I just left Jessica's office and I need to blow off steam. In a good way."

"I'm working at home this morning. I'll put on coffee and ply you with cookies and motherly advice when you get here."

Jo snorted; her mother's advice usually consisted of, "You're a big girl—figure it out." Other than worrying about her adventures while doing research, of course.

Jo walked the six blocks from the subway and left her snowy boots at the door of her mother's Victorian kitchen. Sunlight poured through the big south-facing windows, picking out the facets on the pressed glass sugar and cream set and glancing off the satiny finish of the round walnut table. A plate of peanut butter–chocolate chip cookies sat on an Amish mat they'd discovered at a church thrift shop. Angus lay stretched out on the wide windowsill, purring like a hive of happy bees.

Anna Dace dumped a book of fabric samples on the floor to give Jo a seat at the table. "I heard you come in last night, but Angus and I were too lazy to get up." She poured coffee for her daughter and freshened her own cup. "And then you left so early this morning."

"Jessica is going to be out of town all week— I wanted to sit down with her before she left." Jo took a deep breath. "In a rash moment, I said in front of witnesses I wanted to do a book on bull riding as well as the profile."

"It's about time," her mother said. "I knew someday you would stumble onto something that grabbed you by the ankle and wouldn't let go. So tell me all about your weekend. Your texts and photos tantalized me."

Jo took a cookie from the plate. "I loved Oklahoma City—better known as OKC—and the fans and the cowboys. Tom Cameron arranged for me to have a seat…"

She launched into a rambling account of her weekend, jumping from the cowboys to their wives to the bulls with no attempt at order. She wrote in the same manner, almost stream-of-consciousness for the first draft and then re-arranged the fragments into a coherent flow.

Anna listened without interrupting and then reached over to smooth Angus's fur. "Looks like you'll be spending a lot of time with me, sweetie. Your mama's going on the road again."

"Just weekends, Mom—I'll be home between events."

"You said you sat with the riders' wives. Is your bull rider married?"

"No. And neither is his brother, although I overheard that Tom was engaged once. I guess it ended badly. Of course, I don't need to go into his personal life."

Her mother started to speak and then closed her mouth.

"What? Don't say it." Jo took another cookie. "I'm not getting involved with someone crazy enough to ride bulls for a living. I've been to two events, and Tom took a hit both times. He was out of competition almost a year when a bull fell on him, but he still went back. Does that sound like good relationship material?"

Her mother sniffed but made no comment.

Jo added cream to her coffee and watched patterns form as she stirred. "I'll need to go slowly with this book. The people I've met so far…"

"You think they'll shut you out?"

"Far from it," Jo said. "Kevin McCloud was certainly happy for me to write about his career, but the sailing crowd kept me at a little distance, like some upper-level servant. And the racetrack folks were friendly enough, just so busy I had to step lively to keep out of everyone's way. But everyone I met this weekend treated me like some long-lost cousin or a friend they hadn't seen in a while. I almost feel like a sneak writing about them."

"Jo, most of these people probably come from small towns, like our neighbors near your grandfather's farm. Country folks just don't have that layer of mistrust with strangers. Do they know you're planning a book?"

"I did mention it in conversation with one

rider's wife." Jo laughed. "And a few hours later everyone seemed to know."

"So you're hardly sneaking around. Just be there and listen more than you talk. If you think you're making anyone uncomfortable, back off and explore the subject from another angle."

She refilled their mugs. "Are you planning to write the profile first?"

Jo frowned. "I guess so, but I may have chosen a poor subject. Tom Cameron looked so good on paper—twice a bridesmaid, his brother being a bullfighter..."

"He's uncommunicative?"

"Not really—he's just quiet. I feel like I'm playing a fish on a line—reel him in, let him run..."

"Your interviews work so well because they're not invasive, more like new friends getting acquainted over coffee. Will Tom Cameron let you in like that?"

"I hope so. He's so reticent, and then he opens up with some great personal insight." Tom's words beside Gunslinger's pen leaped to her mind: *I'd ride for free with no one watching... the best eight seconds of your life.* Remembering, she came close to entering his mind; she too lived for those moments of flashing revelation.

"Maybe you could choose someone else if he doesn't work out," Anna said.

Jo snorted. "How would that look? Gee, you turned out to be a dud—I'll find someone better. No, it's Tom Cameron or no one. He's my portal to the whole sport."

"Sounds like an impulsive engagement followed by second thoughts."

"And I'm the one who courted him and then proposed. No, I'll make it work. I've already got the perfect opening, Tom sweet-talking that huge bull that could cripple or kill him."

"Well, I hope you'll still have time to help me—I've got two condos and a town house to prep this week." Anna stood and tucked the tail of her blue polo shirt into her jeans. "Get into your work clothes if you want a paycheck before you take off again."

JO'S LIFE SETTLED into a pattern: days hauling furniture and hanging curtains with her mother, evenings writing ad copy or editing manuscripts and working on her own projects while elbowing her cat off her keyboard. Every weekend she boarded a flight to Sacramento or St. Louis or some other city where she slipped into the backstage world of professional bull riding with scarcely a ripple. Tom had gotten approval for her project, so staff members accepted her presence without question as long as she kept out from underfoot. She used her Nikon for its greater capabilities, shooting hundreds of images at every event, concentrating on the cowboys as they waited to compete and then celebrated or bemoaned the outcome. She didn't try to catch action shots—that wasn't the thrust of her project—but she did capture one heart-stopping moment when the Sports Medicine team knelt around a fallen rider while the whole audience watched in dead silence.

As Jo had hoped, Sophie Haley proved to be the perfect guide precisely because she hadn't grown up in the Western lifestyle. Even after several years living a ranch wife's gritty reality, she still exuded delight in her new life, always excited to share her experiences. The other wives seemed to regard her with amused affection both for her convert's fervor and because of her warmhearted willingness to help in any emergency. And Jo found Mara Veira to be an unexpected asset. Her parents had emigrated from Portugal; she had met her Brazilian husband at a fan meet-and-greet, connecting at once because of her fluency in his language. Now she provided Jo with a link to the dozen or so Brazilian riders.

Tom remained her primary subject. He seemed increasingly comfortable with her, maybe because she had widened her focus to bull riding as a whole. She wondered if he'd forgotten that her first objective had been, as he put it, "to dissect a bull rider." She was glad she didn't seem to be distracting him from his riding. Gunslinger was out of the rotation because of a minor injury, but so far, Tom had ridden every other bull he straddled. The announcers had started using words like *streak* and *gold buckle*.

Jo and Tom had gotten into the habit of meeting after each evening's competition, usually talking about anything but the sport: about their separate histories, his on the ranch and hers growing up on the racing circuit. Somehow reminiscing about her dad with Tom called up only good memories without the final shock of loss. "I had my own team coverall from the time I was seven on—the pit crew treated me like their mascot."

Tom revealed he could recite long passages of Frost and Sandburg, a legacy from his late mother. "She read poetry to us on winter evenings—saving the words in my mind keeps her alive for me."

Some nights they walked for miles along

quiet streets as they talked and other times they simply nursed a single drink in the hotel lobby until they both started yawning.

And on Sundays, like a jet-lagged Cinderella, Jo flew back to her life before bull riding.

CHAPTER ELEVEN

JAKE CAMERON THREW his saddle onto its rack with a grunt. "You got a pretty fair score in that last short round, son. Your streak's what... fourteen rides?"

"Fifteen," Luke said. "But our Tom's not counting."

Tom rapped his knuckles on a stall door for luck. "I don't want to jinx myself."

"I guess having that reporter follow you around isn't doing any harm," his father said.

Tom smiled. Far from it—his riding percentage had never been better. He had started saluting Jo after each dismount, and their late-night gab sessions eased him down from his post-riding high better than his solitary walks had ever done.

"As much time as you spend with Jo, you ought to make an honest woman of her," Luke said. He held up his hands. "I know—you're just friends."

Were they friends? Tom had never really had

a female friend, but he enjoyed a level of comfort with Jo he'd never felt with another woman, except maybe Shelby. And for sure not with Traci. Sadness and regret tightened around his heart.

"Jo's a great gal, but there's no future with her," he said. "She's a city girl to the bone." Although she hadn't said much about New York lately. Of course, she listened a lot more than she talked—probably her way of getting him to open up. The thought bothered him more than he liked to admit.

"I dunno," Luke said. "She seems to fit in like she was born with manure on her boots. The wives and the other riders like her too."

Tom turned away to hang his horse's bridle on its hook. "I'm glad—that makes it easier for her to collect material for her book." He sniffed the air. "Smells like supper's about ready."

They did full justice to Shelby's beef stew with Cajun spices and then sat back with coffee and dried peach pie.

"Will your writer friend show up for the Albuquerque event?" Jake asked.

Tom shrugged. "I guess so—she hasn't missed one yet. We haven't talked about it, but I think she's going to base her book on a full season, since she's been on board since New York."

"You'd like her, Pop," Luke said. "I keep asking her to come home with me, but she just laughs and brushes me off."

"She may not feel comfortable because Tom hasn't invited her," Shelby said.

"Luke's right—you would like her," Tom said. "I guess you'll get a chance to meet her if she comes to Albuquerque three weeks from now."

"That's one we'll never miss," Jake said as he touched Shelby's hand.

"SORRY, BRO." LUKE CLAPPED Tom on the shoulder the next Friday evening. "She wasn't on the flight." His cell phone played a few bars of "Friends in Low Places." He pulled it out and read: Marine needed seat, baby ETA NOW. Next flight arrives 10:32. He grinned. "Good girl!"

Tom relaxed a little but his heart dropped. He acknowledged for the first time he'd come to think of Jo as his lucky charm. He didn't have a coin or a religious medal or special underwear like some of the cowboys did, but he'd been riding lights-out since she appeared on his horizon. Now she wouldn't arrive until tonight's round was long over. He shook his head, angry with himself. He didn't like the idea of depending on anything but his own skill, of needing Jo or anyone as a talisman.

Luke's phone warbled again. "More from Jo." He laughed. "She says you better ride or she'll kick your butt."

So he rode, not his prettiest ride, with a score almost low enough to get him a reride. Luke and the other bullfighters had to work for their pay when his hand hung up in his rope while his boots scrabbled madly in the dirt as the bull spun to shake him loose. But he made the eight seconds and walked away with nothing worse than a sore wrist and ripped jeans where a hoof slashed at his thigh.

He had just enough time to shower and get into clean clothes before Jo's plane arrived. She looked a little tired, he thought, hurrying from the exit gate, but she smiled when she saw him.

"You rode," she said. "Luke texted me. But he said you hung up." She put her hand on his arm. "You're okay?"

Her light touch jolted him. "I'm in better shape than my britches," he said. "Score one for the bull, zero for my Wranglers." He took her carry-on. "Have you eaten?"

"No, I thought I'd wait and grab a bite with you." She looked down. "If that's okay."

They found a 24-hour diner near the hotel and faced each other across the Formica table-top, much like their first meeting in New York City only a couple months earlier.

"I'm glad this is a three-day event," she said, picking at her cheese omelet. "Since I missed the first round. But I know you get twitchy by the third day."

He set the salt and pepper shakers in a tri-angle with the old-fashioned sugar dispenser. "Not so much lately," he said. If he didn't meet her eyes, she wouldn't be able to read his thoughts. "There are more points available with an extra go-round."

She nodded and finished her omelet. "Want to share a piece of pie? The coconut cream looks good."

"Sure." He cleared his throat, nervous as a boy asking a girl to the prom. "Jo—"

Her phone beeped; she glanced at it and grinned. "Hey, my marine got to see his son born. That makes my day." She stuck her phone in her purse. "Sorry, I interrupted you."

"Will you be coming to Albuquerque?" he said in a rush. "My dad and Shelby will be there."

"That's three weeks from now, right?" Her smile warmed his heart. "I wouldn't miss it."

CHAPTER TWELVE

"NINETY-SIX INCHES," Jo said before she yawned.

Her mother jotted the number on a pad and reeled in the tape measure. "Am I keeping you awake?"

"Just barely." She yawned again. "Sorry—what's next, the windows?"

"Next is coffee," Anna said. "We've got till the end of the week to get this house ready. You're practically walking in your sleep. Do you really need to go to every event?"

They settled at the card table Anna had brought into the empty house as a workstation and dug into a box of Italian pastries from the corner bakery.

"I don't have to go, but keeping the same schedule as the riders gives me a real sense of how hard the life is," Jo said and accepted the coffee her mother poured from a big blue thermos. "I've talked to most of the cowboys, and they all say the same thing—the worst part isn't riding or even injuries, it's the travel. They fly in for a two- or three-day competition—if they don't get grounded somewhere by weather in the winter—and risk their lives for a chance at the big money. Plus most of them work during the week, like Tom and Luke do on their family's ranch."

"Pretty much like you, except you're not riding bulls." Anna peered sideways at Jo. "Are you?"

Jo rolled her eyes. "No, Mom—I'm not riding bulls. And I plan to keep going for at least another three weeks, till the event in Albuquerque. Tom's folks are driving down from southern Colorado for the weekend—I promised I'd be there."

"So tell me about last weekend. You said your plane got in late on Friday?"

Monday mornings had turned into debriefing sessions. Jo had discovered from working on previous projects that talking to her mother about her research helped focus her writing; Anna asked questions that readers unfamiliar with bull riding or sailing or horseracing might ask.

"Too bad you don't have time to do any sightseeing on these trips," Anna said when Jo finished describing the most recent event.

"I suppose acting as Tom Cameron's personal assistant takes up most of your time."

"Not too personal—he hasn't needed help covering bruises with makeup since Oklahoma City. I do go along on his PR gigs. He's wonderful with the fans, especially the kids—he's like everybody's big brother."

"He sounds like good husband material."

"For some lucky ranch girl maybe—not for me. I want a guy who comes home in one piece every day at five sharp. I could never marry a cop or a firefighter—"

"Or a bull rider?"

"Especially not a bull rider," Jo said. "Tom's been lucky so far this year, but he could end up crippled in a—well, in less than eight seconds."

"So what about that architect from Georgia you dated for—what was it?—nearly six months?" Anna rummaged through the bakery box and fished out a mini cannoli. "He was certainly reliable. I know he planned to propose—he asked my permission, such a nice old-fashioned gesture."

"Brett was a sweetie, but he hated New York—he couldn't wait to get back to Savannah. I couldn't consider moving so far from... I mean you depend on me—"

Anna set her mug down with a thump. "This

arrangement of ours has worked so far, but if you try using me as an excuse not to build a life on your own, I'll fire you so fast you won't know what hit you. And I'll change the lock upstairs to boot."

Jo stared at her mother goggle-eyed.

Anna's voice softened. "Maybe I'll show up on your doorstep needing to be taken in when I'm old and feeble, but not for quite a while, I hope. You're twenty-eight years old—feel free to leave the nest whenever the notion takes you."

She stood and gave Jo a rare hug. "Break's over. Let's get those windows measured."

JO ZIPPED HER laptop into its case as the plane floated in for a gentle touchdown at Albuquerque International Sunport. She had kept the butterflies in her stomach quiet during the flight by polishing the new material she'd added to her feature, but now they fluttered up at the prospect of meeting Tom's (and Luke's) parents. Foolish of her—not as if they were future in-laws—but she found her hands sweating as she pulled her jacket and carry-on from the overhead bin.

She didn't see Tom or Luke waiting for her outside the security portal; instead a slim woman with dark hair in a long braid and eyes the color of clear water over mossy stones called her name. She offered Jo her hand.

"I'm Shelby Cameron—Tom showed us your picture so I'd recognize you. His dad and I offered to meet you because Tom got tied up doing a TV spot for the local sports coverage." She spoke a few words into her phone and then pocketed it.

"My husband's driving in circles, waiting to pick us up," she said.

So this was the woman Tom and Luke spoke of with such admiration. Jo followed her; from Shelby's straight back and confident walk, Jo had no trouble picturing her turning green colts and problem horses into well-mannered equine citizens.

Luke's Explorer pulled up just as they reached the curb. The rear hatch sprang open; Shelby lifted Jo's bag into the cargo space with a smooth twist of her wrist and then opened the front passenger door.

"Ride up here with Jake," she said. "You'll get a better view of the city."

A wiry man with fair skin and blue eyes turned toward her with the grin she recognized as Luke's own. "Welcome to Albuquerque, Jo. I hope you brought Tom's luck in your pocket."

"Tom makes his own luck," she said, "but I'll be cheering for him." She looked at her watch. "He actually agreed to go on TV?"

Jake laughed. "He didn't exactly volunteer, but he's been leading the pack for three months now—that makes him pretty newsworthy in the sport." He steered onto the highway leading north from the airport toward the city. "If we hustle a little, maybe we can catch Tom's interview—the sports coverage should be on near the end of the five o'clock news."

He pulled up in front of the Marriott nearest the University of New Mexico, where Jo knew the competition would be held. "You gals run up to our room and tune in," he said. "I'll park and be right there."

Shelby laid her hand on his shoulder. "Don't rush," she said.

He covered her hand with his. "Yes, Ma."

She smacked the back of his head, tilting his hat over his eyes. "Don't sass me, cowboy." She climbed out and led the way into the lobby.

"Jake will bring your bag in," she said. "You can register after the news. If you want to watch, that is."

"Of course I do," Jo said. "I can't wait to see how Tom performs without a bull under him."

Shelby clicked on the TV as a blonde in a

tight red dress finished explaining that the weather over the weekend would be unseasonably cold. "Don't put away your down jackets just because the calendar says spring, folks. You can expect fresh snow above 5,000 feet—that should make the skiers happy. And now for the five-day forecast."

"Sports should be next," Shelby said. "Make yourself at home." She hung her wine-colored fringed leather jacket on the back of a chair and sat on the end of the bed. Jake entered a few minutes later and sat beside his wife.

A young Hispanic woman in a formfitting jade-green dress appeared on the screen. "I'm Jennifer Cortez with Sports at Five. The bulls are back in town this weekend, and we have the leading rider, Tom Cameron, here with us this evening."

The camera switched to Tom sitting, apparently at ease, in a canvas director's chair, his hands folded loosely in his lap. Jo stared at the TV openmouthed. She had focused so completely on him as an athlete that his appearance on-screen took her by surprise. In his maroon pearl-snap shirt and black Stetson, he could have stepped off the cover of a romance novel; the faint scar on his cheek only served to enhance his dashing image.

Jo dragged her attention to the content of the interview: Tom explaining how he'd grown up working on the family ranch, that this was his eleventh season riding bulls professionally.

"You've been leading the standings since the beginning of the season," Cortez said. "Who do you see as your main competition?"

Tom smiled. "The bulls. We're all riding for the prize money, but we're competing against the bulls."

"I've heard you have a grudge match with one particular bull." She consulted her notes. "Gunslinger."

"Not a grudge—I love that bull. I'll pick him every chance I get till I get him rode."

A few more minutes of conversation focused on the weekend's event at the University of New Mexico's Wisepies Arena, also known as the Pit, and then the sports coverage shifted to high school basketball.

"The kid did great," Jake said. "Generally nobody can get more than two words out of him when they stick a mic in his face."

"Maybe he's getting more comfortable with being interviewed." Shelby turned to Jo. "He opens up with you, doesn't he?"

"Well, yes, but we just have conversations—I make mental notes to write up later. He understands what I'm doing, but I guess he doesn't feel as much pressure as if I were asking direct questions."

Jake looked at his watch. "Let's have supper so we can get to the Pit early. We'll go to Garcia's Kitchen tomorrow for New Mexican food, but I always take my best girl to Pappadeaux the first night for some Cajun food she doesn't have to cook herself."

"From what Tom and Luke say, she should open her own restaurant," Jo said.

"I don't have the people skills to run a restaurant," Shelby said. "I'll stick to easy clients, like problem horses, and just cook for my own crew."

Jo checked in then allowed Jake to sweep her along with their dinner plans. Remembering what Tom had told her about his family's financial woes, she resolved to pay her own way, but Jake would have none of it. "You're giving Tom's career a nice boost with the article you're writing—his sponsors have got to be pleased. Treating you to a couple meals is little enough thanks."

Luckily Jake had made reservations; even a little before six the restaurant was mostly filled. They shared a fried alligator appetizer and, on Shelby's advice, Jo ordered crawfish étouffée that made her an instant fan of Cajun cuisine. They skipped dessert and made it to the arena well before the opening ceremonies.

"I see now why it's called the Pit," Jo said after the long descent to their seats with the other riders' families.

"More than three stories down from street level," Jake said. "And a long climb back up to the locker rooms after riding."

"I've spotted you on TV sitting with the wives," Shelby said. "And other times I've caught glimpses of you above the chutes.

"I swap off, especially during the three-day events," Jo said. "I get a different perspective that way. I'll sit with you this evening, if that's okay."

"Great," Jake said. "I'll take your spot up top." He stood and started up the steps. Shelby half rose as if to stop him, but then settled back into her chair with a sigh.

"The boys will keep an eye on Jake," she said, "and Doc Barnett is right there. I hate acting like a mother hen, but it's still hard for me to let him out of my sight since his heart attack."

"Tom told me it happened during the blizzard," Jo said. "You must have been terrified."

"Not at the time. When Jake's horse came in

without him, I thought she might have spooked and gotten away from him while he was closing the gate—snow and thunder were hitting us at the same time. I just went into robotic mode when I saw him lying in the snow—check to see if he's breathing, get him on the horse, get him to the hospital alive—but I shook for an hour once the ER crew took over."

Jo had never faced a crisis of such magnitude; she couldn't imagine coping half so well. "Now I understand why Tom told me there's not much you can't handle," she said.

"I guess we never know what we can do until we have to," Shelby said. A few minutes later, she straightened in her seat and waved; Jake waved back from above the chutes. She turned to Jo with a smile. "Now I can enjoy the show."

"Don't you…" Jo hesitated. She'd never had the opportunity to interview riders' parents, an angle she hadn't considered. She changed her question. "Does Jake worry about Tom's bull riding?"

"He does," Shelby said. "We both do, but ranching is dangerous work anyhow. Bull riding just concentrates the risk into eight seconds."

The level of noise from the huge speakers increased as warnings of the coming pyrotechnics flashed, making further conversation impossible.

Jo followed the action on the dirt, but Shelby and Jake held much of her attention. Shelby cheered for the cowboys' efforts on their bulls, but between rides, her head turned toward Jake in his seat above the chutes. Her hands tightened on the day sheet when he disappeared from view for a few moments and relaxed in her lap when he reappeared.

Shelby leaned forward when Tom's turn to ride came, yelling and whistling like the most rabid fan at a hockey or baseball game. When the judges gave him 88 points, the evening's best score, she whooped and hugged Jo before collapsing in her seat to take a long drink from her plastic cup of Coke.

"Sorry," she said. "I do get carried away when Tom makes a great ride like that."

Jake appeared at the end of the aisle and hunkered down at Shelby's side. "Folks behind the chutes were asking who was that crazy lady jumping up and down," he said. "I figured I better get back here before you got hauled out by security."

"Yes, and I saw you up there riding the air bull along with Tom. Don't talk to me about crazy." She sneaked a kiss under the brim of his hat.

"I'm going to that boys' ranch school with Tom and Luke tomorrow," Jake said. "If you're still of a mind to go shopping, maybe Jo would like to go with you."

CHAPTER THIRTEEN

TOM PULLED JO'S chair out for her the next morning when she joined the Camerons for breakfast. "How come you ditched me last night after the event?" he asked as he seated her.

She looked up at him, startled for a moment and then relaxed when she saw he was smiling.

"I didn't want to intrude on your folks' visit," she said.

"I hung out with them maybe half an hour and then went walking. Alone. You've got me spoiled—I missed solving the problems of the world with you."

Jake's voice interrupted before Jo could answer Tom. "So you going to shop me into the poorhouse today, woman?"

"I'll do my best, dear," Shelby said in a saccharine voice. "Jo can encourage me if I'm not spending enough."

Jake gave a theatrical groan. "You'd think just once I could get the last word, wouldn't you?" he asked Jo.

Jo laughed, but with a pang in her heart. She remembered her parents clowning and kidding each other in just the same way, punctuated with hugs and kisses. Marriages like theirs did exist outside her imagination and memory; Jake and Shelby were living proof.

Jake handed Shelby a set of keys. "Don't wreck my rig," he said. "It's got to last us another hundred thousand miles."

"If I recall correctly, you put your truck into the ditch the first time ever I saw you, so don't tell me not to wreck it." Shelby took the keys. "Behave yourself." She turned toward Tom and Luke.

"Don't worry," Tom said. "We won't let him get on any rough stock. You and Jo enjoy your day."

"WHAT ARE THE guys doing?" Jo asked as Shelby started the brown Ram pickup with Cameron's Pride Red Angus emblazoned on its doors.

"They're staging a bull riding and bullfighting workshop at a residential ranch for at-risk youth," Shelby said. "Riders do events like that all over the country—a couple years ago they staged a rodeo for prisoners at a penitentiary in Louisiana."

"So where are we going?"

"One of my favorite places—Santa Fe. It's

less than an hour's drive north. I could bank-
rupt the ranch shopping there without half
trying, but I'm only picking up a special birthday present for Lucy's twenty-first birthday.
A Navajo silversmith who's meeting me there
designed a special bracelet for her. We could
never afford one of his pieces, but I gentled
some mustangs for him a year ago so he's giving me a discount."

"Maybe I can find something there for
Mother's Day," Jo said. "My mom isn't much
for jewelry, but she loves textiles. Do you know
of any good weavers' studios?"

Shelby laughed. "Oh Lord, yes! Jo, we are
going to hit Santa Fe with all guns blazing—
we can window-shop till we drop."

I-25 took them north past numerous signs
pointing to pueblos and reservations. "I wish
we had time to explore off the highway," Shelby
said, "but I need to pick up Lucy's present by
noon—Fidel is making a special trip into Santa
Fe from Taos for me. After that we can just
wander."

Shelby found a parking space in a municipal
lot and slung an intricately tooled purse on her
shoulder. "It's a little walk to the plaza," she
said, "but we won't find anything closer on a
Saturday where I can fit the truck."

"Did Jake really crash his truck the first time he saw you?"

"He really did," Shelby said with a laugh. "On his way home from the Albuquerque event five years ago, as a matter of fact. To be fair, it was snowing, and he braked too hard stopping to give me a ride. It wasn't much of a wreck—he just skidded into the ditch—but he wasn't wearing his seat belt, and he knocked himself out hitting the steering wheel. I managed to back the truck out of the ditch and found a motel a few miles farther north where we could shelter overnight till the snow stopped." She grinned. "I had no idea it was a hot-pillow joint. The clerk probably wondered why I asked for two beds."

"Tom told me why you were hitchhiking," Jo said. "I would have been scared silly."

"I was more mad than scared. I had my big dog with me, so the jerk wouldn't have gotten away with much. We could have sheltered under a bridge until the snow stopped." She shivered. "It wasn't a big storm like the one last spring."

She led the way into an adobe-front coffee shop and introduced Fidel Vigil, the tall man who rose to greet them. "Fidel, Jo is working on a book about bull riding. Tom and Luke are helping with the research."

"We've got some good bull riders on the rez," he said with a laugh. "Too bad they're all nuts."

They sat and ordered coffee before Fidel spread open the green flannel packet lying on the table. "This came out pretty nice," he said. "Of course, you sent me good stones to work with."

A bracelet glowed in the sunlight, miniature silver conchas set with turquoise cabochons and linked with more silver and turquoise beads. Beside it lay a matching pair of earrings.

Shelby clasped her hands in delight. "They're gorgeous," she said. "I couldn't picture what you planned to do with those scraps, but I can see the details from that old necklace. And earrings too—Lucy will be thrilled, especially since they're made from her mother's jewelry." She reached for her purse. "How much do I owe you?"

"Nada," he said. "It was an interesting project. You provided the materials so it was just my labor. I heard what folks went through last spring up in the Animas Valley—let me help you out."

Shelby's head came up. "I can't accept that— I know what your name is worth on a piece of jewelry." She thought for a moment. "That sorrel filly I started for you? I think she has real potential for reining. If you want to haul her to our ranch, I'll finish her for you."

A huge grin split his dark face. "My wife loves that little sorrel—I know she'll be tickled. I'd say I'm coming out way ahead on the deal." He folded the bracelet and earrings back into their wrapper and handed it to Shelby with a bow. "Happy birthday to your daughter."

Jo took one of Fidel's business cards, promising herself something from his website when she could afford it, but meanwhile she treated herself to a double string of turquoise and coral beads from one of the Indian women displaying jewelry on blankets around the central plaza. She found a beautiful wall hanging worked in shades of blue and rose and gray for her mother in a shop featuring the work of local weavers.

Shelby caressed the densely woven textile. "This is from Chimayo, north of Santa Fe," she said. "The weavers there use techniques handed down from the Spanish settlers."

Jo persuaded Shelby to let her pay for lunch at Cafe Pasqual's. "I've always wanted to visit Santa Fe," she said. "Treating you to lunch is little enough thanks for the free tour." She chose the BLT made with chili-rubbed bacon while Shelby ordered a bison cheeseburger with green chili.

"Jake thinks ordering anything but beef is close to treason," she said, licking her fingers, "but I love bison—I tell him it's my Choctaw blood."

They headed back to Albuquerque after visiting a few more shops and galleries. Jo bought a jar of prickly pear jelly and a bag of blue cornmeal muffin mix for her mother, promising herself this wouldn't be her last visit to Santa Fe.

"I'm glad you came with me today," Shelby said as they approached Albuquerque. "I wanted to get to know you—Tom has come out of himself so much since he started working with you."

Jo laughed. "He still seems pretty reserved most of the time."

"Yes, but not so much lately. Something's been bothering him the last couple of years, ever since that bull fell with him and kept him out of competition so long. Not the injury—he's riding better than ever..." She steered around a slow-moving cattle hauler. "I've thought a couple of times he wanted to tell me about it, but then he shies away. Maybe he'll decide to talk to you."

"We don't really discuss personal issues," Jo said. Although she had talked to him a lot about her father. "Tom's not someone you can bully into opening up."

"You are so right," Shelby said, and changed the subject to their plans for dinner before tonight's event.

JO HAD SEEN on Friday how much Jake enjoyed watching the event from backstage, so she gave up her chute seat again to sit with Shelby for Saturday evening's competition. Tom scored 88 points on his bull, but a Navajo cowboy riding as a special invitee turned in a 90-point ride to win the round, triggering a roar of cheering and applause. "There are some top-notch Indian riders," Shelby said. "I think half the Navajo Nation is here tonight."

When the event ended, Jo excused herself and returned to her room. Half an hour later she heard a knock at her door.

Tom stood in the hall, wearing a sheepskin-lined denim jacket; he held out a wool duffle coat. "I'll bet you didn't bring any cold-weather gear, so I borrowed Shelby's. You up for walking tonight?"

"You're still leading in the event, aren't you?" Jo asked as they strode along at a brisk pace. "Even though you didn't win tonight?"

"By less than a point, but there's two rounds

tomorrow. I was glad to see the Tsosie kid win tonight—everybody loves a hometown hero."

"Shelby introduced me to a Navajo silversmith today in Santa Fe—he created a wonderful bracelet and earring set for your sister's birthday. He wouldn't take any payment so Shelby offered to finish training one of his horses in exchange for his work."

"That sounds like a solution she'd come up with. My dad was in a bad way after Mom died," Tom said, "just going through the motions, drinking too much. Having Shelby on the ranch turned him around even before they got married. Now I don't know how we got along without her."

"Seeing her and your dad together reminds me of my parents," Jo said. "They had that same kind of chemistry, like teenagers with their first crush."

"Yeah, I need to get me some of that." She thought she heard a deep undertone of sadness in his voice and shivered. "I guess it's colder than I thought," he said, and they turned back toward the hotel.

JAKE AND SHELBY drove Jo back to the airport after the competition on Sunday afternoon. They were still high from Tom's event win even though he hadn't gotten to pick the now-sound Gunslinger in the championship round.

"We don't get to many events," Jake said. "Too far and too expensive, but we never miss Albuquerque." He took Shelby's hand. "Seeing how I picked up this prize on my way home."

Jo thanked them again for their hospitality, especially the day trip to Santa Fe.

"There's so much to see out here," Shelby said. "I've lived in southern Colorado now for five years, and I've barely scratched the surface. You just can't do much in one weekend."

"She's right, Jo," Jake said. "You need to spend more time out here." He snapped his fingers. "Say, how about you come to the ranch for a good visit? There's a two-week break in the bull riding schedule either side of Easter. Come take a look at our corner of Colorado, maybe get a new angle for your story."

Jo hesitated and looked at Shelby, who gave a little nod. "I'd love that," she said, "if I wouldn't be in the way."

"We'll tell you if you are," Shelby said.

THE LIGHTS OF Albuquerque spangled the early dusk as Jo's plane gained altitude. She leaned back with a deep sigh—a wonderful weekend but she wouldn't get back to her apartment until well past midnight. She had enjoyed spending time with Shelby and Jake and was glad they had been there to celebrate Tom's event win with him.

As soon the plane leveled out she began scrolling through the photos she had loaded onto her laptop. Because Jake and Shelby had insisted she was their guest during the weekend, she planned to thank them by creating an album for them of her best shots.

For the cover she chose a dramatic photo of Tom in the spotlight during the opening ceremonies and ended with a nice shot of him accepting the buckle for the event win even though his scores on his earlier bulls hadn't been high enough for him to pick Gunslinger in the championship round. Her favorite was an image of him leaning over the chute yelling for Deke Harkens to make the buzzer on Gunslinger, and her next shot had caught his expression of profound relief when the bull had tossed Deke at 6.7 seconds.

She included a photo of Tom and Luke in full gear posed with Jake and Shelby in front of a bucking chute as well as one of Luke launching airborne at a bull headed straight for a downed rider. From her chute seat on Sunday afternoon, she had caught a wonderful image of Jake and

Shelby during Tom's ride, Jake cheering and Shelby peeking between her fingers. She chose several more to edit later and closed her computer.

Her phone chimed as she gathered her belongings to deplane—a text from her mother. Have a walk-through early tomorrow morning— come down for coffee around 10:30.

After threatening to fire her, her mother had adjusted her schedule to give Jo Monday mornings off when she arrived home late. To show her appreciation, Jo worked harder than ever, helping Anna measure and paint and haul furniture in and out of properties going on the market.

Her mother hadn't repeated her threat to fire her, but Jo had replayed their brief exchange in her mind repeatedly. At first she had rejected the notion she was hiding from life behind her mother's skirts, but brutal self-examination hinted at some truth in the accusation.

She had dated nice guys who met her criteria for low-risk careers but found their very reliability just plain boring. Even as a small child she had been aware of her parents' romance. They had been like teenagers in the throes of first love, and she had seen the same kind of chemistry this weekend between Shelby and

Jake. Maybe the danger of loss was the secret ingredient for that kind of passion, but was she willing to pay so high a price? Surely there was a middle ground—she just hadn't found it yet.

"I SAW YOU on TV Saturday evening," her mother said, filling Jo's mug and pushing a plate of still-warm applesauce muffins toward her. "You were sitting beside a dark-haired woman wearing a gorgeous turquoise necklace."

"That was Tom's stepmom—his mother died from lupus seven or eight years ago. Shelby's Cajun and Choctaw, with a dash of runaway slave, as she puts it. Jake Cameron picked her up when he saw her hitchhiking in a snowstorm north of Albuquerque."

"On foot in a snowstorm?" Anna shivered. "It's such dangerous country out there."

Jo laughed. "This from someone living in New York City? At least most of the predators are four-legged."

"Was this weekend your last event?"

"Well…" She looked around the kitchen, picturing how it had looked Before—the cracked plaster and eroded linoleum, with layers of grime on every surface. Together she and her mother had scrubbed and sanded and painted until the whole house shone as a testament to love and imagination and elbow grease. She had lived here longer than anywhere else in her life, longer than the four years on her grandfather's farm in Utica. She enjoyed working with her mother, who gave her the latitude to pursue her own writing and editorial work, she occupied a cozy apartment with easy access to Manhattan.

But lately…

Anna snorted. "You're hooked, aren't you? On bull riding."

"I love it. It's crazy and colorful, with characters out of another century. I'll introduce you to everyone when the tour comes to the Garden next January."

"But in the meantime?"

"There's a long summer break starting at the end of May—I'll probably bow out then and finish up with the finals in October." Jo hesitated. "Will Aunt Grace disown me if I don't make it to the clan-fest for Easter? There's no bull riding for two weeks, so Tom's folks invited me to spend some time on their ranch."

"I think you can get away with it. After all, you'll see everyone at your cousin's wedding the weekend before Easter."

Jo moaned and covered her face with her hands.

"You forgot, didn't you?" Anna asked with a little edge to her voice. "We RSVP'd months ago."

How could she have forgotten? She wasn't involved in the wedding party—Jennifer was five years younger and had her own circle of friends as bridal attendants—but she and Jenn's older brother Will were the same age, good buddies and partners in mischief during the years she had lived on her grandfather's farm.

"Don't worry about Easter," Anna said. "I'll cover for you. I'll say you're on assignment— that will impress everyone. Just don't—"

"I know—don't ride any bulls."

CHAPTER FOURTEEN

"The reporter's coming to the ranch over Easter? That is so cool!" Lucy Cameron's voice filled the kitchen as Jake held the phone away from his ear. "I'll bet she knows all kinds of theater people in New York."

"Luce, she's coming for a quiet visit, not to hear you audition. If you start…" He glanced at his wife.

"Emoting," Shelby said.

"Yeah, emoting, I'll ship you back to Boulder for the rest of your break."

Tom stifled a groan. Jo meeting his folks in Albuquerque had been fine—they'd taken to her at first sight—but he wished his dad had consulted him before inviting her to the ranch. He wouldn't mind showing her their spread; she could ride his dad's Thoroughbred gelding Blackjack. With luck the weather would be decent, with no late snow—good thing Easter came late this year. He would take her to the old Cameron homestead with its warm spring.

He jerked his imagination up short. So far he'd managed to keep her separated in his mind from his life outside bull riding; having her here would blur that line. He swore under his breath.

"Tom." Shelby's voice brought him back. "It'll be all right."

He smiled and relaxed. Shelby always seemed to have her finger on the emotional pulse of everyone in the family. His grandmother had been like that, listening without judgment, always coming up with the right words to soothe or encourage or heal. More than once he'd come close to confiding in Shelby about the grief that dogged him from his own past, but knowing her tragic history from before she'd married his father, he'd been afraid of raking up painful memories.

"Yeah, Jo should enjoy the ranch," he said. "Spending some time here will be a nice break from New York City." He'd make sure she had some good stories to tell her big-city friends when she went back to her real life.

THE US AIRWAYS jet coasted in against the backdrop of the Continental Divide and touched down at the Durango-La Plata County Airport. Tom couldn't keep the grin off his face.

No use lying to himself—he had missed Jo last weekend.

She came through the security portal with an answering smile and surprised him with a quick hug.

"I'm so sorry I couldn't be at the last event, but I did watch on Sunday night."

"Then you saw me buck off—end of the streak."

"You don't sound too broken up about it," she said as they made their way out of the terminal.

"The truth is, I'm not," he said. "All the hype about how many rides to set a new record was messing with my concentration. As long as I'm on top when the season ends, the rest is just fluff."

"Gunslinger is fluff?"

He grinned. "I guess I'm allowed one bee in my Stetson." He looked at his watch. "You hungry?"

"Starved! Is it far to the ranch?"

"Too far. We'll grab lunch in Durango." He stopped beside an elderly Lincoln Town Car, its chrome and silvery finish gleaming in the midday sunlight. He opened the door with a flourish. "Your carriage awaits."

Jo laughed in amazement. "Where on earth… This has to be twenty years old."

"Closer to thirty—it's a 1990. It belonged to Shelby's grandfather. She pretty much lived out of it for close to fourteen years, traveling between training jobs."

He stowed her bag in the cavernous trunk and slid behind the wheel. "What do you feel like eating?"

"Anything but wedding chicken," she said. "Mom and I suffered side effects for days."

"How about chicken-fried steak?" Impossible to sneak out of town driving Shelby's car, and Marge Bowman would take his hide off in strips if they stopped for lunch anywhere but the Silver Queen.

"I love chicken-fried steak," she said. "My grandmother used to fix it at least once a month."

Tom found an end space half a block from the Silver Queen to accommodate the huge old car. Marge spotted them as soon as they stepped through the door and trotted out from behind the antique mahogany bar. Tom braced himself; Marge was a force of nature—no telling what she might say.

"You must be that New York writer Jake's been bragging about," Marge said. "Here for lunch? I hope you don't want sushi or a veggie wrap."

"Tom mentioned chicken-fried steak," Jo said.

Marge patted her cheek. "Now here's a smart girl—besides, she could stand some padding on her bones. Go sit—I'll bring you coffee as soon as I put your order in."

Jo finished every bite of her steak as well as a slice of peach pie, earning an approving nod from Marge. "Here's a gal who'll do to ride the mountains, Tom. Bring her back to try my liver and onions à la Marge."

Tom's phone rang as they walked back to the car. "You still in town?" Jake said. "Grab me a keg of horseshoe nails at the Exchange."

"One more stop," Tom told Jo. "And more local color, if my cousin is working today. Oscar represents the Ute side of the family."

Oscar greeted them from his post behind the age-worn counter. "Greetings, writer lady," he said when Tom introduced Jo. He offered his big paw. "Luke told me about you." He turned to Tom. "I've been meaning to call—you feel like doing a little job for the tribe?"

"Maybe, as long as it's got nothing to do with bull riding." The last favor Oscar had asked for the tribe ended up with Tom headlining a full-scale Ute high school rodeo. It had been a great fund-raiser for scholarships but had eaten up time when he'd been needed at the ranch.

"Calving's started," he said. "Dad's counting on Luke and me while we're home."

"A day of your time tops," Oscar said. "And you'll love this project. A couple kids chasing strays up a draw stumbled on some ruins that don't show up anywhere on our map. We sure could use someone to go in and take some good photos."

Tom's interest quickened, but he said, "Oscar, I can think of at least two people in the tribe better qualified than me to do a preliminary survey. Ed Tolkey—"

"Ed just had knee surgery, and Rufus is off visiting kin in Florida. If you could get pictures and some rough measurements, Alene at the Cultural Center can start working up a grant application for a dig. Come on, cousin—I'm counting on you."

Tom turned to Jo. "You feel like toting your Nikon up a cliff face? It won't be ice climbing like you planned, but it might be interesting."

Jo's eyes sparkled. "You bet!"

Tom sighed. "Okay, Oscar, you win. Send me the coordinates. And Dad needs a keg of horseshoe nails."

"Why did Oscar ask you to photograph the ruins?" Jo asked as they drove west from Durango.

"I worked on a dig at Mesa Verde one summer for a special high school project," he said. "I was the lowliest grunt on the team, but I know the basics, especially what not to touch." He glanced at her. "You sure you don't mind?"

"Are you kidding? Getting the first look at undisturbed ruins? People would pay for the privilege."

The barnyard drowsed in sunlight when they arrived at Cameron's Pride, and Ghost's corral gate stood ajar. Stranger dozed beside the barn; he seldom tried to keep up with Shelby these days if she rode beyond the home pasture.

The kitchen was empty, but the scent of meat and spices was escaping from the slow cooker. Shelby had left a note on the kitchen table.

Dear Jo,
Sorry we're not here to greet you. Fence break in the north pasture, a couple dozen head strayed. Ride out with Tom if you'd like to help.
Shelby

"Welcome to the wonderful world of ranching," Tom said with a grin. "You want to rest up or come with me?"

Jo laughed. "What do you think? Just let me

jump into my jeans." She stuck a foot out. "I'm already wearing the right footwear."

DARKNESS HAD ALMOST fallen before Tom and Luke and Jake unsaddled and straggled into the kitchen. Jo and Shelby had ridden back after the cattle were safely gathered, leaving the men to repair the fence. Salad and flour tortillas sat on the table while Colorado green chili steamed in an earthenware tureen, ready to serve in matching bowls.

"Sorry we put you to work right out of the gate," Jake said as Jo ladled chili into his bowl, "but having an extra rider was a big help."

Jo snorted. "I just hung on and let Blackjack do his thing."

"Blackjack's got good cow sense," Jake said, "but he does need someone in the saddle. If you hadn't pitched in, those heifers could have scattered a lot farther before we found them all."

Tom turned to his father after they'd finished eating. "Can you spare me for a day? Oscar ambushed me at the Exchange—he wants me to take pictures of some undocumented ruins kids just found on the rez."

Luke hooted. "See what you get for doing that work at Mesa Verde? You didn't catch me dusting pot shards with a toothbrush."

"Paintbrush," Tom said. "Not toothbrush."

"Sure," Jake said. "This would be a good time of year for it—too early for snakes." He shuddered. Shelby touched his hand.

"Dad's got a bad thing about rattlesnakes," Tom said to Jo. "One almost nailed him a few years ago. I'll check with NOAA—those screws in my leg say weather's coming in."

He rose from the table and crossed to a desk in one corner of the great room to tap a few keys on the computer. "Yep, low pressure system over the Sierras, but tomorrow should be okay to go up the canyons. That will get Oscar off my back."

He hit a few more keys. "Okay, here's the location." He whistled. "No wonder it's gone undisturbed so long. We might need climbing gear." He turned to Jo. "You still game for this? You could stay here and help Shelby work her two-year-olds."

"I'll come with you," she said without hesitation, and his heart kicked into a higher gear.

CHAPTER FIFTEEN

JO ENTERED THE kitchen the next morning dressed for riding, but Tom shook his head. "Those boots won't work where we're going," he said.

"Stir this oatmeal, Jo," Shelby said. "I think my hiking boots might fit you." She returned with a pair of lace-up boots and heavy socks. "Try these."

Jo stamped into the borrowed boots; they fit reasonably well. "So we're not going on horseback?"

"Too far," Tom said, grabbing a notepad from beside the phone. "We're here…" He marked an X. "Here's Mesa Verde National Park, about thirty miles from the ranch by road. The Ute reservation backs up to it—lots more cliff dwellings there, but off limits except with a Ute guide. We're headed just about here…" He made another X. "We'll have to hike in from the nearest fire road."

He rubbed his right shoulder. "I sure hope NOAA is right about that front holding off till tomorrow night."

JO DID HER best to keep up the pace Tom had set, hoping he couldn't hear her panting. They had stopped first at the Ute Cultural Center to pick up a topographic map and then followed a winding dirt road through aspens and sage-brush until it dead-ended overlooking a dry wash. Since parking the truck, they'd been tramping through sand and over rocks and logs for nearly an hour. Increasingly high walls, crenellated like castle ramparts, rose on both sides, damping any breeze and focusing the spring sunshine like a laser.

Tom paused ahead of her and consulted his map. He turned with a grin. "Not much farther. How are you holding up?"

"No problem." She sucked in a deep breath and shifted her backpack. "Are we close now? What does your GPS say?"

"There's no signal for the GPS this deep in the canyon," he said. "I've been following the tracks of the cows and the kids' horses. Here's where they turned off."

She hadn't noticed any tracks; now she saw a confusion of hoofprints leading into a brush-tangled ravine branching off to the right. Broken branches marked the passage of the cattle and horses. A narrow stream flowed from its mouth to disappear under a clutter of boulders and bleached logs in the main canyon.

"The ruins should be on the north wall facing south," Tom said as he led the way up the little watercourse.

Jo followed, careful of her footing on the water-tumbled stones while she elbowed her way through bushes that slapped at her face and tried to grab her hat. She almost fell when she ran into Tom, who had stopped beside a pool maybe twenty feet across fed by the stream they'd been following.

He steadied her with an arm around her waist. "Here's what attracted the cows and game too." He pointed to tracks in the sandy soil surrounding the basin. "Deer, coyote, turkeys... The boys tied their horses here and went on foot," he said, indicating a trampled area near a stunted pine. "Great—if they could reach the ruins from below, they didn't need climbing gear, so we won't either."

He struck off to the right, following signs invisible to Jo, until they came to the base of a cliff, a dead end so far as she could tell.

"And here we are," he said. "I was afraid we'd have to come down from the rim, but this trail should take us right up to the ledge."

She could see no trail, only a massive rock slab leaning against the cliff face.

"Give me your pack," he said, slinging off his own. "This will probably be pretty tight." He took both packs and disappeared behind the slab.

She swallowed hard and followed, trying not to think about snakes and bats and whatever else might hang out in dark places. Loose stones rolled beneath her boots and her shoulders brushed rock; at one spot she had to turn sideways to slither through half crouching.

"You okay?" Tom's voice came back to her like a lifeline.

"Okay," she said, her voice tiny in the claustrophobic darkness. She'd die here before admitting the tight space made her heart race with fear. She squeezed her eyes shut and felt her way as the passage turned, and there was Tom waiting in the sunlight. A gentle path curved upward along the cliff face.

"The ancient ones designed this well," he said. "The path isn't too steep even for children, but a single defender could hold off attackers indefinitely."

He led the way up an easy grade that leveled off on a wide ledge. "Well, now," he said with delighted grin. "I'd say this was worth the climb."

Empty windows and doorways stared blindly at the opposite wall of the canyon. A thread of water slipped across the smooth stone floor to cascade down the cliff face like a silver ribbon.

"This isn't a large complex, probably a satellite to one of main villages—maybe a seasonal camp. We might find signs of cultivation if we climbed up to the canyon rim."

They spent more than an hour shooting detailed photos of the dwellings' exteriors and taking measurements with a long surveyor's tape while Tom described how life had been lived on this high platform. Jo listened, entranced both by the narrative and by his passion for the subject.

"I'd like to get some idea of the interior," he said, unlacing his boots. "Come with me if you like, but don't touch anything, not even the walls."

She swallowed. "Will we find any bodies in there?"

"I doubt it. The people who lived here left under their own steam so far as anyone knows, probably because of drought."

"Okay, then." She removed her own boots and followed him into the first chamber, careful not to brush against the door frame. Tom shone the beam of a flashlight into the far corners and she gasped.

"Bones!"

He hunkered beside the scattered remains. "Animal, not human," he said. "These caves have been vacant for a long time. A cat probably denned up here." He sniffed the air. "But not recently—this is an old carcass."

"Cat? Like a mountain lion?"

"Or a bobcat, although this is a deer femur." He stirred the bones with his toe. "So more likely a cougar."

They moved on through more chambers, finally returning to the ledge overlooking the ravine. Jo shivered; clouds had covered the sun while they had been exploring inside.

Tom looked skyward and frowned. "We need to get out of here."

They laced up their boots and scrambled down the trail at breakneck speed, crashing through the brush along the stream. The first mutter of thunder reached them just as they bolted into the main canyon. To the north, clouds the color of a fresh bruise crouched above the horizon. Another rumble, different in pitch from the thunder, shook the still air.

Tom knelt, laid his hand against the sand,

and then sprang to his feet. He pushed her back toward the ravine.

"What is it?" She peered over her shoulder at the ragged black wave advancing down the canyon floor like an evil army.

"Debris flow—a flash flood's right behind it. Quick, back to the ledge!" He yanked off her pack to carry it in one hand and shoved her ahead of him. "Run, dammit!"

Terror gave her feet wings; the grumble became a growl, louder every second, like a fast-approaching subway train. Water splashed under their boots on the trail and sucked at their ankles by the time they reached the slab. Tom leaped into the notch ahead of her, dragging her upward by one hand. They emerged into daylight to find muddy water laced with debris already swirling halfway up the walls of the ravine. Jo shuddered and followed Tom the rest of the way up to the ledge.

He wiped his sweating face with his sleeve. "Looks like we're stuck," he said. "There may be some footholds cut in the rock to reach the top of the mesa, but the truck's on the opposite side of the canyon. We're safer right here till the water goes down."

She clutched her arms around her body, trying to control convulsive shivering. "What's happening?"

"I'm guessing there was a cloudburst in the mountains that set off the flooding." He dropped their packs to the ground. "We'll probably be able to get out the way we came by morning, but for the time being..." He grinned. "Welcome to Hotel Anasazi."

CHAPTER SIXTEEN

POOR KID—TOM could see Jo was really scared; he was shaking some himself. "I'm sorry I yelled at you, but there was no time to explain."

"How did you know to turn back?" Her voice quavered.

"Those black clouds to the north," he said, "and I could feel the ground shaking, like putting your hand on a rail with a train coming. The grinding sound was the sand and rocks carried by the water. What you saw was miles of debris picked up from the canyon floor and pushed ahead by the water—there'll be a fresh crop of logs in the canyon tomorrow."

And sometimes the carcasses of animals that hadn't made it to higher ground, but she didn't need to hear about that just now.

"If we'd been on our way back to the truck—"

"We might have been able climb high enough, but this way we're safe, and dry except for our feet." He sat on the ground and pulled off his boots and socks. "We can put on dry socks and let our boots air out. I guarantee Shelby put an extra pair in your pack—she outfits Lucy's friends who come home with her from college."

He dragged his pack toward him. "It's way past lunchtime—let's see what we've got to eat."

She was still pale and shivering. He'd seen it many a time, cowboys walking away on rubbery legs from near disaster in the arena to crouch in the locker room speechless and shaking. Heck, it had happened to him more than once.

"Jo," he said. "You need to sit down and take your boots off—now."

She collapsed in an awkward heap and began tugging at the wet laces. He shoved her pack at her. "Put on dry socks and then we'll eat."

He dug into his pack and pulled out foil-wrapped packets, apples and a thermos, silently blessing Shelby for sending a hot drink. He poured coffee and folded Jo's fingers around the cup. "Dad orders this special coffee from New Orleans for Shelby," he said. "Some folks don't care for the chicory, some do. What do you think?"

She gulped the hot liquid and a little color came back into her cheeks. "It's good." She drank again. "It's wonderful," she said, life returning to her voice. "What else do we have?" She began tearing at the food wrappings.

"Whoa, whoa! Remember, this is lunch and supper. Breakfast too, for that matter. We'll be mighty hungry come morning if we eat it all now."

Shelby had sent fat roast beef sandwiches on thick-sliced wheat bread, apples, pickles and a huge slab of gingerbread. A handful of energy bars and a couple of water bottles filled the bottom of his pack under a fleece anorak.

He divided one of the sandwiches with his pocketknife and handed half to Jo with a grand gesture. "Luncheon is served," he said.

He saw with approval she was sipping coffee between small bites of the sandwich, normal function returning.

"Can you call your folks to say we're okay?" she asked.

"I can try. We had no signal on the canyon floor but maybe I can pick one up now we're a little higher." He turned on his phone—only a couple of bars, but he crossed his fingers and keyed in the ranch number. His face lighted when Shelby answered.

"I'm going to talk fast," he said, "in case I lose the signal. A flash flood has us stranded up a canyon. We're safe, but we won't try to hike out till morning. Let them know at the Ute Cultural Center—" He looked at his phone. "Dropped the call." He shrugged. "At least they know we're okay."

He stuck the phone in his pocket. "Let's try to round up enough wood for a fire before it gets dark."

He led the way back as far as the slab and they gathered twigs, pinon cones and small branches lodged in crevices along the path. They returned to the ledge and dumped their trove just as the sun disappeared below the opposite wall of the ravine.

"How many layers are you wearing?" he asked.

"A bra and tank top under my turtleneck."

"Dig out another layer from your pack—you'll need it once night falls."

Jo found a fleece hoodie in her pack. "Do you always carry this much for a day hike?"

"Better to carry more than you need than need more than you carry," he said.

She laughed. "That sounds something to print on a T-shirt." She sobered. "How cold will it get tonight?"

"We won't freeze, but it'll get pretty uncomfortable. We'll be plenty glad to get out of here by morning."

She peered down into the little canyon where only the tops of brush and small trees showed above muddy water streaked with foam and littered with small branches. "Okay," she said. "I can handle that."

Tom wanted to cheer. As Marge Bowman had said, Jo was a girl fit to ride the mountains.

He laid the fire in a sheltered corner of the ledge but didn't light it. It wouldn't provide much heat, but its glow would lend a measure of comfort once night fell. They shared the second sandwich and the rest of the coffee, but he held back the gingerbread for extra calories during the night.

When all light had left the sky, he touched a match to their little pile of fuel and they sat together against the cliff face sharing the gingerbread in small bites to make it last.

"Tell me a story," she said.

He considered her request without laughing. The near escape from the flash flood, their isolation in the ghostly ruins, the great darkness outside their tiny bubble of firelight took him out of himself. Tomorrow he'd be sorry, but tonight he spoke as if in a confessional.

"Once upon a time there was a cowboy. He

was riding bulls pretty good, but he'd racked up enough injuries to make him think about hanging up his rope. He met a girl who said she loved him so he asked her to marry him." If Jo had said a single word he would have withdrawn into his habitual reserve, but she sat without speaking, without even looking at him.

"He bought this girl a ring and told her they would settle down on the family ranch to raise their baby."

He fell silent, fighting the wave of pain that never went away completely.

At last Jo spoke. "How did the story end?"

He gave a short laugh. "Turns out she was in love with the bright lights and the big money, not with the cowboy." He shuddered as if casting out an evil spirit; he couldn't believe he'd spoken so freely.

Jo turned to him at last. "I saw my father die," she said. "I've never told anyone that, not even my mother. I said I was going for a Coke, but I sneaked down to be with my dad's pit crew instead. He was going to win—he was leading by a whole lap. I wanted to be right there when he stepped out of his car."

She clutched Tom's hand. "Another car hit his right in front of the stands. He skidded past me sideways—he looked right at me, I thought. He was fighting the wheel, and then another car hit him. His head snapped sideways like a broken toy, and his car started spinning. I knew he was dead, even before he hit the wall. I ran back to my mom and never told her what I saw."

A drop of moisture hit Tom's hand and then another. Jo made no sound, but tears ran down her cheeks in a silent stream. He wrapped his other arm around her shoulders and they huddled together beside their tiny fire like lost children in an old fairy tale.

CHAPTER SEVENTEEN

BIRDSONG SOMEWHERE BELOW their aerie roused Jo in the gray predawn light. Her back and hips ached from lying on cold stone, but her cheek rested on something warm and solid. She shifted, and Tom woke with a jerk, tightening his arm around her.

"Hey," he said. "Looks like we made it through the night."

Jo sat up and then fell back with a groan. "I'll never again complain about any mattress."

"If everything hadn't been wet, I could have cut some brush to make for a softer rest," he said. "Of course, if everything had been dry, we wouldn't have been stuck here overnight."

"What doesn't kill you makes a great story afterward," she said. She pushed her hair back from her face. "What's next?"

"I'll check the main canyon as soon as the sun comes up." He stood and peered into the ravine. "The water's already gone down here."

Sunlight had made its way onto the ledge by

the time they finished their meager breakfast of energy bars and bottled water. "Wait here," Tom said. "I'll see if we can get out the way we came in."

Jo bit back a protest. She didn't want to wait alone, but she nodded and started packing up the debris from their stay. The sound of his footsteps faded until she could hear only the sound of birds in the brush below and a phantom breeze moaning through the ruins.

His absence seemed endless. Was the main canyon still flooded? Had he fallen into a deep pool and hit his head on a rock? She had almost decided to go looking for him when she heard him returning.

"We can walk out," he said, his face grim, "but it's not going to be pretty."

IT WASN'T PRETTY, not in any way. Sweat and grime caked her clothes and she staggered with fatigue by the time they reached the truck. They had hiked more than three hours over the same route that had taken a third of that time to cover the day before. A pasty layer of silt now plastered a new landscape of logs and small boulders on the canyon floor. Water still stood in depressions gouged out by the swirling current.

In one of the pools... She swallowed hard

and squeezed her eyes shut to block out the sight of the woman's body almost buried in the mud.

Tom slumped on the truck's bumper and punched in 911. "I guess you're missing a hiker," he said. "Female, twenties maybe—it was hard to tell. We had no way to bring the body out, but I can guide a recovery party in." He gave the dispatcher his location and listened. "Yeah, I could see it was a bad one. We nearly got caught too—we spent the night on a ledge up one of the side canyons. We'll wait right here."

He keyed off. "I'm sorry I dragged you through this," he said to Jo. "I guess New York City looks pretty good right now."

Anger burned through the shock. "Bad stuff can happen anywhere. People died in New York City during Sandy because they didn't take the hurricane warnings seriously. We're not lying in the mud like that poor woman because you read the signs in time. So knock it off."

The ghost of a smile flickered across his dirt-streaked face with its shadow of beard. "Sorry, I forgot I was dealing with someone who sails halfway around the world in a little boat."

He tapped his phone again. "I'd better let them know at home we made it out okay." He waited. "Shelby, we're back at the truck, but we have to wait for a search-and-rescue team. We found—"

He listened, sighed. "I'm afraid not. I have to lead them back to a body." He sucked in his breath. "How many?" His shoulders bowed. "Well, at least we've got one accounted for. Look for us when you see us."

He turned to Jo. "Four more hikers are missing," he said.

She stared at him in sick horror. "Four more..." Her stomach churned; she turned blindly toward him and he pulled her into his arms, cradling her against his muddy shirt.

The growl of an engine in low gear announced the arrival of a Ute Tribal Police car. Tom and the officer set off on foot up the wash, soon followed by a Forest Service helicopter. Jo climbed into the truck and closed her eyes, utterly drained. She drifted between sleep and wakefulness, vaguely aware of birds' voices and the sweet spicy perfume of sagebrush on the light breeze. Tried not to think of their grisly discovery in the canyon.

A light tap on the hood jerked her back to consciousness. Oscar Buck stood beside the truck holding a silver thermos and a brown paper bag spotted with grease.

"I heard on the moccasin telegraph what happened to you guys," he said. "I thought you maybe could use a little pick-me-up." He held up the bag. "Coffee and fresh fry bread."

"I could kiss you," Jo said with tears in her eyes. She gulped the hot coffee and tore off chunks of the warm puffy dough, ravenous with the ecstasy of being alive.

Oscar watched with a grin on his face. "I guess that hit the spot," he said. "Did you find the ruins okay?"

For a moment his question outraged her. How could he speak of something so mundane when a woman lay dead just up the canyon, when more hikers were still missing? And then she burned with survivor's guilt at her own primitive joy that she and Tom hadn't suffered the same fate.

"Right where you said to look," she said. "Tom seemed to think it's a significant site. He made measurements and I took lots of photos." She dug her point-and-shoot from her pack and flipped open the little screen.

Oscar leaned close. "Say, you got some great shots! You mind if we use these at the Cultural Center? You and Tom make a great team. He's a helluva bull rider, but he'll make an even better archeologist once he gets back to his studies."

She remembered someone mentioning Tom's attending college. "He was studying archeology?"

"He hasn't gotten that far yet, but he's picked up a bunch of liberal arts credits at Fort Lewis College when he's been out with injuries, plus he's helped out with a couple digs." He laughed. "In his spare time."

Now she understood Tom's intense interest in the ruins; she could picture him teaching with equal passion.

The *thwaup-thwaup* of the helicopter sounded in the distance; half an hour later Tom and the Ute cop reappeared on foot. Oscar met them and they spoke briefly before Tom returned to the truck. Weariness showed in every movement as he climbed into the driver's seat. He drank the coffee Jo poured for him and accepted the fry bread with a nod of thanks.

"They've recovered three bodies, counting the one we found," he said. "Two still missing. The party was out of cell contact just like we were and didn't get the Park Service's flash flood warning." He rubbed his face, smearing the sweat and dirt, and then wiped his hands on his jeans before starting the engine.

"You want me to drive?" she asked. "I napped a little while you were gone."

"I'll get us as far as the paved road, then it's all yours. Thanks, city girl."

THE SUN HUNG low on the horizon by the time Jo parked next to the barn. She touched Tom's arm as he turned to pull their packs from behind the seat.

"What we talked about last night…" she said. His muscles went rigid under her hand. "I was so tired and scared—I don't recall a word we said."

He relaxed and smiled. "Funny thing—neither do I."

CHAPTER EIGHTEEN

SHELBY TURNED FROM the stove when Jo emerged from her room after sleeping for twelve hours. "Welcome back," she said with a smile. "I hope you slept well."

Jo sat at the table and accepted a mug of coffee. "Like the dead," she said and then shivered. Mercifully the drowning victim hadn't invaded her dreams.

Stranger rose from the hearthrug and laid his head in Jo's lap. She stroked his rough fur.

"You've been admitted to the inner circle," Shelby said. "Stranger is always a gentleman, but he doesn't often make overtures like that."

Jo tipped his gray muzzle up to look into his eyes. "How old is he?"

"He has to be about eight. I found him limping along the I-30 in Arkansas eight years ago when he was less than a year old." Shelby fed the dog a scrap of bacon. "I named him from an old gospel song." She sang in a soft contralto, *"I'm just a poor wayfaring stranger a'traveling through this world of woe.* He was my only friend until I met Jake."

Jo filed this information along with Tom's comment that Shelby had lived out of her car for years. "Where is everyone?" she asked.

"I sent Lucy into town for supplies. She got in last night from Boulder after you went to bed. She wanted to wait this morning until you got up, but you need at least one cup of coffee before meeting her."

"What's so awful about Lucy?" Jo asked.

Shelby laughed. "Nothing's awful. I love her dearly, but she's a 120-pound microburst. She'll spin you around and take your breath away when she blows in with no warning. I don't know if Tom's told you about her ambitions..."

"He said she's studying theater arts."

"Jake made a deal with her back in high school," Shelby said. "If she completed one year of college in good standing, he'd stake her to a year in New York or Hollywood. She's kept up her end of the bargain—she's a junior now. It'll be tough after last spring's disaster, but we'll manage somehow."

"Does she have the kind of talent to make it as a professional?"

"We've gone to Boulder half a dozen times to see her perform—we think she's wonderful, of course. But good enough to compete at the next level?" Shelby shrugged. "I guess she won't know unless she tries. Just don't be surprised if she starts quizzing you about the New York theater scene."

"I know actors who show up for all the casting calls and support themselves waiting tables and slicing pizza," Jo said. "I can tell Lucy truthfully it's a tough life. I do have a couple friends-of-friends connections if she decides to come to New York."

"She'll be thrilled for any whiff of the Big Apple," Shelby said. "She was afraid you'd leave after what happened yesterday. Tom told her you had more grit than that."

A glow of pride warmed Jo. "Where is Tom?"

"The guys are out sorting cows. We bring the first-year heifers into the home pasture in case they have problems calving although they rarely do—we breed them as two-year-olds, so they're well grown before they drop their first calf." She freshened Jo's coffee. "Do you feel like working today or do you want to rest up?"

"If Tom can work, so can I—he had a rougher time in the canyon than I did." She wasn't about to admit to the assortment of bruises she'd collected stumbling through the nightmare debris left by the flood.

She screwed up her nerve to ask the question haunting her. "Have they found the other hikers?"

"Yes—one more dead and one alive. A teenage girl in the same party sprained her ankle the day before and stayed in camp. Poor kid, she lost her brother and sister-in-law." Shelby pulled a pan from the oven. "I get so angry—those canyons can be death traps, but people go into them like they're theme parks until a tragedy like this happens. Dangerous enough even knowing the hazards, as you and Tom found out."

She sighed and set the pan on the table. "How about some French toast?"

Jo discovered she was famished; she'd been so exhausted the night before, she'd stayed awake only long enough to shower and then wolf down a bowl of beef stew with dumplings.

"What kind of work can I help with?' she asked after her second helping of French toast drizzled with chokecherry syrup.

"Can you ride Western? I have a couple of two-year-olds ready for an intermediate rider."

"English, Western, bareback… I'm not a fancy equestrian, but I have light hands and I can follow directions."

AN HOUR LATER Jo and Shelby left the corral with Shelby mounted on Smoky, a roan gelding, and Jo on Della, a blood-bay filly. Jo wore a spare hat of Lucy's that Shelby had dug out; she sat a little straighter in the saddle in honor of the hat and her boots. Sunlight poured into the valley like warm honey although the air still held a hint of morning chill and frost sparkled on the grass in shaded spots. Silver mountains loomed to the north and east.

They rode side by side in comfortable silence like old friends with no need for conversation. They skirted a dense thicket along the creek; Shelby reined in where the track made a sharp turn toward a crude gate.

"This is where I found Jake the day of the blizzard," she said. "My world stopped when I saw him lying in the snow—I was sure he was dead. I don't remember now how I got him into the saddle and back to the barn—nothing mattered except he was alive. Luckily the full storm didn't hit until we were almost to the hospital in Durango."

"Losing so many cattle must have been heartbreaking," Jo said, and then she grimaced. "Sorry, bad choice of words."

"It was heartbreaking, but at least Tom and Luke had the carcasses hauled away and burned by the time Jake came home from the hospital. I know I drive Jake crazy with my hovering, but I came so close to losing him. Maybe I'll learn to relax in five or ten or twenty years," she said with a laugh.

She loosened her reins and they rode on. Soon they heard men's voices and an occasional bovine protest. "We'll circle to the outside," Shelby said. "I haven't worked these two much with cattle yet, but it won't hurt for them to get a taste of what it's like. If Della starts acting silly, just ease her away from the action."

Jo nodded and followed Shelby at a walk toward the straggling line of cows guided by Jake and Luke with Tom bringing up the rear. Luke waved, and her heart lifted at the flash of pleasure on Tom's face visible even through the cloud of dust raised by the cattle's hooves.

Caution pulled her up short; she knew she was drifting into dangerous territory. Tom was steady and kind; he had saved her life when the flash flood came roaring down the canyon. She struggled to regain her balance by summoning up the memory of her father's last moments— she could never love someone whose work put him in constant danger—but Tom's face blurred the image.

Della snorted and started dancing under her;

she turned the filly's head away and walked her in a wide circle until the herd passed.

Shelby rode up beside her. "Nice job with Della," she said. "We'll ride home behind the herd so she and Smoky can feel like real cow ponies." They continued to the barn while the men turned the heifers to scatter into the wide pasture along the creek.

Luke rode into the corral just as the rattle of the front cattle guard heralded a vehicle's arrival.

"Heads up," he said. "Hurricane Lucy on the horizon."

A red Jeep Cherokee rocked to a standstill by the kitchen door and a slim young woman climbed out. She spotted the riders in the corral and approached with long strides. She slipped through the gate and shook Jo's hand.

"Hi," she said. "I'm Lucinda Cameron. Welcome to Cameron's Pride."

Jo hid a grin. Everyone referred to her as Lucy, but she doubtless envisioned *Lucinda Cameron* on a Broadway marquee. Her red-gold curls, blue eyes and creamy skin untouched by the Colorado sun might well get her noticed, but she would need more than beauty to build a successful acting career.

Lucy pulled off Della's bridle. "I'm so glad

to meet you, but wow! I thought you'd be older from reading those features you wrote. You've already had such cool experiences."

"I'm working on a pretty cool project right now, with Tom and Luke's help," Jo said.

Lucy laughed. "Isn't bull riding nutty? The cowboys have to be insane—I think they ride mostly for the love of it. A few years ago two former champions retired at the end of the same season. One of them couldn't wait to quit and the other one left the arena in tears after he got off his last bull—go figure."

She sobered. "You must have had an awful scare with that flash flood. Lucky you guys made it to higher ground in time. And then finding a body! Not much like New York City."

"Every locale has its own hazards," Jo said. "I doubt you have many muggings out here. And it wasn't luck—Tom saved us."

Shelby pulled off Smoky's saddle. "Did you get ice cream for the pie?"

Lucy clapped her hands over her mouth. "Yikes, ice cream!" She tossed Della's bridle back to Jo and sprinted toward the Jeep.

Shelby sighed and then laughed. "And now you've met Lucy."

CHAPTER NINETEEN

TOM HOOKED THE top loop of the range gate and mounted to make one last sweep around the herd, checking that all the heifers were accounted for. He took his time riding back to the barn, trying to settle his mind. Despite what he'd told Lucy, he'd half expected Jo to be gone or at least preparing to leave. For a moment he'd mistaken her for Lucy riding with Shelby; the jolt of relief on recognizing Jo had rocked him in the saddle, followed by a dash of cold reality. Maybe she considered him a friend now, a collaborator on her book as well as the subject of her profile, but she had never shown any sign of romantic interest.

Their agreement to bury the revelations shared beside their little campfire didn't wipe her words from his mind. She had bared a secret to him that probably never entirely left her mind. It stood to reason his riding bulls would bar him from any deeper relationship, but he couldn't hang up his rope with the ranch still so deep in debt. Maybe this would be his year for the championship, maybe the next. The million-dollar bonus check plus his season's winnings would pay off his dad's medical expenses and go a long way toward rebuilding their herd. Once that was done, he could get serious about completing his degree while working the ranch at the same time. He would look for a nice girl, one he could trust, someone not pining for city life, have a couple kids...

His resolution folded when he found Jo in the corral brushing down his father's horse. She looked up with a grin.

"I may not know how to work cattle," she said, "but I'm a dynamite groom. Get in line—I'll do your horse next."

"I saw you on Della—you did fine." He swung down from the black gelding. "Blackjack is more what you're used to—Dad rehabbed him after he broke down in a race at Santa Anita."

They finished grooming the horses and turned them out before heading to the house for lunch. Lucy had started an assembly line of hamburgers and salad; they discussed the afternoon's work while they ate.

"I've got a job for you," Jake said to Tom. "How about you guys ride out to the cabin and check the roof since that big wind a couple weeks ago? There should be plenty of shingles in the shed from the repair we did last fall."

Tom turned to Jo. "You ready for more time in the saddle? Maybe an hour's ride each way."

"Maybe you should plan to stay overnight," Shelby said. "Give Jo a real taste of the Old West."

What was Shelby trying to do to him? The last thing he needed was another night alone with Jo.

"I'm up for it," Jo said. "No flash floods, right?"

"No floods," Tom said. She was game, and he loved her for it. "I can even promise a mattress."

"I'll go too," Lucy said. "I haven't been to the cabin in decades."

"Since last October," her father said. "And I think I heard you promise to help Shelby with a 4-H workshop tomorrow."

Her face fell. "Oh pooh! I forgot."

Shelby rose from the table. "You can take a steak from the freezer—you'll have everything else you need at the cabin."

"Okay," Tom said. No way he could get out of it. "We'll ride over to the Buck spread while we're out that way. I want to thank Auntie Rose for sending Oscar with the fry bread yesterday." He grinned at Jo. "Pack your appetite—Auntie Rose will try to stuff you like a Thanksgiving turkey."

"Take a few quarts of applesauce," Shelby said. "They're probably short since lightning hit their apple tree last summer. Tell Auntie Rose to send the boys over to pick from ours come fall—we'll have plenty to share."

TOM AND JO left on fresh horses after lunch. Shelby had asked Tom to give her gray stallion Ghost some much-needed exercise. Jo rode Sadie, a quarter horse–draft cross mare who could and would kick any amorous notions Ghost might have up between his pretty ears.

Tom decided not to look too far down the road—not like Jo expected anything of him. The spring sunshine was warm on his shoulders, he had a fine horse between his knees and a pretty girl riding at his side. He'd be crazy not to enjoy the here and now as long as it lasted.

"We'll visit the Bucks first," he said. "Auntie Rose will ask us to stay for supper, but I want to get back to the cabin before nightfall—stumbling around in the dark trying to light an oil lamp is a pain."

"No electricity at the cabin?"

"No indoor plumbing either, but the privy is just out the back door. We carry drinking water maybe a hundred yards from a spring, and there's a hot spring for bathing."

He treated himself for just a moment to the thought of sharing the little pool with Jo and then hurrying down the path to warm themselves again in front of the fire. He squirmed in the saddle. Shelby had a lot to answer for, setting him up like this.

He reined in at the top of a long hill and pointed to the southwest. "That long ridge? That's Mesa Verde, where I worked on the dig during high school." He reached down to pat Ghost's neck. "This fella came from the band of feral horses wandering around the park. My dad bought him from another rancher for Shelby to train."

"He was a wild horse? I took him for an Arabian, or at least an Arab cross."

"More likely a throwback to the Barbs the Spaniards rode exploring the region," Tom said. "No telling what his bloodlines are, but he does sire nice foals."

They crossed through a big metal gate separating Cameron's Pride from the Buck ranch. The house lay in the next little valley where a stout figure in blinding purple slacks and a red sweater stood in the chicken yard tossing feed to the hens clustered around her feet. Her round face shone with delight when they rode into the yard.

"My favorite boy! Welcome, you and your lady too."

"We're all your favorite boys, Auntie," Tom said, dismounting and returning her hug. "We came to thank you for sending the fry bread yesterday. Jo and I fought over the last piece."

"I knew I should have sent more! Wait, I'll make up a batch right now, just to hold you till supper. We've got lamb stew and tortillas and—"

"That sounds great, but we can't stay. I plan to repair the cabin roof tomorrow and I want to get settled in before dark." He pulled two cartons of applesauce from his saddlebag. "Shelby sent this—she thought you might be short since you lost your apple tree last year."

"That Shelby, such a good-hearted girl," Auntie Rose said. "So good for Jake, my favorite boy."

Tom winked at Jo and she stifled a giggle.

"You have time for coffee and to see who's spending the day with me." Auntie Rose led them into the kitchen of the rambling log house and picked up a pink bundle from a deep box on the table. "June let me keep Autumn Rose for the day while she went into Durango."

"What a beautiful name," Jo said.

"June's other mother-in-law picked it out," Auntie Rose said. "Just before she died last September. She was sure the baby would be a girl."

A tiny fist emerged from the wrappings accompanied by a mewling cry. Tom took the baby from her. "Well, hey, little lady—how about a smile for your cousin Tom?" He cradled her expertly and grinned when she responded with a contented gurgle.

"Not really blood kin," he told Jo. "June's first husband was Oscar's younger brother. She married Delbert Black Horse after Sam got killed working construction."

"Still family," Auntie Rose said. "Still like a daughter to me, and the boys are here helping Oscar almost every weekend." She took a bottle of formula from the fridge and warmed it under hot water before handing it to Tom. "You're such a good hand with little ones, you need to start your own family."

He turned away from Auntie Rose and from Jo's searching gaze, concentrating on Autumn Rose's contented suckling. He would have had a little girl or boy toddling around the barn and corrals by now, already learning to ride… The women's conversation faded out as he focused on the baby's trusting gaze, her warm weight in his hands. At last her brown eyes closed and a bubble appeared at the corner of her rosebud mouth.

"I think she's done," he said and handed Autumn back. "We need to leave so we can settle in before it gets dark."

Auntie Rose laid the baby in the makeshift crib and pulled a foil-wrapped package from the freezer. "Take a piece of my jalapeño cornbread," she said, "and some peach preserves." She took Jo's hand. "You come back soon when you can stay longer. You liked my fry bread, I'll teach you so you can make it for Tom."

CHAPTER TWENTY

TOM RODE AHEAD of Jo when they left the Buck ranch although the track was wide enough for them to ride side by side. His silence walled her out.

Finally he reined in and turned to her with a smile. "Auntie Rose sure took to you," he said. "She doesn't offer her fry bread recipe to just anyone."

"She reminds me of my great-aunt Grace," Jo said. "She's my grandfather's sister. We all run to her with questions from boyfriend problems to career choices. She just listens and nods and everyone thinks she's the seer of the Mohawk Valley."

He laughed. "Just the opposite with Auntie Rose. She talks and talks—by the time she stops for breath, everyone has things figured out on their own. I guess either way works just as well."

Jo wanted to comment on his ease, his total absorption feeding little Autumn Rose, but his cryptic tale told on the dark canyon ledge held her back. Did he have a child somewhere? She had heard no such rumor from the wives and couldn't imagine anything less than his total involvement as a father.

A few minutes' ride beyond the boundary fence brought them to the crest of a rise. A creek roistered through the little valley below; a weathered cabin sat on the opposite bank against a towering cliff that shone golden in the late afternoon sun. Low shrubs beginning to show green hugged the stone foundation.

"There sits the Camerons' ancestral shrine," Tom said as he set his horse splashing through the stirrup-high water.

As they drew closer, Jo saw that although the rough boards were gray with age, the structure showed careful maintenance. After rehabbing the Brooklyn house with her mother, she could appreciate the straight rooftree, the neatly caulked windowpanes, and the level planks in the little porch.

Tom dismounted and led the stallion into the corral; Jo followed on Sadie. He slid the heavy bar to latch the gate before tying his reins to the lean-to forming one side.

"Shelby trained Ghost here," he said. "He tried to make a break for his old range—he would have made it too except Lucy had ridden over to help and slammed the gate in his face." He took a piece of candy from his pocket and handed it to her. "The key to his heart," he said. "Ghost loves licorice."

Jo offered the tidbit on her palm, marveling at the velvety touch of the horse's muzzle. "He has lovely manners," she said.

"Yep, takes some kind of trainer to turn a wild-born two-year-old stud into a gentleman. Shelby gets enough training requests to keep her on the road full-time, but she won't travel unless Luke and I are home so Dad can go with her." A wistful shadow darkened his face. "He and my mom had a great marriage, and he picked himself another winner the second go-round."

He unsaddled Ghost and then Sadie, draping the saddlebags over his shoulder. "The sun will be down before long—we need to get water before dark."

Jo stopped in amazement when she entered the cabin; she might have stepped back in time a hundred years or more. Except for a gas range dating from the 1930s, the interior looked like a movie set from a classic Western. Bunks lined one wall while a wide sandstone chimney with its fireplace anchored one end of the single room. Antique tools and artifacts completed the illusion.

"Like our museum?" Tom asked. "The cabin is Shelby's pet project—she stayed here when she first came to the ranch. She'd been on the run for years from a man who raped her when she was barely twenty and then stalked her because she shamed him in public." Tom dropped the saddlebags on a rough pine table. "The creep tried to kidnap her when she finally got the nerve to face him. He's still in prison and will be for a good long time."

"She told me about finding your dad last year in the blizzard—she's a strong lady."

"My mom was pretty gutsy too," Tom said. "Coping with lupus day to day maybe wasn't as dramatic, but she fought to keep life as normal as possible for us, especially for Lucy. We've got a long line of tough Cameron women in our pedigree. They herded cattle and shot renegades and ran the ranch with children and old men when their husbands were off to the wars. We set a high value on gumption."

Jo was glad she hadn't scurried back to New York's relative security after the harrowing experience in the canyon. The notion had occurred to her.

Tom opened a door to a storage space at the

back of the cabin and grabbed several plastic jugs. "The pump in the sink is just for washing up," he said. "We get drinking water from the spring."

He led Jo out a back door and up a path winding along the base of the cliff. Beyond a rugged outcropping, a natural pool lay in a miniature amphitheater; tendrils of steam rose off the surface in the cooling air.

"An even hundred and five degrees winter and summer," he said. "We've got robes in the cabin if you'd like a soak before dark."

The warm water beckoned irresistibly. "That sounds too good to pass up," she said.

"Fine," he said. "I'll cook supper while you enjoy our spa." He filled the jugs from a tiny cascade falling from the rock face and they returned to the cabin. He reached again into the storeroom and handed Jo a striped towel. "Enjoy. Dinner in half an hour."

He turned away and began unpacking supplies.

Jo pulled sweatpants and a T-shirt from her saddlebag and climbed the path to the hot spring. She acknowledged that she was more than halfway to falling in love with Tom. He was kind, funny, brave and a relentless worker. To those pluses add his love of children, equaling a perfect husband. A big minus: he could be crippled or killed the next time he climbed down into the chute. And he'd shown no more than comradely affection for her.

She shed her dusty clothes and sank chin-deep into the warm water. No breeze stirred; the sky above the little cirque was already purpling toward evening. A few fluting notes of birdsong quavered in the still air. She closed her eyes.

"Supper in a few minutes." A disembodied voice yanked her back to consciousness, kicking and splashing.

"I'm awake, I'm awake!" Over her pounding heart she heard footsteps retreating—she could count on Tom to resist taking a peek, instead behaving like a real gentleman. She stepped from the pool and donned her sweats before hurrying down the path.

Tom was hunkered beside a huge steak over a crude fire pit. He looked up with a grin. "All relaxed? I thought you were planning to spend the night there."

"A good thing you called me—I did drift off."

"If you want, you can check the beans and set the table." He poked at the glowing coals. "I need to tend this fire."

Jo returned to the cabin and stirred the beans simmering on the stove. She found agate-ware plates and mugs in a hanging cupboard and set the table. Oil lamps shed golden light from the mantel; the scent of molasses and bacon rose from the beans. The steak added its own mouthwatering aroma when Tom carried it to the table on a dented tin tray.

"It's not fancy dining," he said, "but steak and beans go down pretty well, as hard as we've worked today."

"As hard as you've worked, you mean."

"Riding one of Shelby's green-broke string counts as work in anyone's book—you did a nice job on Della." He carried an age-blackened coffeepot from the stove to set beside a tin of condensed milk. "I doubt coffee will keep us awake."

Jo ate as if she hadn't seen food in a week, picking up the last crumbs of Auntie Rose's cornbread with a spoon sticky from the peach preserves. At last she sat back, glassy-eyed with repletion.

"I'm ashamed of pigging out like that. As if we didn't have a big lunch just…" She looked at her watch. "Just six hours ago."

"It's the elevation," he said. "I've heard the same thing about sea air."

"You're right—we ate like hyenas on the ocean even when it was easy sailing."

"You can work it off tomorrow running up and down the ladder while I'm shingling."

She managed to stay awake long enough to wash the few dishes before sliding into a sleeping bag on a lower bunk. "This smells heavenly," she said, rubbing her cheek on the flannel lining.

"Shelby planted lavender around the cabin," he said. "She sprinkles the dried flowers in the bags before we shut down in the fall—no nasty cowboy smells."

She chuckled and plumped her pillow. Her eyes stayed open only a few minutes as she watched Tom take a book from an old chest by the fireplace and move a lamp to the table.

THE SOFT CLICK of the door latch woke her; gray light filtered through the south-facing window. She turned in her sleeping bag and glanced at Tom's empty bunk. Through the window she could see him clad only in sweatpants, silhouetted against the pale dawn sky. He raised his arms in a slow sweeping gesture and began to move, half attack and half dance, faster and faster, blurring in continuous motion. At last he stood still, bowed slightly and turned toward the cabin.

Jo caught her breath. He had a beautiful physique, lean and sculpted, but marred by scars on his right forearm, his abdomen, and on both shoulders. She knew he'd also had surgery on his leg. What kind of idiot kept coming back for punishment like that, knowing the next injury could end his career or even his life?

He stopped short when he opened the door. "Hey, did I wake you? I figured I'd be finished before you got up. I lose conditioning if I go more than a couple days without working out." He grabbed a towel from his bunk and wiped the sweat from his face and chest. "I'll take a quick dunk and then fix breakfast."

"Sure, great—no problem." She averted her eyes. "What was that—kung fu?"

"Some kung fu and karate, some tai chi—I put together my own routine. A physical therapist got me doing martial arts to help with my balance a few years ago and I've kept at it." He studied her face; she hoped her feelings didn't show. "I guess it looks pretty strange."

She shook her head. "The moves remind me of Mikhail Baryshnikov. My mom's a big fan so I've seen a lot of his films."

He laughed. "Ballet? Please don't noise that

around the chutes—they kid me enough about martial arts."

"Do you care?"

"Not particularly," he said. "Some guys carry special coins or wear lucky underwear—whatever you think makes you ride better." He picked up his shirt and jeans from an upper bunk. "See you in a few."

CHAPTER TWENTY-ONE

TOM SHIVERED BRIEFLY under the icy waterfall to sluice away the sweat and then eased into the hot spring. What was bothering Jo? She'd covered it well, but something had upset her. Maybe he should have told her he'd be out early, but she'd seemed pretty tired last night and he always looked forward to greeting the dawn alone from the old homestead.

He sank into the warm water, trying to recapture the peace he always felt after completing his routine, but her troubled eyes haunted him. Had he imagined her fleeting expression of… What, horror? Disgust? He couldn't think of anything he'd done to offend her. He could read animals almost like kindred species—the flick of an ear, a ripple of skin—but he had no clue about women.

The scents of wood smoke and bacon frying pulled him from his reverie; he stepped from the pool and dressed before hurrying to the cabin.

Jo turned to him with a wooden spoon in her hand. "My turn to cook," she said. "Bacon and beans okay?"

He relaxed and returned her smile. "Good fuel for roofing," he said. He poured himself a mug of coffee as she set plates on the table and joined him.

When they finished eating, he refilled his mug and beckoned. He would try to make amends for whatever had upset her by sharing his pleasure with her. "The sun's just about to come up."

They sat side by side on the porch steps while the eastern sky turned from aquamarine to peach to gold. Neither spoke, and while they watched, two mule deer emerged from the ravine from which the stream flowed. The shy creatures raised their heads just as the sun winked between two mountain peaks and then they faded back into the brush.

Tom saw tears tracing down Jo's cheeks. "Hey, what's wrong?" he asked. He put an arm around her shoulders.

She shook her head. "Nothing's wrong—it's just so beautiful here." She gestured, taking in the sky and the rolling valley. "This is magical."

He gave her a squeeze and then released her.

"Always seems that way to me—I never get tired of it. But the quiet spooks some people."

"Our neighborhood in Brooklyn is relatively quiet in city terms, but there's always traffic noise. Even on my grandfather's farm we could hear big trucks on the New York State Thruway." She leaned her head back against the porch pillar. "I'm going to miss this when I go back."

He'd be stupid to let himself hope she could be content here, but an image lodged itself in his brain: Jo as his wife, his partner and the mother of his children. He thrust the notion away with almost a physical violence. He'd let himself be fooled once—he wasn't about to make the same mistake again.

Ghost whinnied in the corral and Tom straightened.

A few minutes later a rider appeared from the direction of the Buck ranch. "We've got company," he said. "It's Auntie Rose's grandson Brian."

"Do you think there's an emergency?"

"Nope, he's not riding fast enough. And he's carrying something." He stood as the lanky Ute boy halted his paint gelding at the steps and held out a canvas tote.

"Hey, Tom," he said. "You've got the circus pony here. Cool!"

Tom introduced Jo to Brian Buck. "Brian always calls Ghost the circus pony because he saw Shelby training him from the ground with just hand signals, like a liberty horse." He took the bag. "How come you're not in school?"

"Easter break. Mom dropped me off yesterday when she picked up Autumn. Grandma says you put a spell on her—she's been real fussy lately but not since you fed her yesterday."

"I practiced on you and Sammie when you were babies," Tom said. "And Lucy."

"Wow, Lucy?"

"Yup, when I was younger than you. So if your mom asks you to help with Autumn…"

Brian nodded, his eyes big. "I can do that."

Tom took two Rubbermaid containers out of the bag. "What did Auntie Rose send us?"

"Lamb stew from last night and green chili. And corn tortillas and some prickly pear jelly." Brian grinned. "She sure loves to feed people."

"Thank her for us. Shelby said to send you guys over to pick apples in the fall." He unloaded the bag and handed it back to Brian. "Are you going to stay and help me fix the roof?"

Brian's face fell. "I wish—Mom told me no goofing off till I clean out the chicken coop for Grandma."

"Give me a call when you've finished—maybe we'll still be working." Tom turned the paint's head back toward the creek. "Now beat it."

Brian clapped his heels to his horse's ribs and loped toward the creek with a twelve-year-old's version of a war whoop.

"There goes peace and quiet," Jo said with a grin. "You were babysitting when you were ten?"

"Nine," he said. "Mom had a hard pregnancy with Lucy. She didn't snap right back so I did a lot of holding and feeding. I like babies—maybe I should have studied to be a pediatrician."

"It's not too late for that."

He shook his head. "I've spent enough time in hospitals to know I couldn't stand being penned up like that. I could probably handle teaching. With lots of field trips." He carried the food into the cabin. "The roof should be dry enough by now—let's get to work."

Jo helped drag a heavy ladder from the shed and climbed up behind him. The roof was in worse shape than he'd thought—lucky they'd had no rain or snow since the windstorm. Jo roamed across the roof on her own, tapping on some shingles and tugging at others.

She straightened and turned to him. "If you have something like a clapboard chisel, I can start taking up the bad shingles while you nail down the good ones."

"Check the big toolbox in the storeroom," he said.

She nodded and climbed down, returning a few minutes later with the chisel and two hammers plus a box of roofing nails.

"Don't look at me like I've got two heads," she said with a grin. "I told Luke my mom and I rehabbed our house in Brooklyn. I redid the whole garage roof by myself."

He'd stopped being surprised by anything he learned about Jo, but an unreasonable flash of anger burned his gut that maybe Luke knew her better he did. If he listened to her more than he talked… But that was her job—people just naturally opened up to her. He'd seen it over and over as she chatted with riders' wives and girlfriends, with cowboys and bullfighters and stock contractors and the men who set up and tore down the show. Without pushing, she made everyone feel fascinating and important so they fell all over themselves sharing their life's stories.

He wished again Traci had been half the listener Jo was or that he'd seen through her self-absorption before it was too late.

"Okay," he said. "We'll start at the rooftree and work our way down. Unless you think I'll slow you down."

"Naw, I'm sure we can work together." She stuck her hammer into the loop of a makeshift tool belt she had fashioned from a short length of rope and started prying up the edge of a split shingle.

He shook his head and watched for a moment before tackling the nearest damaged section. Let the games begin.

Before long, his disgruntlement dissolved in the pleasure of a job done well as they replaced old shingles and nailed down loose ones, their hammers playing counterpoint to her tales of repairing hundred-year-old floors and his about his gear bag sent by the airline to Portland, Maine, instead of Portland, Oregon.

Ghost's strident neigh alerted them to a rider's approach; Brian Buck reined in below their perch.

"I came back to help, but I guess you guys

are almost done," he said, a plaintive note in his voice.

"No such thing, buddy," Tom said. "We haven't even started on the back." He winked at Jo.

She looked at her watch. "Since Brian's here, I'll start lunch." She climbed down and took his mount's reins. "Let me take care of your horse," she said. "You can help Tom."

Brian beamed and scrambled onto the roof while Jo tied his paint in the shade and loosened the cinch before disappearing into the cabin.

Without Jo at his side, the work slowed considerably, but Brian made up in enthusiasm what he lacked in skill. Tom kept him busy flinging splintered shingles off the roof, well away from the horses and fetching fresh ones to nail in their place. The sun's warmth grew stronger and he stripped off his shirt; Brian imitated him.

"Chow's on," Jo called from the base of the ladder and then gasped when she saw the jagged scar running from Tom's shoulder blade to his belt. "What happened to your back? Did a bull gore you?"

Tom chuckled. "Tell her what happened, Brian."

Brian grinned over the edge of the roof. "It was my dad and Luke's fault."

"This is one of those stories retold to caution kids," Tom said. "Probably just makes them want to try the same stunt."

"There's always been an eagle's nest up that draw," Brian said, pointing with his chin. "Dad and Luke wanted to know if the eggs had hatched, so they told Tom to climb up because he was smallest and lightest."

"Mama Eagle was not happy," Tom said. "She beat on me all the way down that big old pine and got one good swipe at my back when I hit the ground. Her claws barely broke the skin, but I caught hell when I got home for ruining my shirt."

"And you never ratted on Dad and Luke," Brian said.

"Cowboy code," Tom said with a laugh as he pulled his shirt on.

They sopped up the stew and green chili with the tortillas Auntie Rose had sent and then put the finishing touches on the roof before tightening a few rails in the corral as well. Brian departed only after Tom promised to take him and his brother Sammie fishing up the Animas River once the spring runoff had subsided.

Jo restored the cabin to its preinvasion condition and carried the saddlebags to the corral while Tom saddled Ghost and Sadie. "I closed the door," she said, "but I couldn't figure out how to lock it."

"There's no lock on the door," Tom said with a grunt, hauling up on Sadie's cinch strap. "Anybody wants in that bad, they'd just break a window. And someone lost out here might need shelter." He tied the saddlebags in place and led Ghost out of the corral, closing the gate behind them.

Jo looked over her shoulder as they rode away. "Back to the real world. But I'll never forget this."

"No reason you can't come back." He did his best to keep his tone light.

"Maybe," she said and turned away from the cabin.

CHAPTER TWENTY-TWO

LUKE SNEAKED A second apple dumpling into his dish, dousing it with cream, and then turned to Tom. "Are you getting on any practice bulls before the next event?"

"I should," Tom said. He smiled at Jo. "Kind of slipped my mind, all we've had going on."

"Take a run down to Masterson's tomorrow," Jake said. "You can ride a couple and show Jo how a good stock contractor manages his buckers—maybe she can use it in her book."

"How about it, cowgirl?" Tom said. "Want to visit some bulls?"

"If I won't be in the way."

"Go with him, Jo," Shelby said. "It's a pretty drive through country you wouldn't see otherwise."

Tom pulled out his phone and scrolled to the number he wanted. He laughed when his party answered. "Yeah, it's me. And you're right— I should have called before now. Hey, can you run a couple of bulls under me tomorrow late morning, maybe early afternoon? And how about you roust Pinky out of retirement? I'd like to introduce him to the lady from New York City I'm bringing with me. She's working on a book about bull riding. You can show her what a first-class breeding operation looks like."

THEY LEFT AFTER breakfast the next morning, driving south on Route 140 from Hesperus. The terrain became more rugged, with buttes stretching into the distance, stubby as broken teeth, and deep ravines cutting through geologic strata like a ruined red and ochre layer cake. The La Plata River ran alongside the road in many places, hurrying to join the San Juan.

Shortly after crossing into New Mexico, they emerged into more level country and turned onto an unpaved lane between sandstone gateposts. Half a mile from the main road and over a rise, the ranch house and corrals lay in a valley beside a creek lively with spring runoff from the distant mountains.

A lanky man with a graying mustache emerged to greet them from a long red-painted barn.

"Jo, meet Pete Masterson," Tom said. "He was a top rider when I was just a rookie. Now he's turning out some great bucking stock."

Jo offered her hand; Pete's callused paw wrapped around it like weather-roughened leather.

"Any friend of Tom's," he said in a deep Sam Elliot voice. "I haven't taken any bulls to events this spring, but if I had, I sure would've noticed you." He tucked her hand into the crook of his arm. Tom grinned at her as she let Pete lead her into the maw of the shadowy barn.

The tour ended half an hour later after Pete had introduced Jo to a dozen bulls lazing in roomy stalls or basking in the sunshine. "Of course, I got a bunch more out at pasture, youngsters and retired bulls," he said, "but these guys will be heading out for events the next few weeks. I keep them close since they're in training—special feed, exercise and the like."

"Do all bulls live this well?" Jo asked.

"I can't speak for every stock contractor," Pete said, "but I'd likely take care of my bulls before my wife. If I had a wife, that is." He winked at her. "Which I don't at the moment."

Tom had been following like a silent shadow. Now he chuckled. "Okay, Pete, you've made your run at Jo. Have you got any bulls for me? And how about Pinky?"

Pete released Jo's hand after a final squeeze.

"Pinky's in the small pen behind the chute." He reached into the pocket of his buckskin vest and pulled out a handful of wrapped peppermints. "Have to give him something for his trouble, the old…" He cleared his throat. "Old sonofagun."

Tom and Jo followed Pete toward a long fenced enclosure. "You could have warned me about Pete," Jo said under her breath.

"And ruin his fun? And yours? Pete's all talk, unless he gets a lot of encouragement. But he does go through wives like they've got an expiration date."

Pete stopped beside a fence eight rails high and unwrapped a piece of candy. A huge bull, almost white with stubby curved horns, ambled over and tried to stick his nose between the bars.

"Jo, meet Pinky. He's been retired five years now, good for nothing and living off the fat of the land." Pete opened a narrow gate and led her and Tom into the corral. He gave Pinky the peppermint and handed Jo a second piece. "Give him that and he'll follow you all the way back to the big city."

Jo held out the candy on her flat palm as she would to a horse; the bull lifted it off her hand with a single sweep of his tongue and gave her a melting glance.

"Pinky doesn't sound like an impressive name for a bucking bull," she said. "Not like Gunslinger or Bushwhacker."

Pete chuckled. "No, I guess not. He got caught in a rainstorm when he was barely on his feet. Light colored as he is, he turned pink soaking wet, and the name stuck. But he bucked off some big names in his day."

"Including me," Tom said.

"Say, you want to get on him?" Pete asked.

"Great idea." Tom turned to her. "You could sit on Pinky right in the corral and he'd just stand like a rock, but if Pete doesn't mind putting him in the chute, you can get a real idea what it's like to nod for the gate. Not that we'd turn him out with you on him. You know I'd never put you at risk."

Jo hesitated, her promise to her mother flashing through her mind like the warning before each event's pyrotechnics, but this would be sitting, not riding. "Sure," she said. "Sounds like a wonderful opportunity."

Tom threw his arm around her shoulder in a quick hug. "Good girl," he said. "Pete, get her a vest so she can feel like the real deal."

Ten minutes later Jo stood on the walkway

above the single bucking chute, now Velcro'd into a vest like the ones the cowboys wore in competition. Its light weight surprised her; at the same time, its embrace felt slightly claustrophobic.

Tom had already demonstrated how to step into the chute and sink onto the bull's back. She swallowed and took a deep breath. Pinky had seemed so benign in the corral, but she couldn't see his sleepy-eyed face from this angle, only his massive back completely filling the chute. While she watched, he shifted his bulk and stamped a forefoot.

"You don't have to, Jo." Tom's voice at her elbow brought her back with a jerk. "This was probably a dumb idea."

"Are you kidding? I'm just picking my moment." She was proud her voice sounded normal despite her heart beating double-time. She reached across the chute and stepped onto Pinky's back, easing her weight down until her legs more or less clenched his sides. The bull's skin shuddered as if to shake off a fly; one ear twitched.

She tried to make herself relax, as if she were riding a nervous horse, but the whisper of panic brought on by the vest quadrupled in the confines of the chute. She was trapped in a steel-barred cage with a powerful beast, and this was a tame bull who batted his eyelashes for hard candy.

"Ride's over, Jo." She felt Tom's grip on the back of her vest. "I'm going to help you climb out."

She took in a great gulping breath and grasped the hand he reached down to her. Another moment and she was standing beside him as the chute gate swung open and Pinky ambled out into the arena.

"How on earth do you do it?" She accepted the bottle of spring water he handed her and took a long gulp. "I was this close to freaking out."

"I know," he said. "I was watching your face. I feel the same way. You ever notice how fast I get out of the chute? Bad stuff can happen if you hang around in there too long." He unfastened her vest and slipped it off her shoulders. "You handled it like a real pro."

She watched from just behind the chute as Tom rode two practice bulls with ease. Nothing she had experienced previously on the open sea or galloping down the stretch at Churchill Downs remotely approached the intensity of her few moments spent in Tom's boots. Before today, she had focused on the hazards once Tom nodded to the gate man and on the dangers of the get-off—despite the bullfighters' best efforts. Now she understood the perils he faced inside the chute before the ride even began.

She shivered and took another long gulp from the water bottle.

CHAPTER TWENTY-THREE

JO PEERED INTO the big pot of dirty rice bubbling gently on the stove. She turned toward Marge Bowman, who was setting out peach pies, her contribution to the Easter feast, between pots of geraniums on the window ledge.

"Could you take a look at this?" she said. "It looks awfully thick to me, but Shelby said to keep stirring until the spoon could stand alone."

Marge wiped her hands on her white apron and looked over Jo's shoulder. "It does look pretty stiff, but I don't know that much about Cajun cooking. Just keep everything moving a few more minutes, especially on the bottom so it doesn't burn, and then turn it off and cover it. Shelby can finish it when they get home from Easter services. The boys would probably whup on you if you ruin their favorite dish."

"I'm going to shoot an email to my mom with everything on the menu today," Jo said. "She's spending Easter with her side of our family in upstate New York—they'll be fascinated by who's bringing what to eat."

"You can probably count on Rose Buck for green chili and fry bread," Marge said. "I'm not sure what June Black Horse will bring, but she learned a lot from Rose while she was married to Sam and from Delbert's mother too, so it's bound to be good. Lucy told me she made her mom's barbecued beans…"

"And Jake's been smoking a side of beef ribs since last night. What a combination—Cajun, Ute and good old cowboy cuisine. Plus your pies." She looked at the clock on the mantel. "I'm turning the rice off now—let's have a cup of coffee before the kitchen starts to fill up."

They settled at the oak table, expanded to its greatest dimension, with mugs of coffee and a plate of brownies Jo had made just to say she had contributed something to the occasion. Sunlight streamed through the big window, the clock on the mantel ticked in peaceful rhythm and the fire built against the early morning chill sighed down to embers.

"How the writing going?" Marge asked. "Much more to do?"

"The feature's almost finished. I plan to wrap it up at the finals in October—my editor's fine with that—so it will come out maybe late October or early November. Shelby and Jake get a copy, of course, and I'll send you one too if you like. I changed the focus from Tom alone to include Luke. Once I got to know them, the dynamic was just too good to pass up. I still have a long way to go on the book."

Margie stirred her coffee with unnecessary vigor. "I hope for your sake you did right by those boys—I'll come after you with my meat mallet if you didn't do them proud. The Camerons are about my best friends in the valley. They stood up for me when a lot of people in La Plata County would cross the street to avoid me."

Jo tried to keep a neutral expression—Marge and the Silver Queen were beloved fixtures in Durango. Hard to believe...

"Oh, I know—what could I have possibly done to get myself shunned? It was my husband. He just the same as stole folks' savings and then shot himself rather than face the consequences." Her expression softened. "Charlie wasn't an evil man. He really believed in his schemes—opportunities, he called them—and we never left a town with a dime. He came to Durango figuring to reopen a gold mine up the Animas River, but he never bothered checking all the government regulations before he spent his investors' money on equipment. I sold it all off for pennies on the dollar after he died and gave people back as much as I could scrape together."

"Did the Camerons lose any money?"

Marge snorted. "Jake didn't have two cents extra to risk, what with his wife's medical expenses, but he cosigned a note for me at the bank to open the Queen—that's the kind of man he is. And Tom's just like him."

"What about Luke?" Jo asked with a smile.

Marge laughed. "Luke's a good boy—he's just busy putting in that last crop of wild oats. Something will come along and settle him down one of these days. And Lucy? She started working for me at fourteen, not long after her mother died. Now she can pretty much run the place. I broke my arm pretty bad a few years ago and she managed the whole operation most of her senior year in high school. I'd walk through fire and flood for the Camerons, that's the truth."

The rattle of the cattle guard signaled a vehicle's arrival. A door slammed and they heard Auntie Rose's voice. "If you spill that pot of chili…" Followed by Oscar's low rumble: "Yes, Ma."

Jo grinned. "Showtime."

The kitchen quickly filled; the Camerons

returned from church in Hesperus, followed by June and Del Black Horse with Brian and Autumn Rose and June's older son Sammie, a gangling teenager already showing signs of reaching his uncle Oscar's height. The women performed an intricate dance between stove and fridge and table while the men conferred over the sheet-metal smoker in the yard. Tom took the baby from June, cradling her in one arm while demonstrating bull riding moves to the boys with his free hand.

Jo's writer's mind recorded every detail as she carried bowls and filled glasses: Auntie Rose's magenta-flowered church-going dress, Lucy's bright curls weaving like a flame among the darker-haired Camerons and Bucks, the clatter of voices, deep and high-pitched, the scents of chili and roasting meat and herbs, a kaleidoscope of sensations she would store away for some future writing project.

When Easter dinner finally ended with Marge's pies and a chocolate chili cake June Black Horse had brought, Jo, Lucy and June set about putting food away and cleaning up.

"Could you possibly give me the recipe for that cake?" Jo asked June. "My mom is a great baker—I know she'd love the flavor combination of chocolate and chili powder."

"It should be ancho chili powder if she can get it," June said. "And black coffee. You don't taste it, but that's what makes the cake so rich. Sure, I don't mind sharing."

"And your casserole too, as long as you're being so generous. Was that butternut squash with the beans and corn?"

"Pumpkin, but I'm sure squash would work just as well. My mother-in-law taught me how to make that dish—it's been Del's favorite since he was a kid. She was a great traditional cook, and I learned as much as I could from her before she died." She scooped the pumpkin-bean mixture into a plastic carton. "I'll leave the cake for you guys, but I'm taking this home for Del and the boys."

Shelby appeared carrying Autumn Rose. "I snatched her back before Tom could hide her in the barn," she said, handing the baby to June. "And I think she needs a clean diaper."

June laughed. "I was thinking of leaving her with Tom. She's been teething, but he seems to know how to turn off her cranky switch." She sniffed. "Yep, diaper time."

Jo watched Shelby move around the kitchen with quiet authority, bringing order to the chaos left behind by the feast. Shelby had come to the ranch a stranger and alone; now she appeared to be the lodestar, the true north for everyone's compass. Jo wondered if she could have woven herself so seamlessly into the fabric of life at Cameron's Pride.

After the last guests drove away, Lucy left to spend the evening with her fiancé, Mike Farley, and his family on a neighboring ranch. The men rode out to check on the heifers in the lower pasture while Shelby and Jo fed the horses still in the corral. Stranger stalked beside Shelby like a faithful shadow.

"Has Tom shown you the Cameron burial ground?" Shelby asked. "It's a pretty spot."

She led the way up a footpath to the crest of a little knoll with her dog at her side and opened the wrought iron gate designed around the Cameron brand. Lilacs still in bud grew along the fence while flowering bulbs already brightened many of the graves. Simple upright slabs stood above the earliest burials; rough-hewn sandstone blocks with deeply etched letters marked those from the last hundred years.

Shelby bent to clear a few tiny weeds from the scarlet tulips rioting around Annie Cameron's grave. "Jake told me his wife loved red flowers," she said. "That huge Christmas cactus on the window ledge blossoms like a bonfire for the holidays—he gave it to her the first year they were married. I do my best to take care of Jake and the kids the way she would have wanted." She touched one of the tulips as if it were a baby's cheek. "She seems very close—I like to think she's happy for Jake and me."

She straightened and pointed westward.

Jo followed her gesture to see the riders emerging from the willows along the creek. Beyond them, cottonwoods sheltered the house while the sunset painted the western sky in pink and gold.

Leaving Cameron's Pride, maybe never to return, would be more wrenching than she could have imagined when she first arrived. She had told Tom she loved the energy and diversity of New York City, but life here offered its own challenges and variety. On Friday evening she and Tom had accompanied Lucy and Mike Farley to a performance by a touring dance company at Fort Lewis College in Durango. Afterward they'd gone for dessert at a coffeehouse near the Silver Queen where the guitarist's original songs led Jo to think he'd soon be moving up to a larger venue. She enjoyed the same kind of evening in New York, but here without the dirt and noise and crowding of a subway ride home. And when they returned to the ranch at midnight, she had lingered beside the corrals, marveling at the spectacle of the stars in a sky unsullied by artificial light.

She started from her reverie when Ghost neighed a greeting from his corral; the buckskin mare Luke rode answered.

"Looks like we're back on duty," Shelby said with a smile. "The guys will want to start eating all over again." They left the dead on their quiet hilltop and hurried back down to open the corral gate for the riders.

CHAPTER TWENTY-FOUR

JO WAITED FOR the tiny calf to stagger to its feet and find its first meal before reining her horse back toward the far side of the pasture where Tom and Lucy rode along the willows.

"I found her," she said, throttling back a yell of triumph. "The baby's already up and nursing."

"Good job," Tom said. "That's the last one."

"I think you've brought us luck," Lucy said. "This has been our easiest calving season ever."

"How would you know?" Luke rode up to join them. "You were lazying around Boulder while we were out in all kinds of weather…" He chuckled as Lucy reached across her horse's neck and pushed his hat brim down over his eyes.

"I'm sorry you had to be in on that one bad delivery," Jake said. "We were lucky to save the mama." He reached over and touched her shoulder. "I don't know how things were on your granddad's farm, but with a livestock operation, there's no guarantee of happy endings."

Jo grimaced and instinctively scrubbed her hands together as if the blood and mud still clung to them—too bad she couldn't erase the image of the dead calf from her mind. "Now I understand why you don't breed your heifers till they're older. Will she be able to have more calves?"

"We'll give her a year off," Tom said. "And make sure she doesn't go visiting Oscar's bull again. An older cow would probably have delivered okay, but not a youngster with her first calf."

"So calving is officially over?" Jo asked. "I didn't know I'd be getting a free course in bovine obstetrics as part of my guest package."

"The cool part's over," Lucy said. "Now we have to finish entering all the records in the computer. I'm so glad I'm going back to Boulder tomorrow—I hate that job."

"I'm with you, kid," Luke said. "I'll tag and vaccinate all day long before I wrangle a keyboard."

"I'm pretty good with computers," Jo said. "Maybe I could help, if it's not too complicated."

"Steal that gal's plane ticket and hide her credit card," Luke said. "We're never letting her leave."

Tom smiled. "I'll show you the program," he said, "but don't feel like you have to do it. It's pretty dull work after real cowboying like you've been doing."

They returned to the house and Tom introduced Jo to the computer records listing each cow with its ear tag number. She picked up the rhythm as soon as she learned to decipher the data scrawled in a battered notebook spotted with blood and (she hoped) mud.

She could see why no one wanted the job of entering nearly a thousand tag numbers followed by the calving stats and vaccination records although someone, probably Tom or Shelby, had already made a decent start.

Finally she hit Enter for the last time and sat back with a gusty sigh. "Done!"

Jake stuck his head into the office that also served as her guest room. "You finished the whole log? Girl, I could kiss your boots. That chore hangs over us like smoke from a wildfire. We all take turns chewing at it in our spare time, but it never gets done in one swat like this."

She laughed. "I've seen what spare time looks like on a ranch. You'd better check my work, but it was pretty simple once I figured out Luke's handwriting—everyone else's was easy."

Shelby appeared beside Jake. "I think we owe you some kind of special thank-you for all the help you've given us."

"Like a day off," Jake said. "We've worked you pretty much nonstop since day one. How about a little sightseeing tomorrow? There's the narrow gauge railroad up to Silverton or the cliff dwellings at Mesa Verde. Unless you're off ruins for good and I wouldn't blame you."

"Mesa Verde," Jo said without hesitation. With the right guide.

SHE AND TOM set off the next morning, driving west again as they had in search of the site on the Ute Reservation. This time he turned south where a towering butte marked the entrance to Mesa Verde National Park. Tom stopped first at the park headquarters and got permission to show Jo through some of the sites usually restricted to guided tours or off-limits to the general public.

"I'm a general nuisance here," he said with a grin. "The management has decided it's easier to let me wander around than keep an eye on me."

They roamed first through the exhibits at the

visitor center for a broad overview and then took the road, which climbed in long serpentine curves, gently at first and then more steeply, offering stunning views of the La Plata Mountains standing silver in the spring sunshine.

All day he led her up and down rocky paths and through carefully preserved cliff dwellings, bringing the ancient inhabitants vitally to life with his commentary. Through Tom's eyes, she watched hunters carrying home game and women weaving baskets or harvesting corn and squash on the mesa top while brown-skinned children played among the crops.

They broke for lunch at the café near one of the major cliff dwellings. Tom introduced her to her first Navajo taco, a fluffy round of fry bread heaped with chopped lettuce, tomatoes, pinto beans and shredded cheese and topped with a thick layer of green chili like Auntie Rose had brought for Easter dinner. At the nearby gift shop, Jo bought a cookbook featuring Native American cuisine for her mother and a mystery novel Tom recommended, which was set on the Ute Reservation.

"To read in your spare time," he said with a straight face.

Jo sighed with pleasure and regret when they returned at last to the ranch truck late in the afternoon. "It's been a fabulous day—I hate to leave."

Tom paused with his hand on the ignition key. "If you really mean that, I might be able to get us into the seasonal housing for the night. The full staff won't arrive for another month. Nothing fancy, but better than sleeping on bare rock."

She almost said "No, don't bother," but she caught a hint of pleading in his voice.

"I'd love to stay overnight," she said, and his smile told her she'd made the right decision.

He phoned the park headquarters and was able to pick up a key kept at the museum. "We're staying in one of the rangers' houses," he said "All the comforts of home. But we'd better hustle if we want to get supper before the café closes."

"Will you think I'm a pig if I order another Navajo taco?"

"Pretty tasty, aren't they? Just don't tell Auntie Rose how much you liked it—she'll make you eat one of hers to prove it's better."

"I probably won't get to see her again," Jo said. "I have to fly back in a few more days." Her heart fell with the realization.

"No reason you can't come back," Tom said, pulling out on to the main loop road.

Half a dozen horses straggling across the road saved her from answering. Tom swore and hit the brakes when a gray stallion halted squarely on the yellow line as if to challenge a threat to his little band.

"That stud might be Ghost's daddy," Tom said. "Or maybe his half brother."

Jo snapped a few shots of the stallion and his mares, several heavily pregnant. "I can't believe I got to see wild horses."

"Sorry to bust your bubble. They're wild enough, but they're mostly strays from the Ute Reservation. Tourists love seeing them though."

They ate a quick meal—another Navajo taco for Jo—and picked up fruit and coffee rolls for breakfast. Tom drove to a deserted parking area and pulled hooded sweatshirts from the backseat.

"We're close to 9,000 feet elevation here— it'll get cold as soon as the sun goes down. Bring your camera." He set off up a footpath that wound through wind-stunted pines to a promontory that dropped off sharply to the south and west.

"Just in time," he said, and took a seat on a fallen tree trunk that writhed along the ledge like a crippled snake.

Jo sat beside him and they waited without

speaking as the sun sank toward the horizon. At first she had found Tom's silences disconcerting, so different from urbanites' need to fill every pause with words. Now she found his quiet restful, even companionable.

As they watched, the sky began to glow in shades of gold and rose and magenta. She watched entranced as the cloud patterns evolved, colors blending and changing like oil swirled on water. Purple evening finally claimed the sky except for a ribbon of vermillion along the western horizon as the moon rose above the mountains to the east.

A coyote's quavering call floated up from the depths of the darkening landscape below their aerie, answered by another and then another.

She sighed sharply and blinked tears from her eyes. "Thank you," she said.

"I found this spot the summer I worked up here—I try to watch the sunset from here whenever I can."

"And the sunrise?"

He laughed. "Well, yeah—that too. Want to join me?"

"If I'm not intruding," she said. "I saw some marvelous sunrises and sunsets over the ocean, but the atmosphere here is completely different from sea level."

He stood and held out his hand. "We should head back before full night."

"Are the coyotes dangerous?"

"No, but the path is," he said. "Too easy to sprain your ankle in the dark."

They drove to a cottage furnished with sturdy mismatched furniture and sat at the scarred kitchen table sharing saltines the mice had somehow overlooked and cups of cocoa made from powdered mix.

Jo herded cracker crumbs into a neat pile on her paper napkin. "Mesa Verde is a special place for you, isn't it? The way you lectured today—"

He ducked his head. "I probably bored you out of your mind—why didn't you cut me off?"

"Are you kidding? You made the whole culture come alive for me. Oscar said you'd make a fine archeologist."

He leaned forward, his face alight with eagerness. "Mesa Verde has been studied in depth ever since a couple of cowboys stumbled on it in the 1880s, just like those Ute kids found the ruins last week. We know a lot about the people, how they lived, but there's still so much we don't know. I want to make those discoveries."

"I suppose you've been coming here all your life," she said.

"I grew up seeing Mesa Verde from that ridge above the cabin, but I never got to visit till my eighth-grade class came on a field trip." He chuckled. "The only time I ever got in trouble at school. I wandered off from the herd to explore on my own—one of the rangers finally found me in an off-limits area, sitting in a kiva with a stupid look on my face."

"Only it wasn't a stupid look, was it? You were listening."

His head jerked up in surprise. "How did you know?"

"I watched you today," she said. "Once or twice, I felt like you were listening to someone I couldn't hear."

"A real nut case, right? I'm surprised you were willing to spend the night here. Maybe I'm some kind of flaky ghost chaser."

She took her time answering. "I think you are, but not in a paranormal sense. You feel a strong connection to your heritage, and I think you consider the people who lived here as part of that tradition."

His mouth twitched in a wry grin. "You see too damn much."

She caught herself before saying that observing people was a big part of her job. How cold would that sound?

"But that's why you're good at what you do, right? Reading people?"

She laughed and held up her palms in surrender. "Truce, okay? One of the things I..." She'd almost said "love." "I admire about you is how sensitive you are to everything around you—people, animals, flash floods..."

He groaned. "Terrific—now I'm weird and sensitive too. Just don't spread that around behind the chutes, okay?"

He looked at his watch. "Want to take a little walk? You shouldn't miss looking at the stars from here—we're almost two miles up and maybe sixty miles as the crow flies from the nearest town of any size." He grinned and handed her a sweatshirt. "Come on—the ancient ones won't bother you if you're with me."

A HAND ON her shoulder woke her. "Not long till sunup," Tom said. "You still want to come?"

She groaned. "Gimme five, okay?"

"I'll wait outside."

A few minutes later they followed the same path as the night before, this time in the half light before dawn, and found seats facing east. The mountains of the Continental Divide stood like black cardboard cutouts against the navy-blue sky; the morning songs of birds replaced the coyotes' serenade to greet the growing dawn. The sky brightened gradually until sunlight flashed through a notch between two peaks, lighting the valley below in all its shades of springtime green.

An eagle floated below them, its wings spread wide to catch the breath of the earth warmed by the sun.

Tom took her hand. "Worth getting up for?"

She nodded, not trusting her voice.

CHAPTER TWENTY-FIVE

JAKE HOISTED JO'S bag into the backseat of Luke's Explorer. "You sure you have to leave just yet?" he asked. "We'd sure like to get a few more days' work out of you."

"And I'd love to stay," Jo said, "but my mom has a heavy schedule this week. She's counting on me to help."

She turned to Lucy. "Remember, if you want to visit New York, you're welcome to stay with me. I don't know any directors or producers, but I could put you in touch with people who do."

Lucy hugged her. "I hope I haven't been too big a pest while you've been here."

"No more than a roomful of mosquitos," Luke said, ruffling his sister's curls.

Shelby gave her a brief hug. "You were a big help with my youngsters—you do have good hands. I could turn you into a horse trainer. Come back anytime."

Maybe she imagined it, but Jo thought she

heard *as long as you do Tom no harm* behind Shelby's words.

"Thank you," she said. "I'd like that."

Tom straightened from where he'd been leaning against the vehicle. "We'd better move out if you don't want to miss your plane," he said. He opened the passenger door for her and climbed behind the wheel.

Jo caught a last view of them all waving goodbye, the cattle guard rumbled under the wheels and Cameron's Pride lay behind her.

Tom drove without speaking, and Jo didn't break into his silence. They reached the Durango airport well ahead of her flight time, but Tom braked at the Departures gate instead of parking to walk her into the terminal. He pulled out her bag but held on to it.

"Will I see you next weekend?"

What was he really asking? "Do you want to?"

He looked down at his boots. "Last event you missed, I bucked off."

"Then I'd better show up for the next one," she said.

He still wasn't looking at her, but she could see the smile pulling at the corners of his mouth. "I guess you better."

He passed her bag to her. Their hands

touched for a moment, and warmth suffused her whole being. Lordy, but she was in a bad way!

"It's been…nice," he said. "Having you at the ranch."

"For me too."

He cleared his throat. "Travel safe," he said.

"WELL!" ANNA DACE'S spoon clattered against her mug. "I'm glad you didn't tell me about nearly being caught by that flood. I read about those poor hikers, but I had no idea…"

"That could have been us except for Tom. We didn't get any weather warnings, but he felt the ground with his hand and then told me to start running." Jo shivered. "That cliff dwelling was the eeriest place I've ever spent the night. I'd have been scared spitless if Tom hadn't been with me."

"A good man to have around," Anna said. "The rest of your visit sounded pretty exciting too—sleeping in a pioneer cabin, breaking horses, delivering calves…"

"And listening to Tom's sister fantasize about a career in the theater," Jo said. "I was torn between being a sympathetic ear and explaining the harsh realities of trying to make it on the stage." She groaned. "I told her she could stay with me if she wants to visit New York. Her dad doesn't want to encourage her, but he was grateful I offered."

She broke off a piece of the peach muffin her mother had baked that morning. "You'll have to give me this recipe for Tom's Auntie Rose— peaches are a big crop in Colorado. She's not really his aunt, more a distant cousin on the Ute branch of the family. You would have loved Easter dinner—barbecue, traditional Ute dishes and Shelby's Cajun specialties."

For a moment she was back in the crowded kitchen with Shelby, Lucy, Auntie Rose and June Black Horse. Jo always enjoyed holidays with her mother's kin in upstate New York, but the Buck-Cameron clan had given *extended family* a whole new meaning.

"Are you off again next weekend? You said something about finishing up by the end of May."

Jo took a bite of the muffin to buy time. The feature was finished except for wrapping it up at the finals. She already had enough firsthand material on bull riding to turn out a credible book, but more research would add depth and color. Warring memories jostled in her mind: the strength of Tom's arms around her during the long night in the ruins, his eager mind, his tenderness holding Autumn Rose. And the scars marking his body, inescapable reminders of injuries he had already suffered and dangers he faced every time he rode.

"I'll keep going until the summer break and then follow up at the finals in October," she said. "Want to go to Las Vegas with me?"

"HEY, COWGIRL!" LUKE PULLED Jo into a hearty hug and took her bag. "You ready to rock and roll?"

"Is Tom waiting with the car?"

"Naw, he's back at the hotel icing his foot— a practice bull stepped on it at a friend's ranch. He'll be fine to ride tonight—he just didn't feel like hiking through the airport."

The misgivings that had slept all the way from LaGuardia jumped up and hissed in Jo's ear. If Tom could be injured by a practice bull…

Luke jostled her with a playful elbow. "Come on, it's just a bruise. You never had a horse step on your foot?"

"A half-Percheron on my grandfather's farm, and I was barefoot." She relaxed, just a little. "I just hate to see anyone injured."

"You've been good luck for everyone— nobody's gotten badly hurt since you've been with the tour." He put her bag in his car. "We'll pick up takeout on the way to the hotel and keep Tom company with his protein snacks."

They found Tom hobbling around the hotel room with his right foot in a compression boot. "Just to keep the weight off my toes," he said. "But I don't need my toes to ride."

"You need them to get away from the bull after the buzzer," she said, sharp-tongued in her anxiety.

"Don't worry—Luke and his buddies will take care of me." He punched Luke's shoulder. "Right, brother?"

"Same as always. Sure you don't want some Chinese? We brought plenty."

"Stick it in the fridge if there's any left over—I'll have it later." He turned to Jo. "Guess who's here this weekend."

She guessed the president, the pope and Elvis while Tom shook his head in mock disdain. "More important than any of them—Gunslinger, all rested up and ready for action."

Her heart sank. "Will you have to ride him?"

"If I'm lucky," he said with an edge to his voice.

She slapped a big smile on her face. "I'll be right up there pulling for you to make the eight." She pointed at his injured foot. "Can you warm up with that?"

"Sure, long enough to get my head straight—that's all I need." He slung on his Finals jacket. "See you at the arena."

She stared after him until Luke touched her arm. "Jo, your worrying won't keep him safe. If anything, it messes with his concentration."

"I know—he read me the riot act in Oklahoma City." She brushed a hand across her eyes, trying to erase the memory of his bruised face. "How much longer do you suppose he'll keep on riding?"

"Till he's ready to quit. Could be years, could be next week. A while back he met this gal who was all over him like flies on..." He laughed. "You know what I mean. He said he was quitting then and getting married—he even bought her a ring. Then bang! She was gone and he was riding like the devil was pulling his rope for him. He eased up after I told him he was making my job harder, but then a bull fell with him and he ended up in the hospital with a broken pelvis."

"Why does he keep riding?" she asked. "He's told me he has plans for when he retires. Does the money really justify the risk?"

Luke looked down at his boots. "I reckon it's partly my fault he hasn't hung it up. Tom's always been good with his winnings—he keeps some in savings, but mostly he puts it back into the ranch. Me, I make real good money, but it never seems to stay with me long. A couple years ago an old high school buddy talked me into cosigning for him to open a big yee-haw restaurant and nightclub in Tucson. He's working hard to make a go of it, but I've been pretty much carrying him when I should be helping my own family dig out of debt. The ranch was finally free and clear again from Mom's medical expenses but we took an awful big hit from the blizzard and Dad's heart attack. Now we're back in a deep hole again."

He looked up, suddenly older by a dozen years, a different man from the Luke she had come to know. "Tom will never say it—he's loyal as a good dog—but if he gets hurt bad again, I'll know it's my fault he couldn't quit sooner."

Jo was struck speechless both by the change in Luke's face and by the sadness in his voice. She cudgeled her brain for some comfort to offer, some way to wipe away the sorrow in his eyes.

"I don't think you can shoulder all the blame that he's still riding," she said. "Tom told me himself that making the buzzer on a great bull like Gunslinger feels like the best eight seconds of his life."

"That's so—he reads the bulls better than any rider I've ever seen. He has this connection with them, like respect. I think he understands them better sometimes than he does people. And he does want that gold buckle, maybe as much as the million dollars. He takes pride, Tom does. All kinds of stuff going on in his head, but he doesn't talk much, never has."

A little life came back into his voice. "Me, now—ask me anything. I'll bend your ear till you slam the door in my face." His grin resurfaced and he looked at his watch. "I gotta get moving—not long till showtime."

Jo walked with Luke to the arena entrance and made her way to the concourse. Watching and visiting with the fans, from seniors with canes to babies in arms, made up an important part of her research. She planned to include a sampler of their stories in her book and had gathered a collection of email addresses to contact people for releases.

Several riders were putting in their duty time at their sponsors' booths, autographing hats and vests and programs, posing with fans. The cowboys' accessibility and amiability always impressed Jo, so different from the impatience and downright rudeness many professional athletes displayed toward their fans who paid their exorbitant salaries.

Deke Harkens beckoned when he saw Jo approach the Ariat Boots booth. He counted himself as a special friend because he had first introduced her to Tom. He reached into a tote slung on the back of his chair and handed her a thick cream-colored envelope.

"Dang, I'm glad you're here," he said. "We missed you at the last event before Easter. I didn't have your address so I figured to give you this in person first chance I got."

She weighed the envelope in her hand. "This feels like a wedding invitation."

He beamed. "That's what it is. Me and Mandy have been talking about getting married for a while, but her mom's health just took a bad turn, so we're gonna do it right away so her folks can enjoy it. I sure hope you can make it—you're part of the PBR family."

The invitation touched and flattered Jo. Everyone had been friendly from day one, but being included in a private celebration was a great compliment.

She kissed his cheek. "Thanks, I wouldn't miss it." She heard the shuffle of feet behind her. "I'd better move along—folks are waiting to meet you."

She found her seat in the families' section with plenty of time to chat with wives and girlfriends, including Deke's fiancée, Mandy Franklin.

"You could come as Tom's date, of course," Mandy said, "but we wanted you to have your own invitation. We're putting this together in kind of a hurry, but since we're getting married at our ranch we'll be able to stage a good old-fashioned Texas wedding. I just ordered my dress from Sat'n Spurs—thank goodness they had one I love in my size."

Chatter boiled up about weddings past and future; the other women were all married or in a serious relationship with a bull rider.

Jo didn't contribute to the conversation. She'd never been more than casually interested in the whole wedding spectacle because she'd never met anyone who turned her thoughts toward marriage. Everyone probably speculated about her and Tom—did they or didn't they?—although no one was rude enough to ask outright. For a moment she regretted impulsively accepting the invitation, but Deke had been so pleased to extend it, and the wedding would be a wonderful opportunity to soak up color for her book.

The lights went down followed by the now-familiar ceremony, and there was Tom alone on the shark cage, still leading in the race for the championship. His face was half-hidden by the brim of his black Stetson, but she knew he already wore the look of intense concentration in preparation for his first ride.

The competition began, with only half the cowboys making it to the buzzer. "Tough pen of bulls tonight, folks." Jo sat forward dry-mouthed when Tom's turn came, but he rode his bull with such ease that that his score didn't reflect his ability, landing him fourth in the round.

"Saving himself for Gunslinger tomorrow," the announcer speculated.

Tom lifted his hat to the crowd and disappeared behind the chutes.

Jo stood with her hands on her hips when they all met in Tom's room after the competition. "Did you guys put Deke and Mandy up to inviting me to their wedding?"

"Nope," Tom said.

"Me neither," Luke said. "Deke asked if I

thought you'd like to come and I told him to ask you himself. You going?"

Tom looked up, chopsticks poised above the leftover moo goo gai pan.

"I'd love to," she said, "if you guys don't mind."

"Why should we mind?" Luke raised his Bud Light in a salute. "No harm to having one more pretty girl at a party."

"Mandy's folks have a big ranch in the Texas Hill Country," Tom said. "Her mom just had surgery—she needs to start chemo right after the wedding. This might be their last chance to celebrate for quite a while."

Luke frowned. "I didn't know that."

"Deke told me when he first found out—the Franklins have been good to him." Tom pointed a chopstick at Luke. "Keep it to yourself, okay? They don't want gloomy faces at the wedding."

"I SAW THAT bull on TV Sunday," Anna said when she and Jo met for coffee on Monday morning. "Gunslinger? I thought Tom always rode him."

"Tom's combined scores for his first bulls weren't high enough to give him the first pick in the championship round," Jo said. "He's got his heart set on being the first to ride that bull, so he was half-glad Luis bucked off."

"Only half?" Anna raised her eyebrows in puzzlement. "I'd think he should have been delighted."

"Bull riding is an odd sport," Jo said. "The cowboys ride against each other for prize money, but they're really competing against the bulls. Once the chute gate opens, they're all yelling for whoever's riding to make the buzzer like a big family with thirty-five brothers. And speaking of family, I've been invited to a wedding on a Texas ranch."

"A cowboy wedding? Will the bride wear a sunbonnet and the groom wear a cowboy hat?"

Jo laughed. "Probably no sunbonnets although I'm sure the men will wear their best Stetsons." She clicked a few keys on her laptop. "Here's the website where the bride ordered her dress."

Anna peered over her shoulder. "Those are lovely—I expected leather fringes and six-guns."

"Mandy will be wearing a white hat with a little veil and pearl-toned boots, but no side-arm."

"Are you going with the Western theme?"

Jo sighed and rolled her eyes. "I haven't

a clue. I'll look for something once I get to Texas."

"After Tom picks you up from the airport?" Her mother's turn to do an eye roll. "That's cutting it a little fine."

"He's not picking me up," Jo said. "I plan to fly into Austin a day early and rent a car. I can shop for a dress there and take a look at the country on my way to the ranch."

CHAPTER TWENTY-SIX

TOM TURNED OFF the engine and sat in his truck without moving. He had an uneasy feeling about this whole wedding thing—not exactly bad, just disquieting, maybe left over from the previous weekend. Jo had flown in for the event as she did every Friday, but Luke had taken time off to give a younger bullfighter a chance in the big time. Luke's absence had unbalanced the easy comradeship the three of them shared. Yeah, he and Jo had spent time alone at the ranch, but that had been on his home ground.

Now Luke was AWOL again, leaving Tom to pick up Jo for the wedding alone. He swore under his breath. Some grown-up man he was, twenty-nine years old and scared without his big brother to chaperone him.

Jo answered immediately when he called from the hotel lobby. "Come on up," she said. "I'm just finishing a call with my mom."

He settled his pearl-gray Stetson more squarely before knocking at room 302. When

Jo opened the door, his breath left him like he'd been kicked in the chest by a calf.

Jo peered at him with a frown. "Hey, are you okay? Is something wrong?"

He shook his head, dumb with shock. He was comfortable with her in boots and jeans, but he'd never seen her in a dress. She wore some kind of lacy top with a beaded drawstring at the neck, like old paintings of Mexican peasant girls, and a long skirt, soft and floating in colors like canyon shadows at dusk. With her hair piled on top of her head, a few loose wisps framing her face, she looked good enough to eat. His toes curled in his boots; sweat started under his hatband.

"Do I look okay?" she asked. "I didn't want to go all Western wedding but I didn't want to be too city slicker either." She touched the wide belt at her waist, dark suede with a handsome turquoise buckle. "Is the belt too much? I can take it off—"

"No, don't take anything off." His face felt as red as her lipstick. He swallowed hard. "I mean you look great."

"You look pretty great yourself, cowboy." She gave him a slow once-over and he preened, just a little. Deke had asked him to serve as a groomsman, so here he was duded up in gray

Western-cut trousers cut snugger than he liked plus a ruffled shirt and string tie.

"I look like a Las Vegas poker dealer," he said, tugging at his collar, "but this is what Mandy picked out. I'm sorry I have to pick you up early. The wedding's at six, but Deke asked me to show up way ahead for moral support."

"No problem—I'm sure I can amuse myself." She picked up a tiny purse and a wrap the same material as the skirt. "Where's Luke?"

"Beats me." Anger or maybe panic roiled in his gut. "He flew up to Vegas to meet a friend on Thursday but he said he'd show up in time for the party. I think weddings scare him."

Jo entertained him on the half-hour drive to the Franklins' ranch by describing her first impressions of Texas—brisket and wildflowers, history and honky-tonk. She talked the way she wrote, with keen observations and clever turns of phrase.

They rolled under the wrought iron arch of the Franklin's ranch gate as the sun hung low in the west and a pale moon floated above the eastern horizon. A three-story white house, Tara cross-bred with Southfork, sat on a gentle rise overlooking a glassy lake. Wood smoke, redolent with the scent of roasting meat, drifted through a grove of live oaks and the plink of guitars floated from a white tent in a clearing near the barn.

Deke spotted Tom the moment he stepped from the truck and grabbed him like a drowning man clutching a life raft. "You gotta get me through this," he said in a shaking voice, and he towed Tom toward the bar in one corner of the tent as a bevy of bridesmaids whisked Jo into the house.

Tom was too busy trying to calm Deke down by nonalcoholic means to think about Jo again until he delivered the groom safely to the altar. Deke's expression changed from panic to awe the moment he saw his bride appear on her father's arm, and Tom congratulated himself on completing his mission successfully.

As Deke took Mandy's hand, Tom stepped back and scanned the audience for Jo, finally spotting her near the rear of the tent. She gave him a smile that weakened his knees, and he turned to watch Mandy and Deke, whose given name turned out to be Dexter, recite their vows. Endless photos followed the ceremony. Only when the newlywed's ritual waltzes began was he free to look for Jo.

He found her chatting with Mandy's mother, whose delicate features betrayed a heartbreaking fragility. As if she felt his gaze, Jo glanced over her shoulder with a quick smile. He pantomimed eating and she gave a slight nod. A few moments later she squeezed Mrs. Franklin's hand and rose to join him.

"I'm hungry enough to eat a whole steer," she said. "Or whatever smells so heavenly."

"You won't find wedding chicken here," Tom said, "just brisket and ribs and beans and potato salad and tamales and wedding cake and pecan pie and…"

"Stop, stop!" she said, laughing. "Just feed me before I faint at your feet."

"Find us a seat," he said. "I'll grab some of everything." He loaded two plates and stuck a couple of Bud Lights under his arm, carrying everything to the table Jo had staked out under the oaks. They ate with only appreciative murmurs until she pushed her plate away.

"Now I need to work it off," she said.

"The dancing's started—would that suit you?"

She listened for a moment and wrinkled her nose. "Not really my style." Waltzes had given way to rowdier music for the young crowd. "Could we just walk?"

"Sure, I can give you the tour," he said. "I hiked Deke all over the spread earlier like he was a colicky horse."

The big tent pulsated with light and sound, but only scattered flambeaux illuminated the grove. He led her past the big barn to the lake where the rising moon built a silver bridge across the calm surface. A current of air, too soft to be called a breeze, carried the clean cool scent of water and the perfume of wildflowers along the lake's verge.

They followed a graveled path along the shore. She stumbled a little, and he took her hand but released it when they reached a dock jutting into the water. Here only the thump of the bass guitar drifted through the trees.

Tom stuck his hands in his pockets. "I can't believe the Franklins put this shindig together in just three weeks."

"Never underestimate the power of a determined bride and her mother," Jo said. "It wasn't as hard as a lot of weddings since they didn't have to rent a hall." Her voice softened. "Betsy Franklin is facing a tough battle with ovarian cancer, but she'll have this wonderful day to remember. Not being able to keep up with her work on the ranch bothers her the most, she says. She was a champion barrel racer when she met her husband at the National Finals Rodeo—now she coaches girls in local competitions and sponsors a 4-H group. Plus she raises prize-winning Appaloosas."

Tom smiled and shook his head—a thumbnail bio from just a few minutes of conversation. "You should be some kind of counselor," he said. "You nod and smile and people tell you their life stories."

"Most people just want someone to listen, but I don't have any magic words to give them," she said with a note of sadness in her voice. "I can't even figure out my own life."

The rock music died away and the voice of a solitary fiddle quavered on the night air.

Jo clasped her hands together in delight. "'The Tennessee Waltz'—my grandparents' favorite. Every Saturday evening Grandpa would put that scratchy old record on the turntable and dance my grandmother around the parlor." She curved her arms around a phantom partner and swayed as she sang the opening lines along with the fiddle.

Moving without conscious volition, Tom took her in his arms as if they'd been dancing together forever. Her body molded against his with her breath warm on his neck where he'd opened the top buttons of his shirt after the ceremony. He'd forgotten how good it felt to hold a girl like this, melting into each other in time with the music. Or had pushed the memory away.

The words of the old song came back to him, the lament of love and loss, and his heart turned to stone in his chest.

He couldn't go through this again—he couldn't.

He pulled her closer and bowed his head until his lips touched her cheek.

CHAPTER TWENTY-SEVEN

SHE HADN'T MEANT to entice him; she'd only been acting out the sweet childhood memory of her lanky grandfather transformed by the music into a courtly prince.

Now she floated in Tom's arms, her feet scarcely touching the dock's rough planks. She lifted her face as he bent toward her, their lips not quite meeting. The long touch of their bodies heated her blood and dizzied her like one glass of wine too many and she clung to him as if she might fall without his arms supporting her. His lips traced her cheek and then her neck.

Some deeply submerged vestige of sanity pulled her back from the edge. With supreme effort of will, she put her hands flat against his chest.

"I can't," she said. "I just can't."

His hands stilled on her body. "Yeah," he said. His voice was hoarse, his breathing ragged. "Neither can I. But you better believe I want to."

She swallowed back tears. "Me too, but we could hurt each other too badly."

He still held her but now without passion. "Please don't say never, okay? Just not now."

She nodded against his shoulder.

"Well," he said, brushing a light kiss on her cheek. "We probably should get back to the party." He tucked her hand into his arm and led her back toward the lights and laughter.

Excited voices rocked the big tent just as they emerged from the darkness. At first Jo heard only an indistinct babble and then "Hey, Luke! Way to go, Luke!"

Followed by "Where's Tom? Somebody find Tom."

Luke stood gripping the lead singer's microphone, his arm around a size-two blonde in a skimpy parody of a wedding dress, fluffy veil and all. A diamond flashed on her left hand. He blew into the mike and said, "Ladies and gents, meet Mrs. Luke Cameron."

The crowd went crazy. Tom turned pale. Luke's bride giggled.

Jo shook Tom's arm. "I thought you said Luke was scared of weddings."

"Not scared enough," Tom said, his voice grim.

"Do you know that girl? She looks familiar."

"Her name's Cherie something—she sang

the national anthem in Kansas City. She's been buzzing around Luke ever since, but I had no idea… I should have paid more attention—"

"And done what?" Jo said. "Warned your big brother about designing women? Run her out of town? He's a big boy, Tom—and maybe she really is a nice girl." She tugged on his arm. "Come on, let's congratulate the happy couple."

The reception hit new levels of hilarity with the addition of a second set of newlyweds. Jo danced with Luke, who grinned with manic delight, obviously more than a little drunk. She hoped his bride would stay sober enough to drive them back to wherever they were staying. From the corner of her eye she saw Tom circling the dance floor with Cherie at arm's length, a set smile on his face.

Yee-haw!

Half an hour later she found Tom talking to—or rather at—Luke in the shadow of the barn. She heard him say, "Why all of a sudden? Is she pregnant?"

"Naw, I just got tired of not remembering the names of the girls I woke up with. Cherie's a good kid—give her a chance."

"Are you two headed to the ranch from here?"

"Not right away," Luke said. "We're going on a little honeymoon—Mexico maybe. I'll be working the event the next weekend. I'll take her home to meet the folks after that."

Jo cleared her throat and they turned toward her. "Are you planning on staying much longer?" she asked. She was close to weeping with weariness—the wedding, Luke's appearance with his new wife, and most of all, the wrenching moments in Tom's arms.

"Five minutes," Tom said. He turned back to Luke and gripped his shoulder. "Congratulations, bro. The best of luck to you and Cherie."

Tom didn't talk on the way back, leaving Jo alone with her thoughts. When they reached her hotel he turned off the ignition and took her hand.

"Are you driving back to Austin tomorrow?"

She nodded. "I have to leave here early—I have a noon flight."

He didn't speak for several minutes, only sat running his thumb over her hand, between her fingers. At last he spoke. "Next weekend?"

Here was her chance to make a clean break, to guard against being hurt, to bolt for safety just as she had run in panic from the flash flood. She closed her eyes, reliving the brief moments of passion, the sense of homecoming she had felt in Tom's arms and his superhuman restraint.

"Next weekend," she said.

He kissed her palm. "Travel safely," he said.

"THE WEDDING SOUNDS like a fascinating experience," Anna said during their Monday morning coffee. "Something out of an old Western movie. But you look tired. Are the weekly treks finally catching up with you?"

Her mother was right; she was tired and confused and fearful of seeing Tom again. She realized she had been walking a tightrope for months, balancing between professional detachment and a growing mutual attraction. Now neither of them could deny she had stumbled across the line. How could she face him as if nothing had changed?

"I'm worried about Tom," she said. "He comes across as the responsible brother, but he and Luke really balance and support each other. I wonder how Luke's marriage will change that. He won't be there for Tom in the same way."

"He shouldn't have to be," Anna said. "Tom's old enough to stand on his own. Luke's getting married could be good for both of them." She laughed. "You'd think I know these boys. You've made them very real to me."

"Mom..." Jo played with her coffee mug,

printing damp overlapping circles on her place-mat. "How did you…? Did you ever…?"

Anna waited for her to continue. Most of the time Jo appreciated her mother's hands-off parenting style, but sometimes she wished Anna would at least try to offer advice.

"Did you ever wish Dad would quit racing?" She wanted to kick herself—what a dumb question. Every time a driver died on the track, her mother must have prayed her husband would decide to retire.

Anna stirred her coffee for several seconds. At last she said, "I think you're really asking if I tried to get him to quit." She took Jo's hand. "Sweetheart, if your father had been an accountant or a teacher or a bricklayer who loved his work, I'd have found him just as irresistible. But he was passionate about racing—that's who he was. If I'd asked him to quit, he wouldn't have been the man I fell in love with. Or that you loved, for that matter."

Jo braced herself, waiting for her mother to ask if they were really talking about Tom. Instead Anna pulled a book of fabric samples across the table. "What do you think of this pattern for those dining room chairs in the Park Slope condo?"

CHAPTER TWENTY-EIGHT

TOM HAD DRIVEN the long road home from Texas pretty much on autopilot—a good thing he'd done that stretch of I-40 so many times. The road had seemed endless without Luke in the passenger seat, joking or napping or grousing about the work waiting at the ranch. Tom had managed to work his way through his frustration by the time he hit Albuquerque, but loneliness rode with him all the way to Cameron's Pride.

His unease before Deke and Mandy's wedding had been dead-on, but he couldn't bring himself to regret those minutes beside the quiet lake. He could feel again, as if his heart had started beating for the first time since Traci had walked out on him, scorning him and the life he offered her. Yeah, feeling was painful, but no matter what happened with Jo, he would treasure the memory of holding her in his arms.

Still, he'd be a fool to expect her to show up

at the next event like nothing had happened. More than likely he'd get an email saying she couldn't make it or her mom needed her or that her research was complete, thanks for all your help. From her passionate response, he knew she'd wanted him as much as he wanted her, but she'd made the right decision for them both— no sense setting themselves up for a world of heartache with no happy ending in sight.

He sighed and climbed out of his truck. He had driven out at dawn so he wouldn't be tempted to see Jo before she left for Austin and hadn't stopped for food. He'd grab something to eat now and get to work. A chalkboard beside the kitchen door always listed chores that needed doing; he would pick one that put a horse between his knees.

The quiet kitchen with its generations of family memories and his mom's flowering houseplants that Shelby still tended lovingly all soothed his spirit. He hung his jacket on its hook beside the door and took his phone from the pocket. He'd forgotten to plug it in the night before, and now the no-battery light blinked at him in accusation. He stuck it on the charger; immediately it alerted him that he had a message. His heart began to thud. He had no reason to expect a call from Jo—probably wouldn't be good news if it was from her.

Taking a deep breath, he checked the caller's number—sure enough, it was Jo's. He allowed himself a grim chuckle. She was no coward; she had called rather than send an email. Good for her—cowboy up and get it over with. There wasn't enough juice on the phone's battery to take it from the charger, so he hit Speaker and Play Message.

Her voice filled the room, and his heart. "Hi, Tom—you're probably on the road so I'll make this quick. I'm sorry, but I can't make it on Friday. My mom needs me to help with a big open house on Saturday morning…"

Why not a sick grandmother or even a funeral to attend? He'd hoped for more honesty from her or at least more creativity.

"But I can catch a noon flight to Des Moines and make it for Saturday evening, what with the time difference. Let me know if you can meet me or if I should take a cab." A short pause. "Don't work too hard. Talk to you later."

He reached blindly for a chair and sank onto it. The longing he had beaten down during the long drive home swept over him as relentlessly as the flash flood in the canyon. Jo was coming back. He would see her on Saturday. Beyond that, he wouldn't dare to hope.

So HERE HE stood at the arrivals portal, nervous as a bridegroom, and a lot jumpier than Luke had been, he'd bet a round win. Passengers kept streaming from the Jetway like clowns from a tiny car at the circus—there couldn't be anyone left on board except the crew. He started to turn away—maybe she'd missed her flight or she'd changed her mind at the last minute.

But at last there she was, carrying a baby. She handed the infant to a harried-looking young woman with a toddler in tow. Her face lit when she saw Tom; he could feel a matching grin on his own.

Should he hug her? Kiss her? Sometimes she gave him a friendly hug, no different than the way she greeted Luke. He wanted to grab her right there in the airport and finish what they'd started at Deke's wedding. While he was still making up his mind, she slipped her hand into his and kissed his cheek.

"I watched last night's go-round," she said. "Nice ride." She jostled him with her elbow. "Another score like that and you'll get first pick in the short round. Is Gunslinger here?"

"Not this weekend," he said, throttling back

his emotions. "His owner is saving him for a big event at the end of May."

"Too bad, but he's still waiting for you. I saw Cherie sing last night. Now I remember her from Kansas City—her yee-haw version of the national anthem."

"You mind having dinner with them?" he asked. "Luke wants to show her off to you."

"No, I don't mind," she said. "I know you want to get to the arena early." She touched his arm as he opened the car door for her. "Please be careful."

"Careful doesn't win round money." He looked into her eyes, seeing the worry there. "As careful as I can be," he said and squeezed her hand.

CHAPTER TWENTY-NINE

LUKE AND CHERIE were waiting in the lobby when Tom dropped her off at the hotel. Cherie snuggled up to Luke in the hotel dining room, stealing bites from his plate and almost wriggling with delight when riders who hadn't made it to Deke's wedding stopped at their table to offer good wishes and bawdy advice. Jo wondered how soon Luke would tire of Cherie's clinging and simpering, but maybe her personality suited his own easygoing style, so unlike Tom's quiet intensity.

Luke left for the arena before dessert. "You girls behave yourselves," he said before planting a noisy kiss on his giggling bride.

"Isn't Luke just the cutest thing?" Cherie asked, repairing her lipstick with the use of a tiny vanity mirror. "I'm so glad he's a bullfighter and not a rider. I couldn't stand watching my husband take those awful risks. My daddy got all crippled up riding saddle broncs, and that's nowhere near as bad as bull riding."

Cherie's innocent chatter did nothing to ease the sense of foreboding that had dogged Jo ever since her plane had landed. She had thought long and hard on the flight from Texas to New York after the wedding. The few moments in Tom's arms had shown her what she'd been missing by holding out for safe predictability. If living in fear for his safety was the price of loving him, she would have to pay it every time he climbed down into the bucking chute. Still buoyed by her resolve, she had impulsively left the message on his phone as soon as she got home.

Like most teenage girls, Jo had fallen in love in high school with a nice boy in one of her classes. She and Eric had been inseparable, talking with innocent confidence about forever and happily-ever-after until his father had been transferred to California. They'd corresponded faithfully for a while and then sporadically. They still exchanged Christmas cards, his with photos of his wife and two kids.

She could almost be angry with Tom for sneaking inside her defenses. She had seen him first as an asset to her work and then as a friend and collaborator, valuing his humor and kindness and courage. When she finally acknowledged she wanted him, passion burned hotter than she had ever felt at seventeen. She liked Tom, admired him, desired him. She could love him if she let herself.

Except for his chosen career.

Yes, bull riders did get injured, sometimes badly, but maybe Tom had used up his quota of bad luck. Maybe his rigorous training regimen would protect him from serious harm. And he had all but promised he would hang up his rope for good once he won his gold buckle.

Could she be as brave as her mother had been? She didn't know.

"I said, will you be sitting with the wives tonight?"

Cherie's question jerked Jo back; she made an on-the-fly decision. "I think I'll watch from the chutes tonight and try to grab a few more photos for my book."

"That's okay," Cherie said. "We'll get together at the after-party. You tell Tom good luck, you hear?"

Later while the lights went down for the pyrotechnics, Jo stood waiting along with the small group of fans who had bought chute-seat tickets. Luke saluted her as he and the other two bullfighters ran into the arena. The crowd quieted for the national anthem, and Jo added her own silent prayer during the invocation for everyone's safety.

She mounted the steep stairs to the platform above the chutes and perched in her chair next to the broadcasters' booth, clenching the day sheet in sweating hands. She smoothed the pages and found Tom's name halfway down the list. Was that good or bad? She'd have to wait least an hour for him to ride in the long round, but less time would pass before his second bull in the championship round.

She took deep breaths, trying to relax. She was making herself crazy—she had no reason to believe Tom would be in more danger tonight than at any other time she had watched him ride. For a moment she wished she had chosen to sit with Cherie and the riders' wives, where she could be distracted by their chatter and draw strength from their composure. She shook her head. This was her trial by fire; she had to dominate her fears if she had any hope of being the woman Tom wanted and needed.

"You okay, Jo?" Paula, the staffer she had first met in Oklahoma City put a bottle of spring water into her hand. "You look kind of shaky."

Jo managed a smile. "A little frazzled maybe.

I flew in from New York just in time for the show."

"Yeah, we missed you last night." Paula laughed. "I told the management we should put you on the payroll, as much help as you've been at the PR functions."

Paula's appearance broke Jo's spiraling anxiety. She drank a little water and watched the first riders straddle their bulls. Some made the eight seconds and some didn't but they all walked out of the arena more or less undamaged.

And then it was Tom's turn. He strode along the walkway below her seat; for the first time since she'd been watching him ride, he looked up at her with a grin and a touch to his hat brim. She smiled back and gave him a thumbs-up before sinking back into her chair drenched in cold sweat.

Tom settled his hat more firmly and climbed down onto the back of a brindled bull with its head cocked sideways to accommodate its great spread of horns. The horns were blunted, but they were still formidable weapons, especially against a rider not wearing a helmet. He took a final wrap of the bull rope around his hand, settled his mouth guard into place, and gave a quick nod, wasting no time in the chute.

The bull reared, almost toppling over backward against the gate, and shot forward in a tremendous leap that slid Tom back on the end of his arm. Jo gasped and closed her eyes but then opened them as a mammoth kick rocked him back into position. He broke forward with the bull's next jump, his free arm weaving its elegant pattern above the bull's shoulders and the buzzer sounded, almost drowned out by the crowd's roar. Tom stepped off as neatly as Jo might disembark from an MTA bus.

"That's how it's done, folks." The announcer had to yell over the cheers. "That's why Tom Cameron has been leading the standings ever since the first event of the season. How about 89.5 for that ride?"

Jo wiped sweat out of her eyes, giddy with relief. He made it look so easy she could almost forget the first time she'd seen him at Madison Square Garden, crumpled against the fence just below her seat. One bull down, one to go.

The rest of the long-round rides went by in a blur. She wanted to go to Tom, to tell him what a coward she'd been, to laugh with him over her foolishness, to feel his arms around her. She stayed in her seat, fearing to tempt fate.

Tom chose Doc Holliday for the championship round. "We don't know much about this bull," the announcer said, "except he's kind of mean. He wouldn't be in the short go if he wasn't a rank one."

Jo's comfort level plummeted.

Two bulls didn't buck with much enthusiasm and one fell with his rider, so three rerides would follow Tom's out on Doc Holliday. Jo hunched forward as Tom approached the chute; this time he didn't look up at her. She gripped the railing with both hands chanting "please, please, please" under her breath.

Tom settled gingerly on the bull's back; Deke leaned into the chute with his hands locked on the back of Tom's vest as Doc Holliday tried to lunge forward and upward. She heard Luke call out, "Watch this one, guys—he'll go after you."

Again the quick nod and the gate swung open. The bull stood motionless for a full second and then exploded in a wild bucking spin that threw Tom far to one side, clinging with only a spur hooked over the animal's spine. A quick reverse flung him in the other direction, hanging just above the dirt and still miraculously not touching the bull with his free hand. The buzzer sounded and he fell facedown, covering his head with his arms while Luke and the other bullfighters yelled and waved their arms to draw the bull away.

Doc Holliday lumbered in pursuit of Luke and Tom stood up, dusted his hat and waved it to the crowd.

"That sure wasn't pretty, folks, but Tom Cameron deserves a 95 for pure grit. Let him know what you think of that ride."

Jo screamed her approval along with the rest of the spectators, tears of relief streaming down her face. It was over—her fears had been baseless. Tom waved his hat again and disappeared behind the chutes.

There were just the three rerides before Tom could claim his event-win prizes and then they could all go celebrate—

It happened so fast Jo almost missed it. The second reride went bad at three seconds; the cowboy hit the dirt hard, stunned for a moment, as the bull lunged toward him head down. Luke launched himself at the bull and was sent flying against the chutes, landing on his right shoulder so that his neck bent at a sickening angle. He lay helpless as the bull ground its horns against his motionless body.

She stood frozen, too shocked to scream, as the other bullfighters slapped at the bull while the safety rider dropped a loop on its horns. The medical team including Doc Barnett reached

Luke even before the bull was dragged from the arena.

Tom appeared beside Jo as if by magic and thrust keys into her hand. "The car's in the hotel garage. Find Cherie and bring her to the hospital. I'm riding in the ambulance with Luke." He spun away from her before she could answer and plunged down the steps as Luke was being rolled onto the trauma board with a cervical collar stabilizing his neck.

Jo clutched the keys in one hand with her other fist stuffed against her mouth to keep from sobbing. *Don't think, just do what Tom asked.* She bolted down the opposite steps and raced around the lowest tier of seats to the section where she had seen Cherie earlier in the evening.

"Where's Luke's wife?" she asked Sophie Haley as the announcer promised an update on Luke's condition as soon one was available.

"I don't know," Sophie said. "She left about an hour ago. We thought she was just going to the restroom but she never came back."

"Tom told me to bring her to the hospital." Jo gave Sophie her cell number. "I'll make a quick run around the concourse—grab her and call me if she comes back here."

Her phone buzzed just as she finished searching the last restroom on the concourse. "The event's over," Sophie said, "but Cherie hasn't shown up. Have you heard anything about Luke?"

"No, and I didn't find her either. I'm going to the hospital—send her there if she shows up at the hotel." She disconnected without waiting for an answer.

In her shock and anguish, she couldn't remember what kind of rental Tom had been driving when he had picked her up. She wandered through the parking garage pressing the horn alarm until a gray Honda sedan beeped and blinked at her. She found University Hospital on the car's navigation menu and pressed Go, figuring Luke had been taken to the highest-level trauma center in the area.

Having something to do occupied her mind at some level, but the disaster replayed through her mind in an endless loop, ending with Luke's head snapping to one side exactly as her father's had done. Had he reached the hospital alive? Would he be paralyzed? What other damage had the bull's horns done?

Somehow she threaded her way through unfamiliar streets and parked across the street from University Hospital; on a Saturday night, she found no empty spaces in the ER parking lot. She sat in the car fighting back tears for Luke and Tom and for herself until her phone rang. She recognized Tom's number.

"Where are you? Is Cherie with you?" His voice was hoarse.

"I'm right outside, but I couldn't find Cherie—nobody knows where she is."

She heard him sigh; he sounded weary as death. "Luke made it here alive. Will you wait with me?"

She wanted to run to him, to hold and comfort him. At the same time she wanted to catch the next flight to anywhere.

"Of course," she said. "I'll be right in."

CHAPTER THIRTY

SHE DIDN'T SPOT Tom in the confusion of a busy
Saturday night ER so she asked the clerk at the
main desk for information about Luke Cameron.

"From the rodeo? Are you a relative?"

"His sister," Jo said without missing a beat,
and in a sense she was. She and Tom and Luke
shared a special kinship within the larger family of bull riding.

"He just went up to surgery. I sent your other
brother up to the OR waiting room. Fourth
floor—that set of elevators." She pointed down
the hall and turned to help a frantic-looking
woman supporting a gray-faced man holding
his chest.

She almost backed away when Tom looked
up as she entered the waiting room. His face
was ashen; tears glistened in his eyes. He
reached blindly for her hand, pulling her down
to sit beside him on the tweed sofa. She put

her arm around him, massaging the back of his neck, murmuring meaningless reassurance.

"Have the doctors told you anything yet?" she asked.

"Nobody's had time." His voice shook. "I wasn't watching—did you see what happened?"

The whole sequence flashed before her eyes; she wanted to whimper with horror but understood his need to know. "Luke landed on his head and neck against the chutes and then the bull tried to gore him. The other bullfighters got to him as quick as they could, but he took a couple of hard hits."

"I got there just as the Sports Medicine guys were carrying him off the dirt. Doc was with him. He's the best—he always knows what to do." He tried to smile. "He's saved my butt a few times. I'm sure glad my name's still on Luke's medical card, same as his for me, so I could sign for the surgery permission. Since you couldn't find Cherie."

As if on cue, Sophie Haley stalked through the waiting room door dragging Cherie by one hand. "I found her waiting for us in the hotel bar," she said.

Cherie charged at Tom who had risen to meet her. "He lied to me!" She pounded her fists against his chest. "He said he could take care of me because bullfighters never get hurt." Her blue eyes were huge in her pale face. "This was never supposed to happen!"

Jo wanted to slap her.

Sophie did. "Knock it off! Luke was doing his job, you twit. You'd have seen that if you hadn't been off chasing some guy about a recording contract."

Cherie howled and collapsed into a chair; tears sluiced mascara down her cheeks like tailings from an abandoned coal tunnel.

Sophie turned her back on the spectacle. "Any word yet?"

Tom shook his head.

"Luke's still in surgery," Jo said. "Thanks for bringing Cherie to the hospital." She glanced at the girl whose sobs had subsided to snuffling hiccups. "I guess."

"Let me call Len," Sophie said. "I'll wait with you guys for a while." She jerked her chin at Cherie. "Maybe you'll want me to take her back to the hotel."

She stepped into the corridor for a few minutes in low-voiced conversation and then returned to the waiting room. "I told Len I'd call him as soon we get news." She turned to Tom. "I know you don't eat before you ride—can I get you something from the snack machines?"

He shook his head, but Jo said, "Hot chocolate and some kind of sugary pastry if you can find it. Carbs act as a tranquilizer—I learned that sailing." She sighed. "Get something for Cherie too. We don't need her getting hysterical on us again."

Sophie saluted with the hint of a smile: "Ma'am, yes ma'am! I'll do my best."

Jo turned back to Tom, noticing for the first time he still wore his riding vest. She unzipped it and slipped it off his shoulders. Arena dirt smeared his shirt and jeans; a ragged tear in one shirtsleeve marked a near miss from the bull's hoof.

"Go wash up," she said. "The way you look, the doctors won't let you in to see Luke."

"Restrooms are right around the corner," Sophie said. "I'll show you." She led him from the room.

Jo's knees failed her; she sat with a thump. At that moment, Tom's loss of composure scared her more than Luke's injuries. Could this be the same man who had reacted instantly to the flash flood, yanking her to safety and later directing recovery of the doomed hiker's body? Her mother's voice chimed in her head: *He's not allowed human weakness? This is his brother, almost his twin. No one is brave all the time.*

She gave a startled laugh; maybe her mom helped with advice more than she realized.

"Are you crazy? What are you laughing about?" Cherie had her vanity mirror out, trying to repair her ruined makeup. "What do you care about Luke? You're not even family."

Jo bit back a sharp retort. She cared, all right. And she knew too well the grim future Luke might face. She'd met jockeys who had suffered spinal injuries and wondered how Luke might deal with disability. With his signature good humor? Or would he descend into anger and depression? At least he had a loving family to help him. And a wife. Sort of.

Tom returned with most of the dirt erased from his hands and clothing; he had rolled his sleeves to the elbow to hide the rip. He looked a little calmer, as if facing himself in the mirror had lent him composure.

Sophie arrived with cocoa and doughnuts begged from the OR nurses' locker room. Jo discovered she was famished even though she had eaten a hearty dinner with Luke and Cherie only a few hours earlier. They were devouring the last crumbs when Dr. Barnett entered the room, still wearing a blue scrub suit with a surgical mask dangling around his neck.

He nodded to Jo and Sophie and took a seat on the coffee table facing Tom. "Luke's in the recovery room," he said. "You'll be able to see him in maybe another hour, after they transfer him to the ICU."

Tom opened his mouth but no words came out.

"What were his injuries?" Jo asked.

Dr. Barnett took off his glasses and polished a tiny spot of blood from one lens. "Broken ribs and a ruptured spleen. We had to remove that—it was too mangled to save. And his neck's broken again."

"Again?" Cherie's shriek echoed the shocked protest in Jo's mind. "He's broken his neck before?"

"A couple years ago, in Tucson," Tom said. "We both missed the finals that year."

"I remember," Dr. Barnett said. "You were still in rehab after I fixed your hip."

"So how bad is it this time?"

"It could be a lot worse," Dr. Barnett said. "He's got good reflexes in both feet. I have him in traction and medicated to get the swelling down and prevent further damage. He may need surgery to stabilize the vertebrae, but right now I'd say the odds are good he'll walk away without paralysis." He shook his head. "One of these days his luck's going to run out."

"I get it," Tom said. "I'll talk to him, but you know Luke…"

Dr. Barnett sighed and replaced his glasses. "Cowboys are a special kind of crazy, God bless 'em." He turned to Cherie. "I don't believe I've had the pleasure."

Cherie stuffed a crumpled Kleenex into her purse and offered her hand. "I'm Cherie Cameron, Luke's wife." Her lips trembled. "We got married a week ago in Vegas. We just got back from our honeymoon."

"Congratulations," he said. "I'm sorry to meet you under these circumstances."

Sophie gathered empty cups and crumpled napkins. "I'm going back to the hotel now," she said. "Is it okay if I relay your report on Luke?"

Dr. Barnett looked at Tom who nodded. "Sure, Sophie," he said. "I know you'll get it right."

Cherie jumped to her feet. "I'll go with you—Luke won't know if I'm here or not." She looked away. "I can see him in the morning."

Sophie looked at Jo. "You want a ride?"

Here was her chance to cut and run. Tom sat staring at the floor, apparently oblivious to the conversation. She could give him the car keys…

"I'll wait with Tom," she said and then she saw his shoulders move convulsively.

CHAPTER THIRTY-ONE

Tom knew the season had been going too well. He had been waiting for the sky to fall, but Luke's wreck had hit him like a mugger's attack in a dark alley. Sure, bullfighters got injured— Luke had gotten hurt before—but not as often as riders, considering the amount of time they spent working the bulls close in as they did. They were quick-moving targets and not tied down to half a ton of rampaging bovine. But when they did take a bad hit—

"He'll be fine," he said aloud, like an incantation.

"Sure he will."

He grabbed on to Jo's voice, but then his heart dropped. Before their brief, desperate embrace by the lake, he would have been grateful to have her sitting beside him; he could have clung to her openly, still pretending they were just friends. He had screwed that up by taking her in his arms, by showing her he wanted much more than her friendship. Afterward he'd steeled himself to believe she wouldn't be coming back, and then miraculously she had, giving him another chance.

Until Luke suffered exactly the same sort of injury that had killed her father, right before her eyes, almost close enough to touch. For half a heartbeat, he raged at his brother and then remorse swamped him. All the riders depended on the bullfighters' willingness to throw themselves in harm's way.

At least Doc Barnett's report was balm to Tom's heart. He would make his pitch again for Luke to quit the arena, but he doubted his words would carry much weight. How could he tell his brother to opt for safety while he continued to risk his own life?

"Do you think Luke will retire after this?" Jo asked, as if she'd read his mind.

"Probably not," Tom said with a sigh. "He's a good cowhand, but he just puts in time on the ranch between events. Live fast, die young and make a handsome corpse—that's his motto."

"Not like you."

"Not like me. Once I get my buckle, it's one and done—I'll hang it up for good. That million-buck bonus check would put Cameron's Pride back in the black and take a lot of pressure off my dad. And we'd have three of us working the ranch full-time—three and a half if you count Luke, even if he's still fighting bulls."

He took off his dusty black Stetson and set it brim up on the table. "You ever dream about no worries, no more trying?"

"I think that's called dead," she said with the flicker of a smile. "'Man is born to trouble as surely as sparks fly upward.' My grandmother liked me to read to her from the Bible while she quilted."

"Trouble is better than dead, I guess," he said, "but I get so tired sometimes, like I'm just marking time. Maybe that's why I keep riding—I'm looking for something I can't quite reach."

"Do you know what you're reaching for?" She slouched beside him, legs stretched out, ankles crossed, eyes half closed.

Talking to her was so easy, almost like talking to himself—he would miss that most of all when she left for good. "That story I told you the night we were stranded up the canyon? About the cowboy? That was me, but you knew that."

She made a soft "I'm listening" sound.

"Not long after Dad and Shelby got married, I met this girl. She looked a little like Shelby—long black hair and blue eyes instead of green—probably why I noticed her. She was waitressing in a little café in Kansas where I stopped on the way home from St. Louis— I was traveling alone that weekend. Anyhow, we hit it off right away. Business was slow and we talked for a couple of hours—I was kind of lonesome, I guess. She said she didn't plan on working long in Kansas—she wanted to move to Nashville. She got me talking about bull riding and telling her about California and New York City and New Orleans like I'd visited the promised land. She showed up at the next event and then just kept coming back for more."

Jo took his hand.

If he continued, the pain he had shoved into a box with the lid locked down would escape. He'd have to start over, learning to live with it again, but Jo had trusted him with her deepest sadness. If somehow she decided to stay, there couldn't be any secrets standing between them.

"She wanted to get married," he said. "She was right up front about it. I liked the notion myself—I was getting tired of the partying— but she was pushing too hard. I told her I wasn't ready. That's when…" He took a couple of deep breaths to steady his voice. "She told me she was pregnant." He shrugged. "That clinched the deal for me—I wasn't having my kid born without a right to my name. I bought her a ring and said we'd get married right away. I'd ride till the end of the season and then retire. My dad followed the rodeo when I was small—he was gone most of the time and busted up while he was home. He quit when I was about ten—after that he was the kind of father I plan to be."

He gripped Jo's hand hard. "She got mad when I told her I planned to quit riding and stick to ranching full-time. She said she'd grown up grubbing in the dirt and raising her younger sister and brothers—she didn't plan on being stuck in the middle of nowhere with a baby and a bunch of cows. She threw the ring on the ground and walked out. I figured she'd cool down and change her mind if I could just get her to visit Cameron's Pride—we'd work something out. The next weekend a bull fell with me—maybe I wasn't paying attention—and put me in the hospital for three months."

"And you're still trying to find her."

Even in his misery, he rejoiced that Jo understood him so well. "I started trying to locate her as soon as I came out of surgery, but nobody seemed to know where she'd gone. I've checked every way I can think of in every city we visit, including Nashville, but I've always come up empty—no phone listed to anyone by that name. I even called the police chief in the little town in Arkansas she said she was from, but he'd never heard of a family by that name in his town. I didn't have the money to hire a detective. And I hated to tell my folks I'd been so irresponsible. I tried to make myself believe she'd lied so I would marry her, but maybe she really was pregnant. Maybe she had an abortion or put the baby up for adoption. Or just dropped it off somewhere like an unwanted kitten."

He swallowed hard. "Not knowing chews up my gut—wondering if I have a son or daughter somewhere I'll never know, maybe hurting and needing help. I've never stopped looking for her, because of the baby, but nothing."

Jo laced her fingers through his. "I'll help you."

CHAPTER THIRTY-TWO

TOM'S HAND RELAXED in hers; his head dropped forward, but not before she saw a glaze of moisture in his eyes. His absorption with Auntie Rose's little granddaughter, his kindness with small cowboys and cowgirls at the meet-and-greets all made sense now. She had no doubt he would shower his own children with the same patience and devotion.

But what had she committed herself to? She still teetered on a knife's edge—hang on for the ride or cut and run. She could live out her life without ever meeting another cowboy, planning trips to far away places whenever the PBR came to town.

Coward, a voice whispered in her head. *How can you just walk away? You'll be no different from the woman who broke his heart or from Cherie, for that matter. And what are the chances you'll meet as good a man as Tom? Or ever forget him?*

"Mr. Cameron?" A nurse appeared in the doorway. "You can see your brother now."

He rose, still holding Jo's hand.

"Family only," the nurse said.

"I'm his sister," Jo said.

Tom's hand tightened on hers as they followed the nurse. "Thanks," he said under his breath. "I've never had to visit Luke like this. I'm usually the one banged up, and I was still out of action myself the last time he got hurt."

His fear gave her strength, but her composure evaporated when they entered Luke's unit. For a dreadful moment she was sure Tom, not Luke, lay on the narrow bed. She had mistaken them for twins when she first saw them at Madison Square Garden, but the resemblance had faded in her mind as she came to know them as individuals. Now she could be staring down at Tom, rigidly restrained and tethered to life by tubes and monitors.

She wanted to run weeping into the corridor, out of the hospital and out of the Camerons' lives, never to return. The nurse's words flowed around her—vital signs, level of consciousness—while she fought for control. Only Tom's hand gripping hers kept her in the stark little cubicle.

He released her and bent over his brother, touching his shoulder. "Damn fool," he said.

"You think you're a superhero? I can't wait till you're out of here so I can kick your butt."

The corner of Luke's mouth twitched.

"He's stable and comfortable," the nurse said. "Why don't you go get some rest?"

"Are you sure?" Tom asked. "Maybe I should stay, just in case—"

"I'm sure," the nurse said. "We'll be right here with him, and he'll be more alert in a few hours."

Tom nodded and turned away, exhaustion plain in every line of his face and body.

Jo leaned close and kissed Luke's cheek. "I'll take care of him," she said, and his eyelids fluttered.

She led Tom to the parking lot and opened the passenger door. "I'll drive," she said. "You're dead on your feet."

He climbed in without argument and fumbled with his seat belt. She shook her head in wry amusement—he refused to wear a helmet in the most dangerous sport on earth but never forgot to fasten his seat belt.

At two in the morning the streets were empty; she drove the few miles to the hotel garage only half-awake, by now running on empty herself.

"What's your room number?" she asked. "Give me your key." She could barely hear his mumbled response. She rode up with him in the elevator and opened his door, watching as he entered and stood in the center of the room as if he might stand there indefinitely until ordered to sit or lie down.

She sighed and followed him into the room. "Sit on the bed," she said, taking his hat and vest from him. He let her pull off his boots without protest; she wondered if she should suggest he undress, but decided in his exhausted state it didn't much matter how he slept.

"Lie down and get some rest," she said.

He shook his head. "What if they call from the hospital? Maybe I won't hear my phone."

She reached out her hand. "Give me your phone—I'll listen for a call. You won't be much use to Luke in the state you're in."

Instead he grabbed her wrist. "Please—don't leave."

She hesitated only a second and then sank down beside him. She owed him whatever comfort she might offer, just as he had kept her safe and unafraid in the dark ruins.

"Move over," she said, and then she kicked off her boots.

THE INSISTENT BUZZING dragged her up from a deep well of sleep; she located Tom's cell phone under the pillow and answered with a mumbled monosyllable.

A moment's silence, then she heard, "Is Tom there? This is his father."

She sat up, pushing her hair from her face. Tom slept on without stirring as she slid from under the spread she had pulled over them both during the early morning hours. She tiptoed into the bathroom before answering.

"Hi, Jake. It's Jo. Tom's still asleep—we came back from the hospital around two." She looked at her watch—surely not nine o'clock. Fear struck. "Any updates on Luke?"

"I flew in at seven this morning—Shelby's not happy I took off without her, but I told her to calm down, I'd be at a hospital with plenty of doctors around. I'm with Luke now. He's awake, but he's still fuzzy about what happened. Doc Barnett says that's normal after surgery. Luke's asking about someone named Cherie."

Jo closed her eyes and counted to ten. Just like Luke—he hadn't bothered to tell his folks he'd gotten married. He'd probably planned to show up at the ranch with his new wife and yell "Surprise!"

"I think Tom should tell you about Cherie," she said as she heard a groan and the rustle of bedclothes behind her. Tom reached for his phone, stuffing his shirttail into his jeans with his other hand.

She heard him say "Dad?" as she laid his car keys beside the TV and let herself out of the room.

CHAPTER THIRTY-THREE

BACK IN HER own room, she was so eager to peel off her rumpled clothes, she almost missed the folded pages from a hotel memo pad, slipped under her door. She read the round schoolgirl script:

> Dear Jo,
> I'm sorry to bother you, but I know Tom doesn't like me much anyhow, especially after the way I acted last night. I hope Luke's all better this morning but I can't go see him. Hospitals scare me so bad I was about ready to throw up. I'll wait at the hotel if he's getting out pretty quick or maybe I'll go back to KC. He knows where to find me there. Please tell him I love him but I'm just no good with sick people.
> Yours truly,
> Cherie

Jo's phone rang while she was still trying to digest Cherie's note; she recognized the number from Cameron's Pride.

Shelby's voice, quiet but vibrating with concern, greeted her. "Jo, Jake just called me. Are you still with Tom?"

"I'm back in my room for a shower and fresh clothes. I'm sure he'll be going to the hospital as soon as he gets cleaned up—we just collapsed when we got back way after midnight."

"Will you be going to the hospital with him?"

Jo shrank from the idea of visiting Luke again in the ICU—the shock of picturing Tom in his place was too fresh in her mind. "I hadn't planned—"

"I wish you would," Shelby said. "I know Luke's wreck is hitting Tom hard. You've been good for Tom. I watched you two together while you were here—he was more at ease than I've seen him in years."

Just as Tom had relaxed in her arms last night, almost instantly asleep. "If you think I can help..."

"You've developed a connection with him I don't believe he's had with anyone else," Shelby said. "Please stay at least until the situation stabilizes."

Jo admired Shelby, knowing how she had won out over tragedy, and valued her regard. "Of course. I'll go with him," she said. She had to give Tom Cherie's note anyway.

A knock sounded on her door as she was combing her damp hair back into a ponytail. Tom stood outside, freshly shaven in clean shirt and jeans, but with arena dirt still in the creases of his boots.

"I tried calling you—" he said.

"I was probably in the shower. Are you on your way to see Luke?"

"Will you come with me?" His need spoke in his eyes.

"Of course, if you want me to."

He took her in his arms in a quick hard hug and then led the way toward the elevators.

JAKE ROSE TO meet them when they entered the ICU waiting area. His face creased with a smile when he saw Jo. "Shelby call you? I told her she should talk to you."

Jo answered his smile. "She's quite a lady, isn't she?"

"Whoa, you better believe it," he said. "She's got me broke gentle for sure. So who's Cherie?"

Tom sighed. He'd already read Cherie's note. "You better sit down, Dad," he said.

Jake scanned the note for himself after Tom told him about Luke and Cheri's surprise appearance at Deke and Mandy's wedding reception.

"Poor kid," he said. "I don't know if Las

Vegas wedding vows include 'in sickness and in health,' but I doubt she thought she'd be in for this kind of trouble."

Jake's compassionate take on Cherie's defection shifted Jo's view of last night's scene in this room.

"Should I try to get her here, do you think?" she asked.

Jake shook his head. "It won't hurt to talk to her, but if she can't, she can't. Lord knows I sat in enough hospital waiting rooms with my first wife, fighting the urge to bolt for the high country. We'll tell Luke the truth, that she's too upset to see him all banged up like he is."

"Her number is probably in Luke's cell phone," Tom said. He looked at Jo. "Maybe you could call her just to find out her plans."

Like it or not, she was unofficially part of the Cameron support system. "I'll try to reach her when we get back to the hotel," she said, bowing to the inevitable.

Jake looked at his watch. "It's been an hour since I saw Luke," he said. "You guys can probably look in on him now."

Tom took Jo's hand, the haunted look back in his eyes, and pushed his way through the door to the ICU.

Luke's appearance was less shocking this

morning. Daylight diluted the eerie glow from the monitors that had lent a ghostly hue to his face the night before. The traction harness restraining his head and neck still gave him the look of a prisoner on the rack, but his eyes were open and clear.

"Hey, bro," he said. "Gonna kick my butt, are you?"

Tom cuffed him lightly on the arm. "The first chance I get, but I'll let you get on your feet first."

Luke's eyes turned to Jo. "Thanks," he said. "I heard what you told me last night."

She shrugged and smiled. "Just for the hospital records, I'm your sister."

"I never doubted it," he said. His eyes shifted back to Tom. "Where's Cherie?"

Tom glanced at Jo as if to say, *You're good with words*. And, taking a deep breath, Jo thought, *Shelby, you owe me for this*.

As Jake had said, better to stick as close as possible to the truth. "She was here last night while you were still in the recovery room, but she was practically in hysterics so we sent here back to the hotel. I haven't talked to her this morning."

Luke closed his eyes for a moment; a ripple of sadness crossed his face. "I can't say I'm surprised," he said. "She's a good kid but I suspect she's a little short on gumption."

Dr. Barnett appeared and lifted the sheet off Luke's feet. "Wiggle your toes," he said, and he nodded in satisfaction when Luke complied. "I'd say you got away with it this time, but one of these days I won't be able to put Humpty Dumpty back together again."

Luke grinned at him. "Sure you will. How long do I have to stay rigged up like this?"

"Till I'm happy the swelling has gone down, and then you'll wear a collar 24/7 for the foreseeable future. You still may need surgery to stabilize the vertebrae. Plus you're still post-op from abdominal surgery. Are you having much pain?"

"Naw, you know me—no brain..."

The doctor snorted. "That saying was originated for you." He replaced the sheet over Luke's feet. "You can probably leave the hospital in a couple more days, but I'll want to see you in my office to evaluate the neck injury." He turned to Jake, who had joined them. "Do you guys think you can ride herd on this maniac long enough for him to heal up?"

"If I can't, my wife can," Jake said. "She green-breaks mustangs—Luke won't be much of a challenge for her."

Dr. Barnett chuckled and left to write new orders.

"Did Tom tell you about your wife?" Jake asked Luke. "It would have been nice if you'd told us you were getting married."

Luke had the good grace to look embarrassed. "I'm sorry I didn't let you guys know, but it happened kind of fast, Las Vegas–style, and then we took off for Mexico last week. I figured we could all get acquainted after the event. And yeah, Jo told me what happened last night. I expect Cherie will jump on a bus and just keep going—good thing I didn't get too used to having her around. Maybe she'll get a few bucks for that rock I bought her."

A nurse entered the unit. "Luke needs to rest," she said. "You can visit him a little later."

Jo kissed his cheek. "Like I learned from the sailing crowd, keep the pointy end up."

He grinned. "Too bad I didn't marry you. See you on down the road, okay?"

"Count on it," she said.

Back in the waiting room, Jake spoke to Tom. "I want you back at the ranch to help Shelby. I'll stay here until Luke can be discharged so I can make arrangements to get him home."

"I'll see if Cherie is still at the hotel," Jo said. "If you'd like me to."

Jake scribbled a number on a small notebook taken from his pocket. "Give her my cell number. I'll be glad to meet with her if she wants, but my gut tells me Luke's right—he's probably seen the last of her. Are you headed back to New York?"

"I do have to go," she said, not looking at Tom. "For now."

He held her by both shoulders. "You're welcome anytime at the ranch—I reckon you know that. You stepped up like a real Cameron."

She nodded without answering, touched by the warmth and kindness the whole clan had shown her.

"I'll stop by again before I fly out," Tom told his dad. "Come on, Jo—I'll drive you back to the hotel."

He didn't speak until he had parked in the hotel garage and turned off the engine. "I was pretty stressed out last night when we first visited Luke," he said, "but I know you were too. You were seeing me laid out like that instead of him, weren't you?"

One of the things she loved most about Tom was his sensitivity to those around him. "It was pretty shattering," she said. "When Luke hit the chute, it was just like watching my dad's crash

again, and then seeing him so hurt and helpless... That could have been you."

"It has been me," he said. "And it might be
again. You're plenty brave, but I won't ask you
to go through that if I get hurt again." His jaw
muscles tensed. "Like Dad said about Cherie,
if you can't, you can't—there's no shame to it."

He was offering her an honorable way out if
she chose to take it.

"Don't ask me to decide this minute," she
said. "All this with Luke and Cherie—I'm so
mixed up."

His lips twitched in a sad smile. "Enough
to mess with anyone's mind." He climbed out
and opened her door. "Let's go look for the
runaway bride."

As Jake had predicted, Cherie was gone. Tom
persuaded the manager to let him gather Luke's
belongings, including his cell phone. He gave
an exclamation of satisfaction when he found
Cherie's number on Luke's contact list.

"I should call her," he said. "Maybe if I'd
been more welcoming, she wouldn't have
bolted like this."

"Or maybe she would have," Jo said. "She
and Luke haven't been married long enough to
build any kind of foundation, and some people just can't handle a crisis. Would you like

me to try getting in touch with her? Since she felt more comfortable leaving the note for me. I can tell her Luke's going to be okay and give her your dad's cell number."

"Sure, why not?" he said. "We've imposed on you for everything else." He wrote both numbers on the pad beside the bed.

"Want to hear something funny?" he said as he handed her the note. "When you first asked if we could do the profile, I warned the family we might all have to get involved with the project. Now it turns out you're the one who got sucked into our troubles. Has that ever happened before with your research?"

For a moment his question stung her, but it was a fair one. As a journalist, she should have remained detached, purely an observer. She had crossed that boundary long ago; she could rewrite the whole narrative as a memoir.

"I never tried to write about anyone like your family before," she said. "You've all made it pretty hard to stay an outsider. Bad journalism maybe, but it's been a wonderful experience."

He nodded as if he understood and let the subject drop.

They stopped once more at the hospital on their way to the airport; Tom went inside briefly and came out to report that that Luke was sleeping with Jake napping in a chair at his bedside.

"Shelby must be going nuts with your dad so far away," Jo said.

"As nuts as she ever gets," Tom said. "Doc Barnett knows about Dad's heart attack last spring, but I dropped a word with the nurses too. Just in case."

Tom drove on to the airport and pulled up at the Departures gate.

"Wait with me," Jo said.

"I'll turn the car in and meet you inside."

Tom picked up a gate pass then they went through the security check together and found a quiet corner in the airport bar. New lines of stress marked Tom's face but his hands no longer shook as they had the night before.

"There's just a few more events till the summer break," he said. "I guess you won't be attending."

"I need to step away," she said. "This has been some kind of wild ride. I have to stand back and take a deep breath before I make a stupid decision that will hurt us both."

"Fair enough," he said, but his face fell. "I'm glad one of us still has a little sense."

"One thing I promise—I will start looking for Traci," she said. "I'm not an investigative reporter, but I'm a dynamite researcher, and I know people who know people. Send me anything you can remember about her, never mind how minor it seems—previous jobs she might have held, her favorite foods, where she liked to shop... Give me the last date you saw her, her full name, the town she said she was from, even if it's bogus. People trying to disguise their identity usually use the same initials—she might have grown up someplace with a similar name. Do you have a photo?"

"Maybe somewhere on my phone, although I deleted most of them," he said. "Luke probably has some on his—he took pictures of us at a couple different events."

"It's probably a long shot to find her," she said, "but I'll do my best. If you do have a little boy or girl somewhere, they deserve to have a dad like you."

He sat without speaking, obviously struggling with emotion. "I can't tell you what that would mean to me," he said at last. "Even if you never find anything, I'll be eternally grateful to you for trying."

She stood as her flight was announced. "One more thing—you need to tell your dad and Shelby the whole story," she said. "You've done the hard part, telling me. If I have any luck you'll want them to know everything. And if you want me to start making inquiries, it won't be a secret much longer."

"I know that," he said. "Talk to whoever you need to. I've held back on this too long already."

He walked with her to her gate and said, as he had at Deke's wedding, "Please don't say never, okay?"

"I won't—I'm with you all the way, no matter what I find. Just give me time."

"All the time you need." He smiled. "And I promise I won't run off and get married in Las Vegas." He put his arms around her and she clung to him as she had beside the quiet lake, as if she would never let him go. He kissed her palm when he released her and then walked away without looking back.

CHAPTER THIRTY-FOUR

"Jo, I'm so sorry about Luke," Anna said as she smoothed a strand of hair away from her daughter's face. "I saw the whole thing on TV. I'm glad you were able to help out."

Jo shivered. "Saturday night was pretty grim. Tom took it hard, of course, but this isn't the first time Luke's broken his neck. He'll probably go right back to bullfighting as soon as the doctor clears him."

"And then to have his wife run out on him— that must have been devastating."

Jo laughed. "Maybe not so much. I got the impression they really hadn't bonded that strongly, but Luke can be just as private as Tom, in his own way. Tom doesn't talk much and Luke hides behind all his talk." She recalled Luke's moment of rare candor regarding his regrets for not helping with the ranch's money troubles. "He and Tom are like opposite sides of the same coin—maybe that's why they're so close. If that makes any sense."

"That's what makes family relationships so interesting," Anna said.

"It's going to get more interesting," Jo said. "Like a fool, I volunteered to try and contact Luke's wife, figuring she might talk to me since she left me that note."

"Do you have any idea where she might be?"

"Not a clue—all I have is her cell number, so she could be anywhere. I called yesterday and left a message, but she hasn't gotten back to me."

"What do you plan to say? Is Luke angry she left? And does he want her back?"

"I don't know, so I can't tell her," Jo said. "I'll just tell her what the doctor said and give her Jake's phone number—she'll have to take it from there."

"Try her right now," Anna said. "Maybe you'll get lucky."

Jo sighed. She really didn't want to talk with Cherie, but she had promised. "If she doesn't answer this time, I'll leave another message, but I'm not chasing her indefinitely."

She punched in the number Tom had given her. The phone rang three times—four, five... She readied her message about Luke's condition when Cherie answered with a tentative note in her wispy voice.

"I guess Luke must hate me," she said after Jo identified herself. "I bet he never wants to see me again."

This was the conversation Jo didn't want to have. "I really don't know what he's thinking," she said. "He was still kind of groggy when I left. His dad asked me to let you know Luke's going to be fine—I guess a broken neck sounded worse than it turned out to be in his case. The doctor said he probably won't have any permanent disability."

She heard a gulping breath and then a loud sniffle. "I'm so ashamed," Cherie said. "I just couldn't stand seeing Luke hurt. You think he'll ever forgive me?"

Jo's heart softened; Cherie's fears were no different than her own, only more honestly expressed. "I think you need to call him," she said, her voice gentle. "And you don't need to be afraid to talk to his dad either—you'll never find anyone kinder than Jake Cameron. Good luck to you and Luke."

She sat in a reverie after the call ended, starting when her mother spoke her name.

"You handled that just right," Anna said. "I'm proud of you."

"I'm not very proud of myself," Jo said. "I'm

just as big a coward as she is where Tom is concerned."

"Maybe, but you stuck it out when he needed you. You might get stronger with practice. Will you be going to the next event?"

Only fair now to fill her mother in on her relationship with Tom even though the details might bring back painful memories. "I can't see Tom for a while," she said. "The night of the wedding we went for a walk down by the lake. Someone was playing 'The Tennessee Waltz' and we started dancing all alone in the moonlight…" She flushed and looked away.

Anna touched her hand. "Sweetie, I remember what it's like, wanting someone that way. I went to the stock car races at Watkins Glen with a date…" She smiled. "I can't even recall the poor guy's name. The minute I saw your father, I knew I'd do anything to be with him. The risks in his work just made our time together more precious."

"Then you were braver than I am. I almost thought I had the guts to love him in spite of the danger until I saw Luke in the ICU. I almost lost it—he and Tom look so much alike, all I could see was Tom lying there. You must have felt the same way, worrying about Daddy."

"Actually, I never really thought about your

father being badly injured," Anna said. "In his day, drivers were more likely to die than be injured. Either he would be fine or he'd be dead. He beat the odds for a long time…" She looked down at the colored pencil she'd been using to sketch a detailed floor plan. "And then the odds beat him."

She looked up and continued. "But I agree with your decision. If you can't accept Tom as he is with a whole heart, let him move on. Either take him or turn him loose, and don't spend too much time making up your mind." She laid the pencil down. "So I guess you'll have a lot of free time on your hands now."

"I won't be traveling, but I'll be working on another project," Jo said. She told her mother about the quest she had undertaken for Tom. If she planned to start making inquiries and searching public records, his almost-marriage wouldn't be a secret for long. Besides, Anna was an avid mystery reader; she might have some good ideas about possible avenues to explore.

Anna regarded Jo with exasperation when she finished her tale. "And you're afraid to marry Tom because he might get hurt riding bulls? A man who cares this much about a kid he's not sure exists? But you'd be fine with him working every day with cattle and horses and blizzards and rattlesnakes and flash floods. Me, I'd take my chances. If you don't want him, I'll grab him myself." She grinned. "I can picture myself as a cougar."

Jo knew her mother was trying to lighten the mood, but she was determined to finish what she'd started and own up to the secret she'd carried for fourteen years.

"One more thing," Jo said. She closed her eyes, seeing her father's crash as if it were yesterday, seeing Luke as his shoulder and head struck the steel chute gate. "I saw Daddy die. I was right by the rail, on my way to watch the finish with his pit crew."

Anna covered Jo's hand with hers, which had started shaking. "I knew where you were headed, sweetie, but I didn't think you'd gotten close enough to see the crash. You think I'd let a fourteen-year-old girl run loose in a big crowd like that without keeping track? Your dad's pit crew always let me know the minute you showed up—I knew you were safe with them. You were such an independent child, and then a teenager—I did my best to keep you safe without smothering you. After your father died…"

"I turned into a horrible little witch, didn't I? I hated you for letting Daddy go on racing."

"I knew you did," Anna said. "That was the main reason why I moved us back to live with Grandma and Grandpa. You didn't hate them, and I knew you'd forgive me eventually, even if you never understood how it was with your father and me. And now maybe you do."

"I wanted to tell you that I saw Daddy's crash," Jo said, "just to make you as miserable as I was, but I could never get the words out. I told Tom about it that night we spent in the old ruins—lifeboat mentality, I suppose. Now I can talk about it without giving myself nightmares." She gave a humorless laugh. "Except now I'll probably see Luke breaking his neck instead of Daddy."

"Or maybe you won't see either one," Anna said. "But this search you're doing for Tom—what if you find his fiancée and she does have his child? What if he decides he should be with her? He may not marry her, but he sounds like the kind of man who would take on the responsibility no matter what."

"Believe me, I've thought of that," Jo said. "I spoke up purely on instinct when I said I'd help, but how could Tom and I go forward now that I know there's a woman who might have his child out there somewhere? We both have to deal with that possibility."

"Times like this, I think maybe I've done a pretty good job raising you," Anna said. She pushed her chair back. "I think some exercise would be good for you. I've got three big rugs to load in the van plus six dining chairs and a kitchen table. What do your cowboys say? Let's git 'er done."

A FEW DAYS later a long email from Tom arrived—everything he could remember about his brief relationship with Traci O'Hara. He hadn't spared himself (or Jo) by glossing over details she would need to pinpoint a possible pregnancy and delivery date from the time of conception. At the same time, she could tell he'd been naively trusting, accepting Traci's word that she was taking the necessary precautions.

I partied some like most of the dumb young bucks out on the road for the first time, but it felt kind of lame to me—all the girls seemed pretty much alike except for their hair color and where they came from. I think the cowboys were all the same to them too. I was ready for something more serious by the time I met Traci. She could probably tell I was an easy mark.

He had included several photos from Luke's smartphone. One struck Jo as particularly poignant: Tom with a sheepish grin on his face, his arm around a striking brunette whose blue eyes stared into the camera with a hint of pleading. The picture was high-res enough for Jo to crop for a useable headshot to show for identification purposes.

I think she grew up in Arkansas—she talked a lot about taking the bus to visit her grandmother in Little Rock and she said she worked there as a waitress one summer before she graduated high school.

Jo's mother pounced on the reference to high school. "I see all these ads online for year books. Ask Tom if he knows what year she graduated."

JO CALLED TOM that evening. He must have recognized her phone number; he picked up with a soft "Hey."

Ten in New York, eight o'clock at Cameron's Pride. She could picture Tom relaxing after a hard day's work hauling feed or maybe tagging calves. Shelby and Jake would be cleaning up after supper, kidding each other about women's work and sneaking quick hugs between the table and the sink. At that moment Jo would almost have sold her soul to be there, walking out with Tom in the cool evening to check the horses before bedtime, stopping in the fragrant darkness of the barn for a long deep kiss.

She cleared her throat. "Hey yourself, cowboy. I got your file, but I've got some questions. You're pretty sure Traci graduated high school? Do you know what year?"

"Matter of fact, I do. She had this old Chevy Malibu she drove to events—she said she liked to drive and she was afraid to fly. She had the tassel from her graduation cap hanging on the rearview mirror—I'm pretty sure the little charm said '06."

"Now the hard question," Jo said. "Do you remember the colors in the tassel?"

A long silence, and then Tom said, "Red for sure and white or maybe yellow."

Jo pumped her fist in triumph; the search had just narrowed considerably. "Tom, I could kiss you!"

She heard his soft chuckle. "I can be in New York by tomorrow evening."

She almost told him she'd be waiting at the airport. "Not just yet," she said. "Let's chase down this ghost first. When's Luke coming home?"

"He and Dad got in this afternoon. He's all rigged up in a fancy collar for six weeks and then he'll see Doc Barnett about maybe needing surgery on his neck. Luke says he hated to come home—he misses all the nurses and therapists. Dad said he would have needed bear spray to chase them off."

"I can just imagine," she said. Luke had probably been swamped with female attention. She wanted to talk longer, to hold on to the sound of Tom's voice, but she said, "We'll get on the high school angle tomorrow—I'll keep you posted. Don't work too hard."

He laughed. "You know what it's like here, short-handed like we are. Feel free to come help anytime—you were turning into a pretty good cowgirl."

CHAPTER THIRTY-FIVE

"I WISH YOU'D told us all this at the time," Jake said. "Maybe we could have helped. I guess you were distracted, what with rehab and all."

"I wasn't distracted," Tom said. "I thought about it day and night, but I was ashamed I'd gotten into a mess like that, and then her disappearing... I was barely hobbling around with a walker, half-crazy that I couldn't go look for her. I didn't much want her back, but I'd have given marriage my best try for the baby's sake. If there ever was a baby. I remember Grandpa Bert saying a man should never put in a crop without getting title to the land first."

"I'd have tracked her down for you," Luke said from his seat in the big leather recliner. "What else are big brothers for? She might have shown up next on the pro rodeo circuit."

"I never thought of that," Tom said, "although she kept talking about Nashville—she was always wheedling to sing the national anthem. I guess she thought marrying a bull rider might get her foot in the door with country-and-western producers."

"That sounds like Cherie," Luke said. "And good luck to her."

"So now Jo's trying to track this Traci down for you," Jake said. "You've got a good girl there, Tom."

"I don't have her—I may never have her," Tom said. "She can't get past her father dying like he did. I think she was starting to come around, and then she saw Luke's wreck from right above the chutes. It took a lot of guts for her to even come to the hospital." Jo's face when she saw Luke in the ICU, the sick look of shock, played vividly in his memory. "I guess she understood how much I needed her there with me."

"Give her time," Shelby said. "She's got to work it through at her own pace. I think this search she's doing will be good for both of you, even if she never gets the answers you want."

Jo's FIRST CALL came that evening, the first of many. Tom held his phone even after she hung up, trying to keep the sound of her voice in his mind a little longer. He hated her knowing about his weakness, how he had behaved irresponsibly with a woman, but he had tried to do the manly thing. Traci had discarded him just like she'd tossed the ring at his feet. Finding out if she'd really been pregnant and learning the fate of the baby might lift the burden his heart had carried every day for more than two years. Jo's three words spoken without hesitation—*I'll help you*—made him love her even more than he had before.

After that they spoke nearly every day. He called her from the saddle, checking the fence line or riding drag behind slow-moving cattle, from airports and hotel rooms and from the old Cameron homestead, where he'd lain awake listening to her breathing quietly in her sleep. She called him after every round of bull riding to congratulate or commiserate, sometimes offering spot-on observations about his performance if he failed to make the eight seconds.

And he did buck off more than once—no more nonsense about a streak. To be honest, he was almost glad Jo was half a continent away, cheering him on but giving him space to make his best run at the championship. He'd meant what he had told her: once he snagged the gold buckle, he would never straddle another bull.

He collected the usual sprains and strains and bruises, a couple of cracked ribs at the Colorado Springs event, but nothing that kept him from getting on his next bull. He got used to Luke's absence—the other bullfighters were just as able and dedicated—and found himself included in the other riders' family groups as if he were a married man with his wife home tending the ranch while he was on the road.

The first half of the season ended in May with his razor-thin lead still intact and Gunslinger still unconquered, although Tom had tried once more to ride him. He planned to compete at a few major events through the summer—the Calgary Stampede, Frontier Days in Cheyenne, the Pendleton Round-Up—hoping to increase his lead, but with Luke still laid up, he needed to spend most of his time helping his dad at the ranch. Heaving bags of feed and minerals and wrestling calves for branding and castration posed their own hazards, but he would hit the second half of the season in better shape than any gym workout could deliver.

Jo called the night before he left for Cheyenne. He thought he heard a new note of tension in her voice and asked if something was troubling her although he hated to hear her answer.

"Mom and I watched *8 Seconds* last night," she said. "I watched it in January before I came to the event at the Garden, but I'd forgotten Lane Frost died at Frontier Days."

He closed his eyes in frustration; he didn't need to deal with her fears as well as his own. No bull rider who walked past the bigger-than-life statue of Lane Frost in Cheyenne ever forgot his death there, his heart shattered by ribs broken from a sweeping blow of the bull's horn.

"Jo, you've been with the tour long enough to know that kind of injury isn't likely to happen now," he said. "Cody Lambert was Lane's traveling buddy—he developed the vest we all wear because of the way Lane died."

"I know, but the movie was so real..."

"Yeah, I watched the movie just once—it creeped me out how much Luke Perry looks like Lane. I was just a baby when it happened, but we all feel like we knew him." He took a deep breath. "Look, Frontier Days is just another event—it's no more dangerous than any other. Cheyenne puts on a great show—you'd love it." He almost said, *I'll take you there someday.*

He heard a tiny sigh. "Okay, good luck and be careful."

He answered as he always did. "But not too careful."

She managed a laugh. "I know—careful doesn't win round money."

WHEN JO CALLED the first week in August, her voice vibrated with barely suppressed excitement. "I think I've found Traci's hometown."

Tom laid down the fence stretcher he'd been using and wiped his sweating hand on his jeans. "She said she grew up in Spring Hill, Arkansas."

"How about Spring Hill, Texas? You assumed Arkansas because of her trips to Little Rock. This town is close to I-30 and just across the border from Arkansas but nowhere near the town where you spoke to the police chief. She could easily have gotten on a bus there for Little Rock. And the school colors are red and gold. I've been trying to get in touch with someone at the high school, but all I get is an answering machine. I suppose everything's shut down for the summer."

He bowed his head against the fence post, his emotions too powerful for speech. "I don't know how to thank you," he said at last.

"Don't thank me yet," she said. "All I've found is a possible starting point. I've got my mom looking at the yearbook pictures for 2006, trying to find a face to match your photo. She's always my sounding board for my writing, so I put her to work on your search."

"Sorry to be such a bother..."

"Don't be foolish—we're both glad to do whatever we can to help."

She ended the call as she always did: "Be careful and don't work too hard."

CHAPTER THIRTY-SIX

JO FLUNG HER phone on the sofa in disgust. "I'm convinced the school department in Spring Hill, Texas, doesn't really exist," she said to Angus, who wound around her ankles in sympathy. "I've left six messages to call me back, and now I can't even get an answering machine."

She retrieved her phone and hit the speed dial to reach her mother. "Are you up for a quick trip to Texas?"

"Texas," her mother said. "In August. Sure, count me in."

TWO DAYS LATER their flight landed in Texarkana. The sun bleached all color from the flat landscape; heat shimmered off the tarmac in undulating waves.

Anna wiped sweat from her forehead. "I can't imagine anyone choosing to live here," she said. "Even the trees look exhausted."

"Maybe that's why Traci was so anxious to

get out," Jo said. "At least we'll have AC in the rental. With luck, we won't be here more than a day."

They drove the forty-plus miles from Texarkana to Spring Hill, Texas, and stopped first at the address listed online for the local school district headquarters. The door of the low brick building was locked, with a curling notice taped to the inside of the door's glass stating no one would be in the office until August 15. Jo copied the barely legible emergency number and dialed it while she and Anna took refuge in airconditioned comfort at Swanny's Café.

A recording of a woman's voice with a flat nasal twang informed her that nobody was home—try again later. "So much for dealing with an emergency," Jo said.

"You folks looking for somebody?" Their waitress, Ruby according to her name tag, stood at their table with their BLTs and iced tea ("All we got is sweet").

"Yes, ma'am." Jo had picked up the habit of saying ma'am and sir from the Southern-tier cowboys. "We're trying to locate someone who grew up around here, a young woman named Traci O'Hara. It's kind of important."

"Lizzy and Cora O'Hara live south of town,"

Ruby said, "but they're a couple of old maids—they're both in their sixties."

Anna dug out the photo Jo had enlarged from Tom's snapshot. She handed it to Ruby. "Have you ever seen this girl?"

Ruby set the pitcher on the Formica-topped table and perched purple-rimmed reading glasses on her nose. She studied the picture.

"That's Terry O'Meara," she said at last. "Frank O'Meara's older girl. I'm not surprised she took a new name—nothing about Frank O'Meara she'd want to keep. She stuck it out here just long enough to graduate high school and then lit out. As far as I know, she's never been back."

She handed the photo back to Anna. "You don't want any truck with Frank O'Meara. He's about the meanest man ever lived in this county, and we've had some mean ones. He worked his poor wife to death like she was a mule and tried to do the same with his kids. The boys ran off as soon as they were old enough to hold their thumbs out on the interstate. The girls…" She shook her head. "Who's looking for her?"

Remembering Jake's advice regarding Luke's wife, Jo twisted the truth as little as possible. "She was engaged to my brother," she said. "She told him she was pregnant but then she ran out on him. He was in a bad accident right after that and wasn't able to look for her in person so I said I'd try to find her."

"I never heard anything about her having a baby," Ruby said, "but she's been gone from here maybe seven or eight years now. You might try talking to Sally-Ann—that's Terry's little sister. If she's kept in touch with anybody, it's Sally-Ann."

She pulled a pencil from her frizzy blond updo and drew a map on a paper napkin. "She and her husband have a mobile home just off the state road. I'd go now if you're going, before Darrell gets off work at the paper mill. He's not a bad sort, but Sally-Ann won't be able to get a word in edgewise if he's there."

After finishing off lunch with excellent pecan pie "made with nuts from just down the road," Jo and Anna followed Ruby's map to a pink-and-white double-wide trailer with a satellite dish on the roof. A gas grill sat under a huge tree Jo recognized from Deke's wedding as a live oak. A camo-painted ATV hunkered under a lean-to; Jo saw no other vehicle. A brave mass of scarlet and purple petunias planted in a white-painted tractor wire bobbed in the wind.

"Are you sure it's safe to get out?" Anna asked. "They might have a mean dog."

"I don't think so," Jo said as a lean tan-and-white hound emerged from the shade under the trailer and stretched lazily fore and aft. "You wait here, just in case."

She parked the car in the shade and knocked on the flimsy door hard enough to make herself heard above the subdued roar of the air conditioner. The hound stuck his wet nose in her hand.

The young woman who answered the door could have posed for the picture taken with Tom—blue eyes, dark shoulder-length hair with a slight wave—but ten years older. And this was Traci's—Terry's, she corrected herself—younger sister. A baby, possibly a year old, rode on her hip while a toddler of indeterminate sex peeked from behind the limp skirt of her flowered sundress. Inside, an older boy, maybe five or six, stared at cartoon images on the wide-screen TV.

Jo introduced herself and gave Sally-Ann the same explanation she'd given Ruby.

The girl's lip curled. "Took his own sweet time to come looking for her, didn't he? It doesn't matter now—Terry's dead."

Jo steadied herself with a hand on the door frame, shocked. "You're sure?"

Sally-Ann shrugged. "Sure enough as not to matter. I'm the only one in the family Terry ever kept in touch with. She always sent Christmas presents for Darrell Junior…" She jerked her head toward the boy watching TV. "Nothing much—she didn't have money to spare—but she never once missed. When two Christmases went by with not a word from her, I knew she was gone."

"I'm so sorry," Jo said. "You two must have been close."

"She was awful good to me when we were growing up," Sally-Ann said. "She took beatings Pa would have laid on me. I got married when I was sixteen to get away from him, and she left as soon as she graduated because I was already out of the house. She used to tell me once she made it big in Nashville, she'd send for me to come live with her." She chuckled. "I just let her talk, and I wouldn't leave Darrell. He brings home his paycheck faithful as clockwork and doesn't knock me around like my old man did. And he loves his kids."

"Do you know if she had a baby?" Jo asked. "She told my brother she was pregnant."

"If she did, she never told me, but she wouldn't

want word of it to get back to Pa." Sally-Ann shivered. "I wish I could get farther away from him than I am, but all Darrell's family lives right around here, so he'd never move. Anyway, he's big enough to back Pa down."

"Can you think of anyone else who might know more about your sister?" Jo refused to let her best lead slip from her grasp.

Sally-Ann sighed. "Maybe. She had a roommate in Nashville last I heard from her. I've got the address somewhere—course I don't know if she's still there." She thrust the baby into Jo's arms. "Hold Justine while I look."

The little girl stared up at Jo with trustful eyes. The teddy-bear pattern on her cotton sleeper was faded almost beyond recognition, but the garment was spotless and a sweet clean-baby fragrance rose from her hair.

Sally-Ann returned with a dog-eared index card. "Terry said to let her know if Pa died—she swore she wouldn't set foot back in Texas as long as he was alive." A brief spasm pinched her features. "I wrote my phone number on the back. I've got about all I can handle with my three, and there's no one else in the family I'd give a puppy to raise, never mind a baby, but you do find out Terry had a kid, call me, okay?

So I'll know." Sally-Ann handed over the card. "Good luck."

Jo returned to the car. "Sally-Ann thinks her sister is dead—she hasn't heard from her in more than two years. But I have to find out for sure." She handed her mother the card. "Next stop, Nashville."

CHAPTER THIRTY-SEVEN

COMPARED WITH EAST TEXAS, Tennessee looked like the Garden of Eden. "You can see Opryland off the left side," a flight attendant informed them as the plane banked for its final approach to Nashville International Airport. Jo looked down at the sprawling complex of gardens, glass-domed buildings and parking lots with tour buses lined up like beached whales. She wondered how many young dreamers had beaten their hearts against those ramparts in vain like moths against a windowpane.

They picked up another rental car but crept through rush-hour traffic to their hotel rather than search at once for the address on the card. "I have an idea Terry's roommate might not live in the best section of town," Jo said. "We'll be better off trying to find it in the morning. I am going to check with the police. They might have some record if she really is dead—it isn't likely a woman her age would die of natural causes. And they might know if she left a baby behind."

"You can take care of that on your own," Anna said. "I'm missing my daily dose of Judge Judy."

Jo shook her head in amusement; for years her mother had been a slavish devotee of the sharp-tongued TV magistrate. She got directions at the concierge desk for the police headquarters and walked the few blocks from their hotel. She repeated her tale to the officer on desk duty, asking for information about Teresa O'Meara or Traci O'Hara. After she waited a few minutes on a hard plastic bench, a woman introduced herself as Detective Plunkett and took her to a cramped cubicle.

"You're inquiring about Traci O'Hara's death?"

Jo's heart sank. "So she is dead?"

"I'm afraid so." Plunkett consulted a file she held. "About eighteen months ago—a mugging gone bad. She was serving drinks and singing for tips at a club on Broadway." She wagged her head in regret. "Another Grand Ole Opry star who never made it. A druggie who worked in the kitchen followed her when she got off work and tried to grab her purse. She resisted and hit her head when she fell. She was still alive when the manager found her an hour later, but she died in the ER. What's your interest in the case?"

"I've been trying to help a friend locate her," Jo said. "I spoke with her sister in Texas just yesterday. By the way, she was born Teresa O'Meara. Her sister was sure Terry was dead when she didn't hear from her two Christmases in a row."

She handed Plunkett the photo printed from Tom's phone. "Are we talking about the same person?"

Plunkett studied the picture and nodded. "I'm afraid that's her, all right."

Another young life lost as needlessly as the hikers caught by the flash flood. Jo quailed at the thought of how the news would distress Tom despite the heartbreak Traci had caused him.

"The man in the photo is my friend who's looking for her," Jo said—one thing to cook up a bogus story for the general public but a bad idea when dealing with the law. "He asked her to marry him after she told him she was pregnant and then she took off with no word where she was headed. He would have tried to find her right away, but shortly after she left, a wreck put him in the hospital for several months."

Plunkett looked up from making notes. "Auto accident?"

"A different kind of wreck. He's a bull rider—"

Plunkett groaned. "Oh Lord, one of those. I went to watch bull riding here last summer— those guys have got to be nuts."

"I can't argue with you," Jo said with a laugh. "He wants very much to find out if Ms. O'Hara did indeed have a baby and, if so, what happened to it."

"Your friend have a name?"

Jo had warned Tom his name would come up at some point; he'd said to go ahead, whatever it took. "His name is Tom Cameron," she said.

Plunkett's eyes widened. "Hey, I saw him ride last year. So now he's looking for his kid?"

"He's looking for the truth, one way or the other." Jo gave her the address copied from the card. "Here's the last address her sister had for her. I was planning to look up her roommate tomorrow."

Plunkett looked at the address. "Hold off on that—this is what we call a neighborhood in transition. Some good folks are moving into that area, but there's still some not so good. Let me make a few phone calls. Will you be in town a couple days?"

Jo handed over her business card. "As long as it takes," she said.

Jo's PHONE RANG just before noon the next day. "Ms. Dace? Detective Plunkett here. I have some information for you if you want to stop by headquarters again."

This time an officer escorted her to a conference room of some sort with a much-abused leather sofa and a long utility table surrounded by a few scarred wooden chairs. Plunkett sat at the table across from a middle-aged woman with no-nonsense shoes and tired eyes.

"This is Blanche Carter from the Tennessee Department of Children's Services," she said. "Why don't you give her the full rundown about your search?"

Jo went through the whole story again. "Tom Cameron fully intended to marry Ms. O'Hara and retire from bull riding to raise their baby on his family's ranch in Colorado. Apparently his plans didn't suit her and she left without giving him any idea of her destination. He recalled she had mentioned Nashville a number of times, and then I got the address here from her sister."

She leaned forward in entreaty. "He's a good man who wants to take full responsibility for the welfare of any child he may have fathered."

Ms. Carter took a file folder from a plain black computer case and opened it. "Traci

O'Hara did have a baby while she was living here in Nashville," she said. "She shared an apartment with another young woman who watched the baby in the evenings while she worked. When Traci was killed, her roommate brought the baby to Children's Services because she had no idea how to get in touch with Traci's family or the baby's father. According to the roommate, Traci had originally planned to give the baby up for adoption and then changed her mind."

Jo now had all the major pieces of the mystery. She had found Traci and her baby, but she still didn't know how the story had ended. "Was the baby adopted?" she asked.

"We have a good system here in Tennessee," Ms. Carter said. "In a case like that of Traci O'Hara's baby, first we check the Putative Father Registry to see if anyone is claiming paternity. Meanwhile, the child is placed in foster care for at least six months with a family who wishes to adopt—we monitor these placements very carefully before moving forward with permanent adoption. After an adoption has been legalized for one year, we won't open the case again. It's a slow process but one that's geared toward the ultimate welfare of the child."

Jo could scarcely bear to ask the next question. "And how far into the process is Traci's baby?"

Ms. Carter paged through several sheets in the file and then closed the folder before answering. "If Mr. Cameron had come looking to claim his child in another six months, he would've been out of luck."

The social worker took a manila envelope from the file and handed Jo a photograph. "Do you see any family resemblance?"

Jo stared openmouthed at the baby's picture. "Oh my God," she said. "Let me show you something." Her hands shook as she scrolled through the photos on her phone, taken during her visit to Cameron's Pride. At last she found the one she sought and passed the phone to Ms. Carter who showed it to Detective Plunkett.

"Remarkable," the social worker said. She slipped the photo back into its envelope and handed it to Jo. "I imagine you'd like to take this with you. Is Mr. Cameron now married?"

Time for her to cowboy up. "No," Jo said, "but he soon will be."

"And his wife would be willing to accept his child from a previous relationship?"

"Oh yes!" She had found Tom's child for him, somehow making it hers as well. "Yes, she'll welcome his baby."

"I see," Ms. Carter said, smiling.

Jo held the envelope as if it contained a map to buried treasure. "Would there be any harm in my contacting Ms. O'Hara's roommate? The woman who brought the baby to you? I'd like to fill in some of the blanks between the last time Tom saw her and when she died."

Plunkett and Ms. Carter exchanged glances. Carter shrugged. "I can't see how it could hurt. She has no legal standing and she's not actively involved with the child."

She consulted the file and wrote a phone number on a page torn from a legal pad. "Her name is Marcy Liddel. This is the last contact number we have for her—I don't know if it's still good. She called regularly at first—she seemed fond of the baby—but we haven't heard from her in almost a year."

She gave the page and her card to Jo. "The child is in a safe, loving foster situation, but of course ideally she should be with her own relatives if they're able to raise her properly."

"She'll be welcomed into an extended family that's been part of Colorado history since prestatehood days," Jo said. "The Camerons can give you references ranging from their relatives on the Ute Tribal Council right up through the governor. Tom has tried to find his ex-fiancée, but from what you've told me, she was already dead before he could start making a good search."

"Too bad he didn't find her in time, but who knows what the outcome would have been if he had," Plunkett said. "Apparently she had her own agenda. You càn try contacting Marcy Liddel by phone. If you don't have any luck, call me and I'll arrange for an officer to go with you to the address you showed me."

Jo checked her purse to make sure she still had Plunkett's card. "Neighborhood in transition, right?"

MARCY LIDDEL RETURNED Jo's call the next morning. "You want to talk about Traci? There's a coffee shop across the street from the police headquarters—it's always full of cops, so I guess it's a safe enough place to meet. I'll be there at eleven-thirty."

Jo looked at her mother and did a silent fist pump of triumph. "How will I recognize you?"

"Just look for a red mop on a black handle." Marcy said with a laugh.

Half an hour later Jo slid into a booth opposite a woman in her early thirties. As Marcy Liddel had said, Jo had no trouble spotting her mop of tomato-red dreadlocks, a striking contrast to her ebony skin.

"So why are you interested in Traci?" Marcy asked in a gravelly voice. "Is Missy okay?"

"Missy?"

"Traci's little girl. Isn't that what you're here about?"

Jo had been ready to start her spiel again, but the set of Marcy's mouth, the shadow in her eyes, stopped her short.

"Missy's fine," she said. "I haven't seen her in person, but the case worker says she's in a good foster home with a family who wants to adopt her." She had made a copy at the hotel of the photo she'd been given. She slid it toward Marcy. "Here's a recent picture."

Marcy studied the photo as if memorizing every feature. "I loved that little girl," Marcy said. "I was with Traci when Missy was born and I took care of her about as much as Traci did. She was the best baby—I'd write music in the evenings with her tucked up on my lap because I hated to put her down. I wanted to keep her after Traci got killed, but I didn't know how to arrange it. I went to ask for help—I should have known better. I've got a record for weed, nothing heavy, but they took her away from me."

She clutched the picture with both hands. "Can I have this?"

"It's yours," Jo said. "Traci was your friend, wasn't she? Not just a roommate."

"We made a perfect team," Marcy said. "I can write songs, but I've got a voice like sandpaper on a screen door. Traci couldn't write a note of music, but boy, could she could sing. I was working days in an insurance office and she worked evenings putting my songs out there while I took care of Missy. Like I said, a perfect partnership. She was just starting to get noticed—she got a couple gigs singing backup for big names at Opryland. She'd say, 'I can smell it, Marce—my big break is just around the corner.'" Marcy shrugged. "Maybe it was."

A waitress appeared at their table; Jo ordered coffee and Marcy asked for a Coke.

"So if you're not here about Missy, what do you want?"

"Did Traci ever tell you anything about Missy's father?" Jo chose each word with care. Maybe Marcy would tell her something to ease Tom's pain when he learned of Traci's death.

The waitress set their drinks on the table; Marcy stripped the paper wrapper from her straw and took a long drink of her Coke before answering.

"At first she acted real mad when she talked about him," she said. "How he wanted to stick her off in the middle of nowhere so she'd never have a chance to catch her big break. But after Missy was born, I think she came close to calling him a couple times. She said he was a good guy—he deserved to know he had a kid—but she was afraid he'd pressure her to go back with him or try to take her baby away from her. I would have tried to contact him after they wouldn't let me keep Missy, but I couldn't find his name anywhere in her stuff and she didn't put it on the birth certificate either."

Jo showed her the photo of Traci and Tom she had displayed for Detective Plunkett. "This is Missy's father," she said. "His name is Tom Cameron—he's a professional bull rider."

Marcy studied the picture. "No way—Missy doesn't look much like Traci except for her blue eyes, but she sure doesn't look anything like him."

Jo found the picture on her phone that had convinced the social worker. "Do you see a resemblance here?"

Marcy's skeptical scowl dissolved and tears starred her eyes. "Oh yeah—that's my little doll-baby, all grown-up."

CHAPTER THIRTY-EIGHT

JO AND ANNA flew home to New York the next afternoon. Tom was riding in Oklahoma that weekend; Jo called as usual to wish him luck but told him nothing of her travels to Texas and Tennessee. On Saturday, she called Cameron's Pride. As she had hoped, Shelby answered.

A long silence followed Jo's recital. At last Shelby said, "You're sure?"

"You won't need to ask after you look at the photo—I'll send it as soon as we finish talking. But should I tell Tom? Right now, I mean. I think it eases his mind that I've been looking for Traci—he can concentrate on riding bulls. If I tell him what I've found…"

"I would want to know everything instantly," Shelby said, "but that's a mother's point of view. I don't know if Tom told you—I got pregnant when I was raped. I would have loved my baby anyhow, but I miscarried at about six months— I never even got to hold him. If I had a second chance…"

Jo could picture her staring out the big kitchen window, her mind and heart far back in time and distance.

"But I think you're right," Shelby said. "Another few weeks won't make a difference, especially now that Tom's making such a strong run at the championship. Let me talk to Jake—I'll call you back this evening."

JAKE CALLED JUST before the event in Oklahoma was scheduled to begin. His voice shook with emotion. "Whatever happens with you and Tom, you'll always be part of our family," he said. "When I looked at that little face…" He was silent for several moments and then cleared his throat. "Tom's going to take it hard when he hears about Traci or Teresa, whatever her name was—he'll blame himself somehow. So yeah, hold off telling him. Let him ride his bulls. If he wants to throw a fit that we didn't tell him sooner, I'll take the blame."

Jo smiled; she had a hard time imagining Tom throwing anything resembling a fit. "Okay," she said. "No one knows but you and Shelby and my mom. I was glad to have her along on this hunting trip—I might have gone up like a balloon without her to hold me down."

Her elation dissolved at Jake's next words.

"When do you plan on seeing Tom again? The phone calls are good, but it's been a long summer for him."

Her first sight of Luke lying unconscious in the ICU flashed through her mind, the instant conviction that the broken body wasn't Luke's, but Tom's. "Maybe soon…"

"Hey, I shouldn't have asked. When the time's right, you won't even have to think about it. And thank you again for what you've done for us. Just tell us who to contact—we'll take it from here."

Anna joined Jo to watch the Oklahoma event on TV, marveling as always that every rider wasn't carried out on a stretcher. "And these men get patched up and come back for more. They must share some common mental aberration."

"I stopped trying to figure it out months ago," Jo said. "These cowboys seem like nice sane guys, some of them with wives and children, completely normal until they climb into the chute. They may say they're riding for the money, but I can't think any amount is worth the risks they take." She laughed. "But what do I know? I'm just praying Tom wins the championship this year. He promised me he'd retire as soon as he gets his gold buckle."

"And you don't plan to see him until he does?"

"I still get panicky when I think about watching him ride in person." The remembered anguish flared in her chest. "I was a mess that whole last event. I was so sure Tom would be injured—I was ready for it. I practically collapsed with relief when he rode without getting hurt. I can't live on that kind of roller coaster. And then seeing Luke injured just the way Daddy was—he could have died..." Jo scrubbed at her eyes with her palms. "I haven't worked up my nerve yet, but Jake says when the right time comes, I'll know."

Anna gave her a quick hug. "Come on downstairs and tell me what you think of the new brownie recipe I made for the open house tomorrow."

Jo CALLED TOM after the last round of the last event of the regular season. "So you're taking the next three weeks off before the Finals?"

"Well...not exactly," Tom said. "I'm ahead by just a couple hundred points—I'll probably hit at least one minor league event and try to pad my lead. Winning this year means a lot to me." He hesitated. "Will you be at the Finals?"

"I really should come, to finish off the feature…"

"Then do it," he said. "Stop running away, Jo."

His quiet intensity moved her more than open pleading could have done. "I will, I promise. Just give me—"

"I know, give you more time." His voice dropped. "Well, hope I see you in Las Vegas."

THE PHONE RANG the next Sunday morning; Jo recognized the number at Cameron's Pride. She expected to hear Jake's voice or Shelby's, but Luke greeted her.

"Doing better than I deserve," he said when she inquired about his recovery. "I'm home minding the ranch this weekend—Dad and Shelby are in Nashville again. It's been some kind of trick to keep all this from Tom. And, say, I need to thank you for calling Cherie after I got hurt."

"Did she ever get in touch with you?" Surely Tom or Shelby would have told her if Luke and Cherie had reunited.

"She's called a couple times," Luke said. "She apologizes all over the place, but she's never said anything about coming out here. I'm not in any shape just now to go chasing after her—to tell the truth, I'm kind of out of the notion. Maybe we'll get back together and maybe we won't. I'm not pushing one way or the other. But why I called—Tom needs a hand. He's just down the road from you—"

"Down which road?" Why would Tom be anywhere near New York City?

"He rode at an event in Newark this weekend," Luke said. "A bull got a little wild in the chute last night and knocked him around some so he spent the night in the hospital, just for observation. And he's got a cracked bone in his ankle, no big deal. But he could use some help getting to the airport. They're giving him a hard time about being discharged with no one with him."

Her decision came so effortlessly she was ashamed she had hung back so long. Jake had been right: when the time came, she would know. "Tell me which hospital," she said, "and I'm on my way."

She called her mother while she grabbed her purse and the keys to the van. "Want to ride to Newark with me?"

CHAPTER THIRTY-NINE

"PLEASE TURN LOOSE of my jeans," Tom said through gritted teeth. He tugged on the legs of his Wranglers; the stocky red-haired nurse kept her hold on the waistband. At least he'd managed to find his shirt and briefs before she caught him getting dressed.

"The doctor hasn't discharged you yet," she said, "and you can't leave without a responsible party with you. You've had a concussion—"

"I was out maybe thirty seconds, tops—"

"Plus I gave you pain medication just an hour ago that could affect your balance—"

"I didn't take it." Although he could sure use a handful of Advils right now. The headache that had pretty much disappeared during the night was back and had brought buddies with it.

"Mr. Cameron, please get back in bed. I'll try to find the doctor—"

"Get back in the bed, Tom."

He almost toppled over in shock at hearing Jo's voice.

"Now, please." She took the jeans from the nurse. "He won't be leaving alone—I'll be with him. Can you get me a pair of sharp scissors or maybe a knife?" She inspected the jeans. "He can't get these on over his splint—I'll have to open up the seam."

The nurse grinned. "I'm sure I can find what you need."

Jo turned back to him. "Tom Cameron, you're a fool and I'm a bigger one. Now lie down like a good boy."

He sank back against the pillows; he would have jumped out the window if she'd told him to. "How did you know—?"

"Luke called me. I got here as fast as I could—luckily there's no traffic on a Sunday morning."

"I've got a two o'clock flight—"

"We'll cancel it," she said. "You're coming home with me, at least overnight."

"Dang, you're bossy."

She gave him a smile that spread pure joy through him. "You don't know the half of it."

An hour later he was dressed and scrawling his name on multiple discharge forms. Jo hefted his gear bag to her shoulder as an orderly arrived with a wheelchair.

Tom grabbed the crutches the nurse had brought. "I don't need a wheelchair—"

"Stop wasting time and get in the chair—I've got someone downstairs waiting to meet you."

THE RIDE IN the van from Newark to Brooklyn wasn't much fun; maybe he'd taken a harder hit than he liked to admit. Jo and Anna helped him up the three porch steps to the bright downstairs apartment. He stood swaying a little in the spacious front hall while they discussed sleeping arrangements.

"Do you mind keeping Angus company upstairs?" Jo asked. "Tom can have your room and I'll pull out the sofa in your office."

He started to protest, and they both turned on him. "Hush," they said in unison.

He grinned. Maybe he'd been better off with Nurse Ratched.

Jo served him lunch, a grilled cheese sandwich with tomato soup, as he sat with his leg propped up on the Victorian sofa in the sunny parlor. Funny, he remembered his mom giving him the same thing when he was sick as a kid—must be some universal remedy, like chicken soup. He was pretty tired by the time he finished eating and didn't put up much of a fight when Jo insisted he stretch out for a nap on the bed in her mother's room.

A low pulsating rumble woke him in near darkness; a heavy weight sat on his chest. He opened his eyes and found himself eyeball to eyeball with the biggest feline he'd seen since he'd caught a bobcat raiding the chicken house.

"I sure hope I'm not hallucinating," he said.

He heard swift footsteps outside the bedroom door left slightly ajar. Jo entered and scooped up the long furry body. "Angus, shame on you! I'm sorry," she said. "He must have sneaked down the back stairs to the kitchen. Do you like cats?"

"That's at least two cats," he said.

"Just one Maine Coon, but he is a big boy—eighteen pounds of love." She snuggled Angus under her chin. "You're lucky—he seems to like you."

"Is not getting along with Angus a deal breaker?"

She frowned at him; in the dim light he wasn't sure whether or not she was serious. "It is," she said.

He reached up both arms. "Come to papa, Angus."

She laughed and dumped the cat on the far side of the bed before sitting and taking Tom's hand.

"Listen," he said, "I need to tell you—"

"No, you listen—ladies first." She twined her fingers with his. "You're a bull rider—that's what you do. I can't..." She looked away and took a deep breath.

Here it comes. A cold sweat broke out on his body. She could have at least waited till he was standing up.

"I can't ask you to stop being who you are, any more than my mom could ask my dad to stop racing. And I won't make us both miserable by whining about it. You ride as long as you need to—I'll be right there yelling for you to make the buzzer."

Maybe it was a good thing he was lying down. He let out the breath he'd been holding in a long whistle. "Dang if you haven't beaten me to the punch," he said. "I wanted to make my best run at the championship and I've done that. My winnings for the year won't clear the ranch's debts completely, but they've made a good dent. And with luck I can still pull in some big money in Las Vegas. Win or lose, the finals will be my last event."

She bowed her head; her tears fell on his hand.

He pulled her down beside him on the bed so that she lay with her head on his shoulder.

A headache still lurked behind his eyes and his right leg throbbed like a son of a gun, but he'd never felt better in his life. He tightened his arm around her shoulders, and she lifted her face to meet his lips.

The kiss ended an eternity later as if by some inaudible signal. "After the finals," he said, and she snuggled against his side with a soft murmur of contentment while Angus purred and butted his head against Tom's arm.

THE THOMAS AND MACK CENTER in Las Vegas throbbed with anticipation; this was the last ride of the last round of the last day of the PBR Finals.

"This is it, folks," the announcer said. "It all comes down to this one ride. You've seen Tom Cameron cover his bulls all week with a splint on his leg—that's real cowboy grit. He's already got a $250,000 check in his pocket for the event win. If he can get past this last bull, he takes it all home—the gold buckle and the million-dollar bonus. And you all know the bull he'll be facing."

The crowd howled, nearly lifting the roof off.

Tom stood above the chute and tightened the thong around his riding glove one last time. Across the arena, he could see Jo's mom and

Luke seated with his dad, Shelby and Lucy. He looked over his shoulder at Jo perched beside the broadcast booth and blew her a kiss. She caught it to plant on her lips before giving him a thumbs-up and a big smile.

He reached down into the chute, stroking Gunslinger's neck. "This is it, buddy—this is our last dance. It's been great knowing you." One last ride, win or lose.

He eased onto the bull's back and fitted his glove into the handle as Deke pulled his rope and Len Haley gripped the back of his vest. Hat jerked down hard, mouthpiece in place— he took a deep breath and nodded.

The power of Gunslinger's first kick had Tom looking at the rafters; the leap that followed shot both his boots up alongside the bull's ears. He was riding the wave, matching Gunslinger jump for jump—

The bull spun hard to the right, flinging Tom outward like a fastball from a major league pitcher. He hit the dirt and rolled to safety as the bullfighters dashed in to intercept the bull.

The buzzer sounded.

"And this year's World Champion is Luis Veira," the announcer yelled as Brazilian flags blossomed throughout the arena.

Tom scrambled to his feet and limped over

to Luis in time to shake his hand and help the other riders carry him on their shoulders to receive the trophy.

He stood back and looked around the arena. Hard to believe he was seeing it for the last time as a competitor—eleven years of his life, since he was a green kid just out of high school. He should be feeling a greater sense of loss.

Instead a profound peace settled on his heart as Jo slipped her hand into his. "Great ride, cowboy," she said.

He smiled down at her. "It has been. Say, your mom's here—how would you feel about a Las Vegas wedding?"

"Are you kidding? And cheat Auntie Rose out of seeing her favorite boy married? She'd never forgive us. I'm sure we can throw something together at Cameron's Pride."

She tugged at his arm. "Too bad about the gold buckle, but I've got a different kind of prize waiting for you."

He didn't try to quiz her as they made their way back to the hotel. The lobby was almost empty—most of the fans were still at the arena celebrating Luis's win. They rode up to the suite he'd reserved for his family.

Jo led him to the sofa and sat on the coffee

table facing him. His heart began to pound; he had no notion what might be coming next.

"First, I found all this out about two months ago," she said. "I told your dad and Shelby— we all agreed keep it to ourselves until after the finals. Blame us all—it seemed like a bad time to distract you from your riding."

She took his hands in both of hers. "Mom and I went to Spring Hill, Texas, after I told you about my hunch back in August. I found out Traci did grow up there—her real name was Teresa O'Meara. She did go to Nashville—"

"Was?" Ice lodged in his chest. "You said, 'was.'"

"She died in Nashville about a year after she left you, a mugging gone bad, the police said. Before you really had a chance to go looking for her. I'm so sorry."

He looked down, swallowing hard. Yeah, Traci had handed him two years of sadness and frustration and heartbreak, but now he remembered her smile and her vitality, her appetite for life. If she had stayed with him...

Jo pulled a photo from an envelope on the coffee table and handed it to him.

He glanced at it. "A picture of Lucy when she was a baby," he said. "So what?"

"That's not Lucy," Jo said in a soft voice.

He looked again and stopped breathing. His hands shook so badly he almost dropped the photo. His knees would have failed him if he'd been standing; he couldn't speak past his heart in his throat.

Jo pulled him to his feet and led him to one of the closed bedroom doors. A middle-aged woman he'd never met sat reading by a dimmed light. She put down her book and gestured toward a portable crib in one corner of the room.

He grabbed Jo's hand. This couldn't be happening, not after the months and years of wondering, of shame and sadness and needing to know. He crossed to the crib and looked down at the sleeping child.

"It's Lucy," he said in an awed whisper. "About the same age I started riding her around in front of me in the saddle."

The woman stood beside them. "I've met your sister," she said. "Your father told us there's always one red-haired Cameron in every generation. I guess your daughter drew the lucky card."

He wrapped his arms around Jo, tears running down his face unchecked. "Who needs a gold buckle when you've given me this?" he said in a choked voice.

"Becoming an instant mom scares me silly,"

Jo said, "but you and Auntie Rose will help me get the hang of it, right?"

He tightened his embrace, rocking her in his arms. "Of course we will," he said.

Missy smiled in her sleep.

* * * * *

*Don't miss the next book in
Helen DePrima's
CAMERON'S PRIDE miniseries,
available February 2017!*

WESTERN WP PROMISES

YES! Please send me **The Western Promises Collection** in Larger Print. This collection begins with 3 FREE books and 2 FREE gifts (gifts valued at approx. $14.00 retail) in the first shipment, along with the other first 4 books from the collection! If I do not cancel, I will receive 8 monthly shipments until I have the entire 51-book Western Promises collection. I will receive 2 or 3 FREE books in each shipment and I will pay just $4.99 US/ $5.89 CDN for each of the other four books in each shipment, plus $2.99 for shipping and handling per shipment. *If I decide to keep the entire collection, I'll have paid for only 32 books, because 19 books are FREE! I understand that accepting the 3 free books and gifts places me under no obligation to buy anything. I can always return a shipment and cancel at any time. My free books and gifts are mine to keep no matter what I decide.

272 HCN 3070 472 HCN 3070

Name	(PLEASE PRINT)	
Address		Apt. #
City	State/Prov.	Zip/Postal Code

Signature (if under 18, a parent or guardian must sign)

Mail to the **Reader Service:**
IN U.S.A.: P.O. Box 1867, Buffalo, NY 14240-1867
IN CANADA: P.O. Box 609, Fort Erie, Ontario L2A 5X3

LARGER-PRINT BOOKS!
GET 2 FREE LARGER-PRINT NOVELS PLUS
2 FREE GIFTS!

HARLEQUIN®

super romance®

More Story...More Romance

REQUEST YOUR FREE BOOKS!
2 FREE WHOLESOME ROMANCE NOVELS
IN LARGER PRINT
PLUS 2
FREE
MYSTERY GIFTS

٭٭٭٭٭٭٭٭٭٭٭٭٭٭٭٭٭٭٭٭٭٭

HEARTWARMING™
٭٭٭٭٭٭٭٭٭٭٭٭٭٭٭٭٭٭٭٭٭٭

Wholesome, tender romances